HEAD FIRST

Bennett Security Book 2

HANNAH SHIELD

Cover design by Damonza

Editing services by The Wicked Pen

Published by Diana Road Books

Edgewater, Colorado

HEAD FIRST

*L*ana Marchetti smoothed her fingers through her hair. She looked down at her sweater, wondering if she should change. Was it sexy enough? Too sexy? Did it smell? She checked, and decided she was okay.

Her hands fluttered at her sides as she walked back and forth across the living room carpet. She could still hear Max talking quietly to his sister Aurora in the next room. Sweet, strong, handsome Max.

Her body flushed, realizing that he would come back out here soon. He'd say goodnight to his little sister, tuck her in, and then he and Lana would be alone.

Alone. Together. She and Max.

"Relax," she whispered to herself. "You're going to get sweaty."

She'd already made the decision. Tonight was the big night. And when she set her mind to something, she always made it happen.

Tonight, she would finally lose her virginity.

Max Bennett just didn't know it yet.

This was already a lucky night. A once-in-a-lifetime kind

of night. Max was here visiting Aurora, and Lana's parents were out of town, and Lana had finished her finals a few days earlier than expected. Otherwise, her parents would never have consented to Lana and Max being unsupervised in the house together.

Not because of any specific concern on their part. Lana was the typical overachieving good girl. President of her senior class in high school, valedictorian, already committed to a pre-law major now that she was in college. She'd never once gotten caught undressed with a boy, never snuck out. Lana knew she was attractive because people constantly told her. *Goodness, so pretty, and smart, too? You must have all the fellows chasing after you.* Thanks, Grandma.

But instead of showing interest, guys her age seemed intimidated by her. She'd never even had a boyfriend. Hence her persistent virginal state at nineteen, even with the sex-fest going on around her in her dorm.

Max Bennett? He was a Green Beret in his twenties, back in West Oaks for leave. Max was also the sexiest, most absurdly masculine man Lana had ever seen. Just looking at him made her so turned on, she thought she'd spontaneously orgasm.

Lana had started out as Aurora Bennett's babysitter, way back when Lana was just fourteen. Max had already been enlisted. Then, the Bennett family hit hard times. It was a long, complicated story, but eventually, little Aurora had ended up living with Lana's family instead of her own. Which meant that Max came here, to Lana's house, to visit Aurora whenever he got time off.

Usually, Lana's parents were around to keep a watchful eye on the sexy soldier in their midst. But at this moment? They'd planned a weekend getaway, thinking Max would be here with his little sister alone.

But what they didn't know couldn't possibly concern them. The door to Aurora's room snicked closed, and Max emerged from the hallway. There he was, in all his gorgeous glory. Six feet of hardened muscle beneath his T-shirt and cargo pants. Thick, defined biceps, narrow waist. His dark hair was buzzed close to his scalp, which only emphasized the angular bone structure of his face.

Every inch of her skin flushed with wanting him. It was almost painful. But she was nervous, too. There was so much of him. Was he big *everywhere*?

If she kept having thoughts like that, she'd pass out from a lack of oxygen to the brain.

"Is Aurora asleep?" Lana asked, relieved that she sounded fairly normal.

"Yeah, she went out quick. She was already halfway there when I carried her in. I guess I kept her up later than usual."

Aurora was thirteen now, a bundle of eye rolls and sarcasm. But she acted much younger around her brother. Aurora saw her own family so rarely that she needed Max to baby her a little.

"She was so excited to spend time with you," Lana said. "Been looking forward to it for months."

"I guess it's good to be missed." Max smiled, like maybe he knew that Aurora wasn't the only one happy to see him. His gaze brushed down her body for a brief second, so quick Lana almost didn't catch it.

Max had never flirted with her before tonight. Never let his eyes linger too long. The last time he'd visited, just six months back, she'd been in high school. And he was ever the upstanding, honorable kind of guy, even though she'd had ample fantasies about *him*.

But tonight, he'd paid her a lot more attention. Asking Lana questions about college, about his sister's progress at school. He'd grinned at her in a lopsided way that made her stomach tie itself into knots. Part of her had worried she might have imagined his interest.

But she hadn't. He'd just been checking her out.

Game on. Let's do this.

"Should we finish the movie?" Lana asked, hoping he didn't notice she was a bit breathless. "Aurora's seen it before, anyway. She won't mind."

There was that grin again. "We can. Sure."

They sat on the couch in the living room, leaving a couple of feet between them. As if Aurora was still sitting there as a buffer.

Lana started up the movie again. It was a superhero adventure, a DVD that belonged to her dad, but she was actually enjoying it. It turned out that watching men in capes jump around New York City was a pretty good time.

But she was watching the man beside her instead of the movie. Max took up her peripheral vision. The cushions compressed beneath him, his legs spread wide as he relaxed. She'd been smelling him all night, a woodsy combination of pine soap and spicy aftershave, but sitting this close to him was like being surrounded by a dense forest. She inhaled deeply, thinking of the last picture he'd sent Aurora of him in his camo gear. *Mmmm.*

Max's arm dropped into the no-man's-land in between them. Her eyes fixed on this new invasion into her territory, and the last thing she wanted to do was retreat.

Did he want to get closer to her? When was she going to get up the nerve to make some kind of a move? Or maybe she should just wait to see what he did first. She didn't want to seem too eager. What if he didn't like that?

Max picked up the remote and hit pause on the movie. She jumped a little, turning to look at him.

"Sorry," he said. "I was just thinking about something Rory said earlier. She mentioned some kid's been bothering her at school? She told me she didn't want me to talk to the principal, but what do you think?" His look of anxiety was sweet.

Lana found her voice. "She was getting bullied by another girl. The same thing happened to me at her age. My mom had a conference with her teacher, and it seems to be getting better. I've been checking in with her about it. She's been great, otherwise, so I don't think you need to worry."

He seemed contemplative. "You know her really well. Better than I do."

"You can't help being gone."

"Yeah, I know that, but I still stress about how she's doing. It's a relief that she has you watching out for her."

Her insides warmed with pleasure at his attention. Lana turned to face him more directly and tucked one knee beneath her on the cushion. "My parents and I love having her here. Aurora makes me crack up every single day. And I always wanted a sister."

Oh my god, no. Why did you call her a sister? He's her brother. And that would make you… Ew. No. Take it back.

"I just mean, Aurora's amazing."

"She's definitely special." Max lifted his fingers and nudged Lana's knee. "I'm grateful she has you in her life."

Lana took a moment to respond, still focused on the fact that he'd touched her. "I'm grateful for that, too."

"Just wish my own parents made an appearance around here more often. Rory said it's been a few months since she's seen them."

Lana nodded sadly.

He bobbed the remote in his hands. But he didn't turn the movie back on. "You must be a lot busier now than you used to be, with school and all."

"Yeah, I'm not around as much. If the commute wasn't so long, I would just live at home." She was going to college in Los Angeles, a sea of traffic away from West Oaks, though not so far in miles. "But I get back here multiple times a week. We always have Friday night dinner together, and I talk to Aurora on the phone pretty much every single day." Just in case he worried that Aurora didn't have enough support.

But Max didn't take up the subject of his sister again. Instead, he kept asking Lana about herself. Which was something else he'd never done much before.

"You have time for yourself too, right? You must have a boyfriend or something."

"Oh, no," she stammered. "No boyfriends. Or anything else. I mean, I would like a boyfriend, theoretically. I like boys. Er, men. I like men." *Someone please stop me. Help.*

Max frowned, tilting his head. But his frown still looked like a smile. He perused the length of her again, but more slowly this time. His gaze might've been a blow torch for the way it was setting her on fire.

"Trust me, Lana. The guys like you back."

Her face flushed.

"Have you just not found the right one?"

She'd had plenty of dates, but they never seemed to go anywhere. "I'm not really sure what guys want." That bit of truth had just slipped out. But she was curious what he'd say in response.

"Men are pretty predictable." Max laughed, turning away. Like he was embarrassed. "It can't be that hard to figure out what they're after."

She crossed her arms. Was he laughing at her? "I want the same thing."

His eyebrow arched, and his focus moved slowly back to her. "Do you, now?"

"So, I guess the problem is me."

Why did she ever think this would work? Why would a man like Max want *her*? She could write an essay analyzing a Hemingway short story in her sleep. She could outline an entire mock trial argument on her bus ride to class. But when it came to sex, she was utterly hopeless.

Lana started to get up, but Max's large hand rested on her shoulder, gently lowering her back down.

"Look, I think the issue is that guys aren't sure what *you* want. Everyone expects a guy to make the first move, and that can be nerve-racking. Especially when they aren't sure if it'll be welcome."

Her brows drew together as she considered his words. "So, they're afraid of getting rejected? It's an ego thing?"

"Not exactly. Not always. They don't want to get slapped in the face. But much worse would be if they misread a situation and made a girl do something when she's not ready."

Was Max talking about the guys she normally dated, the guys she met in class?

Or was he talking about himself?

She planned her next words carefully. "How do I let a guy know that I'm interested in…" She swallowed. "In him?"

"There are plenty of ways." His voice had gone low and husky. He was staring down at the remote control in his hands. "You could just tell him. Or better yet, show him."

Her heart raced. Her chest was tight, and she struggled to breathe, as if she'd just run a mile. Her nerves couldn't take much more of this.

But he'd essentially just told her that nothing would happen if she didn't move first. Which implied that he *did* want her to make a move. On *him*.

She'd been captain of the chess club in high school. Because, *of course* she had. Making the first move had never been a problem then. In her intro political science class, she never hesitated to raise her hand.

Max switched the movie back on. Villains in bright costumes resumed their rampage through Manhattan. He seemed to be absorbed in the story, but a muscle in his jaw kept pulsing. That arm remained on the couch cushion, just inches away from her.

Lana rubbed her hands against her jeans. *Okay. You want to finally lose your V-card? Then woman up. Here goes nothing.*

She reached over and rested her hand on his arm.

The explosions and shouting continued on the screen, but Max had gone still.

Lana brushed her fingertips along the inside of his forearm, tracing the sinewy veins and muscles. She couldn't help licking her lips. How could a few inches of arm be so sexy? The way the muscle flared out at the elbow, then back in near his wrist. The strength that must be contained in that one small area alone.

Maybe she had an arm fetish.

Or perhaps it was just a Max Bennett fetish.

She laced her fingers between his. Max clasped hers firmly back, which was exactly the encouragement she needed.

Lana got up onto her knees and leaned over to kiss his neck. The woodsy scent of him was intoxicating. So manly, with some indefinable quality underneath that made desire throb at her core. Her lips moved to his chin, enjoying the friction of his stubble.

A moan came from deep inside his chest. It was a desperate sound. And she had brought that out of him.

Max's nostrils flared as he looked over at her. What she saw in those dark irises took her breath.

Hunger. Pure and simple. Like he wanted to devour her and all his control went into restraining himself.

Yes, she wanted to shout. *Don't hold back. Take me. Have me.*

In one movement, he scooped her up and pulled her toward him. Not quite in his lap but balanced on his thigh. He dipped his head, and his mouth met her collarbone with surprising gentleness. His tongue slipped out, tasting her skin.

"Do you like that?" he murmured.

"Yes," she choked out. *Yes, yes, yes.* Was it possible to die from sexual tension? Because her brain was short-circuiting. Her hands found his chest. Beneath the fabric of his T-shirt, he was a wall of hot muscle. She felt his heart beating under her palm.

"Tell me what you want," he said. "I need to be sure. I need to hear you say it."

"I want you."

Finally, his mouth claimed hers.

Chapter One

*L*ana paced across the carpet in her office. Her morning had started off so well. She was a couple of weeks out from her next trial, and she'd *almost* gotten her prep work under control.

Then she'd checked her email and found the little present that the defense attorney had dropped off during the night.

She pressed the handset of her phone against her ear. "What the hell is this piece of trash you just filed?"

"I assume that's a rhetorical question," Paxton Wayfair said. "You're the one who concealed important evidence from my client."

Lana wanted to throw something. She looked around at her paper-strewn desk and cluttered bookshelves. She managed to restrain herself, if only because she wanted her anger to leave some kind of mark. In her messy office, nobody would even notice.

"Your client is a cold-blooded murderer," she said.

"So says the corrupt prosecutor and her lapdog investigator. I'm going to prove you're both liars."

Lana clenched her fist. The cordless phone creaked under the pressure.

"But we could avoid all this unpleasantness if you'd offer my client a deal. He'd be willing to plead to receipt of stolen property. One year of probation should do it."

"How do you sleep at night, you son of a—"

"Temper, temper, counselor. The judge already warned you to be civil to me."

Lana hung up on him. The plastic handset slammed so hard into the cradle she wondered if she'd broken it. The District Attorney's Office still had old phones from the early two-thousands. Glamorous, it was not.

Usually, she kept a cooler head. She saved her ire for interviewing suspects in an interrogation room whenever she was called upon to work with the local police department. But this case felt personal for her in a lot of ways.

Lana was the Assistant District Attorney for West Oaks County, California, a picturesque seaside enclave on the outskirts of the Los Angeles metro area. They only had a few violent crimes a year. But in a couple of weeks, wealthy playboy Ryan Hearst would go on trial for the murder of Heather Barnes, a local teenage girl, back in 1998. The girl's death had gone unsolved for decades, thwarting every attempt to find a new lead, until Lana herself started working on the case in her spare time.

She'd asked her old friend Max Bennett to help investigate.

Since he'd left the army, Max had started Bennett Security, the top private security company in their region. Moonlighting as an investigator wasn't his daily gig. But she and Max had known each other forever, and they'd worked together on a handful of cases before.

Then, Max had found evidence to blow the Barnes case wide open. Hearst's arrest came shortly after. Lana had been looking forward to prosecuting that scumbag for a long time.

Of course, Hearst hired thousand-dollar-an-hour attorneys from Los Angeles to defend him. Paxton Wayfair, the man she'd just hung up on, was the worst of the lot.

Lana had plenty of good friends who were criminal defense attorneys, but Wayfair wasn't one of them.

And now this, right on the eve of trial. Wayfair had accused her of personal misconduct.

An inappropriate intimate relationship with her so-called investigator, Max Bennett, the motion had said.

Wayfair didn't know how comical that accusation really was.

The phone rang again, and Lana grabbed it. "If you think I'm even going to consider offering a plea——" she began, belatedly noticing the caller ID.

Wayfair's name wasn't there. Instead, it said, *Unknown Number*.

She heard heavy breathing on the line.

Not again. She was so sick of this.

"I don't know who you are, or if you work for Wayfair. I don't really care. But if you think you can intimidate me with these pathetic tactics, you've got another thing coming."

Still, the person on the other end of the line said nothing. Only breathed.

A chill ran down her body, straight into her feet.

Lana had to be tough as a litigator, especially as a woman who wasn't even thirty yet. But these calls unnerved her. The guy—it had to be a guy—had called five times in the last month. Always when she was alone at work.

Never said a word, just breathed fast. Panting.

Disgust flashed through her, making her stomach curdle. "Why don't you come to my office next time. Do your little creeper act in person. I'll shove my fist down your throat, you mouth-breathing mother——"

Then she noticed that her door had just opened. Max Bennett stood there, hand on the doorknob, his eyes widening.

"Um, so, put me on your do-not-call list," she choked out, and hung up.

Max came fully into the room and closed the door. "Who was that?"

"Telemarketer? Or maybe a prank call." She sat down, gripping the chair to hide the shaking in her hands. "Who knows."

"A prank call? People still do those?"

"Apparently so."

She took a deep breath, trying to calm her nerves. She didn't want him to know about the calls. Max had an overprotective streak as long as the Pacific Coast Highway.

Once, she might've welcomed that kind of attention from Max. Now, it was way too complicated.

Besides, the creeper probably worked for Paxton Wayfair. She wasn't going to let Wayfair get under her skin. "What can I do for you?"

Max didn't usually come all the way to the District Attorney's Office. They conferenced by phone or at his plush company headquarters.

"You texted? Said there was an emergency?"

"Right. Of course, I did. Sit down." If only so she didn't have to keep staring at his long legs and trim stomach in that tailored suit. She'd thought he looked good in his army fatigues, but businessman Max was somehow even hotter.

He took a seat across from her. Her government office was a sad comparison to Max's fancy one across town, with its big computer screens, glass walls and ocean views. Yet the man looked gorgeous, even amidst tacky outdated furniture. Max looked good *everywhere*.

Her life would be so much easier if she could stop noticing that.

"Hearst's lawyers have filed a new motion. They want to keep you from testifying about the evidence you found, plus disqualify me as the prosecutor. All based on 'newly discovered evidence,' or so Paxton Wayfair claims."

"At least he doesn't do things half-assed. What is this new evidence?"

"He claims that you and I are…" She averted her eyes. Lana had thought she'd been through enough courtroom confrontations that she couldn't get flustered anymore. But this subject was proving her wrong.

"Sleeping together," she finished. "And that I seduced you into framing his client, all so that I could make a name for myself as a prosecutor."

Max sputtered a laugh. "Us? That's…" His face was turning red.

"Completely ridiculous. I know."

"Why would anyone even think that?" His voice had gone strangely high-pitched, which might've been funny in other circumstances. Usually, Max had the kind of smooth baritone that made men listen and women dampen their panties. "You and I, we're…practically family."

The muscle in her jaw tightened. "Just what I was going to say." Which was a bald-faced lie. Whatever she felt for Max, it wasn't familial. But he, on the other hand, seemed horrified by the very idea of them as lovers.

You didn't used to feel that way, she said silently.

She and Max did have a history, as much as he clearly wished to forget it. An ancient history. It was not something they talked about. *Ever*.

"You don't think the judge will buy it, do you?" Max asked. "She already denied their last motion to suppress the evidence."

"This new motion is baseless. But I'm worried the judge will grant a hearing, which will only give it oxygen." Judge Vaughn couldn't decide to scratch her own butt without holding a hearing about it first. "I'm sure Wayfair just wants to make me squirm. And waste my time. I don't have an army of junior associates doing trial prep for me, unlike him."

All she had was her second chair, Trevor Allen. He was helpful and good with victims, but Trevor wasn't exactly headed for the Supreme Court.

She rested her forehead in her hands.

Perhaps she shouldn't have asked for Max's help with the case. If she'd found some other investigator to nail Ryan Hearst, this wouldn't be happening.

"How can I help? Should I kick Wayfair's ass?"

Lana sighed, lifting her head. "Sign an affidavit that Wayfair's accusations are pure make-believe?" It was a written statement under oath that she could attach to her opposition brief. Hopefully, Judge Vaughn would be satisfied, and that would be the end of it.

"Of course."

She typed up a quick statement and printed it for his signature. After they'd finished, he said, "If the Judge does grant a hearing, when will it happen?"

"Probably in the next few days? It'll be fast, otherwise we'll have to move the trial date."

"Just tell me the day and a time. I'll be there whenever you need me."

She ignored the flutter in her chest. As usual, he was clean shaven, his dark hair expertly cut, no doubt at an expensive salon on Ocean Lane. If only she could see him as some kind of unofficial sibling or cousin, the way he now seemed to think of her.

If only she could forget what they'd once shared.

"I really appreciate your time." Lana kept her tone professional. "Thank you."

"It's no problem at all. I'm sure you'll have no trouble thwarting Wayfair's latest stunt, and you'll be back on track in no time. Since I'm here, should we talk about my testimony for the trial itself, too? I thought you had a few more things you wanted to go over since our last prep session."

She made a show of organizing a stack of papers on her desk, even though she would probably need a dumpster to work her way through all this mess. Literally and figuratively.

"Not now. I have to go speak to the victim's sister. I need to prepare her if she hears about Wayfair's motion. Whenever there's something unexpected with the case, she gets understandably upset."

"You want me to come with you?"

"I've got it." But she appreciated his offer. Her annoyance at him faded. As it always did. "I'll call you when I have an update."

"What about dinner tonight?"

She looked up, her eyes meeting his dark ones. "What?"

"We could do trial prep over dinner later. Since you're busy now." He just shrugged, like his suggestion meant nothing. Like she and Max had dinner together alone all the time. Just a couple of old friends, drinking wine outside work hours, with no Aurora or anybody else to provide a buffer. No awkwardness.

No awkwardness at all.

"Actually, scratch that, I just remembered I have a prior obligation." He stood, digging his hands into his pockets. "Another time. Let me know about the hearing?"

"Right. I will." She put on her best poker face until he left.

They might've grown up in the same neighborhood in West Oaks and shared a certain history. But it was far wiser, both for her career and her heart, to hold Max Bennett at arm's length.

Chapter Two

*M*ax left the District Attorney's Office, biting the inside of his cheek. What had he been thinking? Asking Lana to have dinner with him, like that was something they did? Like it wasn't the worst idea he'd had since… Jeez, since the last time he'd gotten too close to her.

Wayfair had accused them of having an inappropriate relationship. Hell. The man didn't know the half of it.

Max couldn't believe he'd gotten so embarrassed in front of her. He was usually unflappable.

He'd spent over a decade in the military, many of those years in Army Special Forces. Getting accepted among their ranks had been the honor of his life, especially since he'd done it at a younger age than the typical Green Beret.

For the last few years since his discharge, he'd been building a multi-million-dollar company, not to mention a lucrative commercial real estate portfolio. He wasn't easily intimidated. Not by terrorists with guns, not by hot-shot investors, not by arrogant clients or mouthy lawyers.

No one.

But there was something about Lana that made him a

touch unsteady. She'd always had that effect on him. Usually, he managed to hide it better.

He'd been babbling like an idiot, just because some sleazy lawyer made up a story about them being...

God, even thinking the word made his skin flush with heat. Lovers. About them being *lovers*.

He hadn't allowed himself to think about Lana that way for a very long time. At least, not for more than a moment or two, and not in any detail. Because those kinds of thoughts would lead to daydreams, and then to outright fantasies. Which was pointless, since it wasn't something he could ever act upon.

Not again, anyway.

Three nights. They'd shared three incredible nights back when she was nineteen. It had happened a decade ago, while he was on leave. Not something he was proud of. Then he went back overseas, and she got on with her life, just as she should. He hadn't done too much damage, thank god.

He got into his car and drove back to the Bennett Security headquarters, determined to put Lana out of his mind for now. She would let him know when he needed to do anything else for her case.

A few hours later, he was seated at his desk, elbows resting on the surface, fingers tented together.

"So, where do you see yourself in five years?" He blinked at the man across from him, drawing a complete blank when he tried to come up with the guy's name. He glanced down at the resume sitting in front of him. "Albert," he added, even though there had already been a conspicuous pause.

Albert launched into an explanation of his ambitions. But Max could hardly concentrate on a word the man was saying. He really didn't give a shit about Albert or his career path, no offense to the poor kid. It was nothing personal. But his resolve not to think about Lana was proving ineffective.

Lana had been really upset, and for good reason. Paxton

Wayfair was trying to make a fire when there wasn't even smoke. He'd already tried to argue that Max didn't follow the proper procedures when he'd secured the evidence against Ryan Hearst. A necklace that had belonged to the woman Hearst killed. That necklace was the key to Lana's entire case.

Wayfair had struck out on his first attempt to suppress the evidence, so he'd concocted this absurd conspiracy theory that Max and Lana were secretly plotting together to frame an innocent man.

It couldn't possibly work.

Max had half a mind to call up that asshole lawyer and tell him where he could shove his opinions. But Lana probably wouldn't appreciate that.

She'd frown at him with that lush mouth of hers. Then she'd narrow her large brown eyes. He didn't like to see her worried, but angry? Angry Lana was extremely sexy. She'd been assertive even when she was younger, but she'd really come into her own since graduating law school and joining the DA's team.

Sometimes Max wondered if she'd taste the same. If she'd moan the same way she did all those years ago.

I want you, Max. I want you inside me.

"That's why I think I'd be a great fit here at your company," Albert said.

"Huh?"

Max remembered where he was—in the middle of interviewing the most nondescript job candidate in history. He'd zoned out thinking about Lana.

And now he had a semi. Wonderful.

"Yes, thank you, Albert." Max stretched a hand across the desk, which was slightly awkward. But no way was he going to stand up and raise the flag. "Why don't you head downstairs and see if Sylvie has any more questions for you? If not, you're free to go."

Get ahold of yourself, Bennett. Max closed his eyes.

After a few minutes had passed, Max went downstairs to find Sylvie, his top data analyst and computer expert. She was also his resident hacker, although they never used that term in mixed company.

"What did you think of Albert?" he asked. "Please tell me you were paying attention when he was talking, because I only got about a third of it."

"He's smart, and he did well in school. Knows how to code. And we *do* need someone. Desperately."

His company had been growing fast, and his employees couldn't keep up with all the work. They had multiple positions to fill.

"But?"

"Albert seemed a touch sensitive when I quizzed him about his weaknesses. And he mentioned 'work-life balance' more than once. This place will eat him alive."

Max laughed. "I'm not that hard to work for, am I? We all have lives outside this office."

Sylvie fixed him with a wry stare. "You're my boss, so I'm not going to answer that."

He rolled his eyes. "Okay, fine. Have someone send Albert his rejection and schedule the next interview. We'll find a new coder. Or we'll clone you."

"A plan A, and a plan B. I like it."

Max left Sylvie to her work. He walked around the open workspace, checking on the rest of his team.

He was proud of what he'd built here. Bennett Security had three main divisions: Sylvie's group, which handled coding, technology, and data analytics. Then his sales team, which designed custom security set-ups for wealthy clients all over West Oaks and the wider Southern California area. And finally, his bodyguards, who provided in-person protection for those same clients when needed.

Sylvie helped on the research side. Max himself had a private investigator license, and he consulted with local and state law enforcement on occasion. Not because it made the company any money, but because Max wanted to give back to his community. He had tremendous respect for the West Oaks Police Department and District Attorney's Office, especially since Lana had become the second in command there. If Max could help make their limited resources stretch further, he'd do it.

Max never expected any of his employees to work harder or longer hours than he did. But Sylvie was right. He was a demanding boss, and if he wanted to keep the amazing team he'd built, he would have to make sure they didn't get overworked. They needed to fill those open positions soon. And he would have to take an updated look at their salaries compared to the market, and maybe allow an extra day off here and there. It wouldn't hurt.

He didn't need days off, but not everyone was like him.

Max didn't take vacations because he couldn't stand to be still. He always had work on his mind, and he felt useless if he wasn't pursuing a goal.

Unfortunately, despite his company's success—or even because of it—Max wasn't sure lately what his next goal should be.

Back when he was in the military, he'd spent his leave times worrying over his sister Aurora. But now that Aurora was grown, she didn't appreciate his interference. So, he was keeping a more respectful distance and trying to trust her to manage her own affairs.

Maybe that explained his lack of focus lately. Aurora didn't need his help anymore, and the company had met this year's projections already.

He needed a new project. Something challenging that would keep his interest.

Max's phone dinged. It was their front-desk receptionist. Max's own assistant had recently gotten married and moved across the country. That was another of the positions he needed to fill.

"Call for you on line two," the receptionist said. "Mrs. Haber."

Haber. Max had a quick flash of memory from the last time he had seen the woman. She was one of those clients who paid enough to get him to make house calls, instead of someone else on his sales or tech team.

He jogged up the stairs to his office, which sat above the open workspace. He had glass walls so that he could check on his team below, and enjoy the panoramic ocean landscape in the windows that took up one side of their building.

"Mrs. Haber," he said after pushing the button for line two. "Always a pleasure. How can I help?"

"A pleasure indeed. But why so formal? You had no problem calling me Julia before."

True. He'd let himself get informal in other ways with her, too. Which had been a terrible idea. But Max had an impulsive streak, especially when it came to women. He'd always had trouble thinking straight when all the blood rushed out of his head and into his dick.

He wasn't completely out of control, of course. He never slept with women who were otherwise attached or under the influence. And like any successful entrepreneur, he'd learned how to work around his weaknesses.

"Are there any problems with your system?" he asked.

She laughed breathily into the phone, which she probably thought sounded seductive. She was a lot more enticing in person. And extremely clear about what she wanted, which had always been a turn-on for him. That explained how he'd ended up screwing the divorcee against her kitchen counter.

But only after making sure that she understood it couldn't happen again. He was a no-strings-attached kind of guy. And from the minute she had unzipped his pants, he'd already

known that no more than once would be the best policy with
Mrs. Haber.

Would zero be better? Absolutely. But he couldn't be a
saint all the time. If he didn't allow himself the occasional
impulsive decision, he would probably never get laid at all. His
schedule didn't allow for going out to bars or clubs. He had no
patience for apps, either. When he met a willing and attractive
partner, he usually jumped on the opportunity. He wasn't
going to apologize for it. He had no regrets.

Well, except where Lana was concerned… But he'd been
younger then. More reckless.

"My system could use a tune-up," Julia said, with more
innuendo than you'd find in the beginning of a porno. "I was
hoping you'd be able to stop by again for a visit."

Inwardly, he groaned. He would have to be careful. Even
though she had readily agreed to his terms, some people
thought they could renegotiate.

"That is very tempting, Julia." He threw in her name to
soften the blow. "But as I told you before, I can't get involved
with clients. You were the single exception, but it was a one-
time deal. Our lives are both so complicated. I'm sure it's for
the best."

She sighed. "Yes, you're probably right. But if you change
your mind…"

He extricated himself from the phone call as quickly as
possible after confirming that her security system was
working just fine. But he went ahead and scheduled a tech to
check up on it. One of the women who was already
married. He didn't want Mrs. Haber to get her claws into
anyone else.

Max prided himself on knowing what other people
wanted and figuring out how to deliver it. That was true
whether he was making a business deal, working with a client,
or on his knees in the bedroom.

Yet he knew his limits.

He'd told Mrs. Haber what she needed to hear. But he'd been honest about having rules.

He called it the "rule of three."

No more than three nights with any woman, ever. Sometimes it was two, and often he allowed only one. As he had with Mrs. Haber. But after three nights, that was it. The end. Hard stop.

Otherwise, things got messy. People developed feelings. Drama started. His selfishness and unavailability would rear their ugly heads. Three nights guaranteed that he wouldn't mess things up too badly. There were never any tearful break-ups because there was nothing to break. His partners knew what they were getting ahead of time.

All in all, Max was comfortable with his life. He wasn't cut out for extended romantic entanglements, and that was okay with him. He wasn't capable of giving himself to another person the way a relationship required.

Besides, three nights were usually all he needed to get even the most alluring woman out of his system.

Except for Lana.

Lana.

Just her name made his breath skip.

He still wanted her, even all these years later. But it was no coincidence that he'd only spent three nights with her—because she was the inspiration behind his rule in the first place. The exception that proved its necessity.

So many times, he'd wondered what might have happened if he'd tried with her. If he'd given a real relationship a shot. Back then, he'd been in the service, but the long distance wasn't the issue.

The real problem was, he never should've slept with her in the first place. He'd known in his gut that he could end up hurting her. He *would* have if he'd kept seeing her. And hurting Lana was something he never could've forgiven himself for.

Chapter Three

*L*ana walked along the beach with Claire Barnes beside her. It was an especially gorgeous day, the wind calm, the air cool. Lazy sunbathers lay out on the sand.

Claire turned her face up to the sky. "I miss my sister the most on days like this. Heather felt like she belonged at the beach. She was becoming a pretty impressive surfer, actually. I remember one of the times that I found her living right off the boardwalk. It seemed dangerous, but she didn't care. All the activity and people made her feel so alive."

Heather Barnes had died in 1998. Her body was found on a deserted beach, just a few miles away from where they were standing. Whenever Lana met with Claire, they came to the ocean. Heather had spent so much time at the beach, both in life and in death. Maybe Claire felt closer to her sister here. Lana had met enough victims and their families to understand that healing could be found in unlikely places.

Claire seemed to be taking the news about Wayfair's new motion pretty well. Especially considering the judge had just granted a hearing.

"The hearing will be in a couple of days," Lana explained. "I'll text you the specific time and location."

"Will Ryan Hearst be there?"

Hearst was out on bail. The judge had denied Lana's request for electronic monitoring, and there was no way the police could devote the resources for full-time surveillance. But officers from West Oaks P.D. and the surrounding areas were volunteering their off-duty time to watch Hearst, unofficially. They'd catch the man if he tried to leave town.

"Defendants can choose to appear for legal motions, but his lawyer said Ryan wouldn't be present. Probably because Paxton Wayfair wants to focus this on me and Max Bennett more than on Hearst himself."

Claire nodded. She was a social worker, so she had dealt with plenty of legal cases in her career, too. Though not so personal as this one.

"Can I come?"

"You're welcome to come. But Wayfair is just doing this to mess with me. There's almost no chance the judge will agree with him." It wasn't easy to disqualify a prosecutor for unproven allegations of misconduct. And Wayfair had no real evidence.

"But there is *some* chance." Claire hugged her arms around her middle.

"I guess that's true. But even if the Judge grants the motion, we'll appeal."

"I can't accept that all the work we've done would be for nothing. Especially when we know that he did it. He killed Heather, and he almost got away with it. Maybe he still will."

"I'll do everything in my power. I promise, Claire."

They kept strolling along the path. But now that they'd been walking a while, the sun was getting hotter. Unrelenting.

Ryan Hearst, then a local teenager, had been a key suspect from the beginning. Claire had seen Heather get into Ryan's car on the night that her sister died.

The next day, surfers found Heather's body. She'd been strangled and severely beaten. It had been a vicious act by someone who wanted Heather to suffer.

When the police knocked on Ryan Hearst's door, his wealthy family hired the best lawyers. While he admitted he'd given Heather a ride, no physical clues came up to link him to Heather's death. Nor did any witnesses place him with her at the time of the murder. The DA back then chose not to pursue charges, claiming a lack of evidence.

But Claire had never given up hope. She'd continued to contact law-enforcement officials every year, even after Heather's case went cold. She often spoke about Heather's favorite necklace, the one the girl always wore, yet had been missing from her body.

Finally, Claire found Lana's phone number. The two of them bonded over being West Oaks natives, when so many people here came from other places and bought second homes that they only visited during the peak season or weekends.

Dozens of investigators had looked into the case over the years. Lana made no progress until she called Max Bennett for help. When Max got involved, he studied every detail anew. He would come to Lana's office to pour over the files and ask probing questions.

Then suddenly, earlier that year, Max had gone quiet. At that point, Lana had wondered if Max had forgotten the case altogether. He was busy with his company. That, she understood. But she'd also seen him on Ocean Lane on several occasions, each time with a different woman on his arm. He was a grown man in his thirties, so of course he didn't need to explain his behavior, least of all to her.

But if he'd decided to just drop the investigation into Heather's death, Lana had believed that she deserved to know. Her annoyance had turned into simmering anger by the time he'd finally called her up.

"Lana, I'm at the Hearst residence. Ryan's sister let me

inside. I've already called this in to the police, but I think I've found the necklace that belonged to Heather Barnes."

Shocked, Lana had rushed to the scene, along with West Oaks detectives and patrol officers. They took the necklace into evidence. After analysis at the crime lab, forensic experts found Heather's blood embedded in the hinge and chain of the necklace.

That new piece of evidence was all it took to start the ball rolling toward Ryan Hearst's prosecution for murder. After over twenty years of waiting, Claire would finally see her sister's killer in court. It wasn't a slam-dunk case by any means. But Lana had worked hard to build a solid case against the man.

"We'll get this sorted out," Lana said to Claire. "And we'll make sure you get to tell Heather's story."

∼

WHEN LANA GOT BACK to the office, she stopped at the district attorney's open door and knocked on the frame.

"Stephen?"

"Lana, come on in."

Stephen Abrams stood up and offered his hand, smiling. He was in his sixties, with a full head of white hair and a trendy pair of glasses from Warby Parker that he updated frequently. Stephen had held various public offices in West Oaks before becoming DA, including mayor. He was the kind of beloved local politician that could do no wrong.

But unlike some, Stephen deserved his reputation. As mayor, he'd helped to make criminal justice reforms before the idea hit the mainstream. He'd also been a great boss to the women who worked for him, which was a big reason that Lana had taken this job in the first place. She'd turned down offers from bigger cities to work for Abrams on her own home turf.

"There've been some developments in the Hearst case. I thought I should let you know." Lana came into his office and closed the door.

Stephen sat down and listened thoughtfully as she explained Wayfair's latest motion. He barely raised an eyebrow at the subject matter, though his frown did express his concern.

"Now that Judge Vaughn has granted the hearing," he said, "do you feel equipped to handle it? Would you rather have someone else step in since you're personally a subject of Wayfair's motion?"

"Absolutely not, sir." She almost never called him that, but she wanted to make sure that he understood how serious she was about this. "It's my case. I'm going to see it through to the end."

"I assumed you would because I know you. But I just wanted to make the offer. There are plenty of attorneys who might prefer a neutral third-party to get involved if they were in your shoes. I can see benefits to going either way, but this is your call. I trust you completely."

"Thank you. I really appreciate that."

He tilted his head in acknowledgment. "On a much more positive subject, people have been asking me for my thoughts on the election primary coming up later this year. They expect me to put my seal of approval on whoever's going to run to take my place. I'd really like to tell them it's you."

Until recently, Stephen had no intention of retiring anytime soon. But in the last year, he'd developed health problems that had prevented him from trying many cases. So, he'd put Lana, his second in command, essentially in charge of the entire office. He'd been giving her the most high-profile cases and grooming her as his successor.

It had been a coup for her to become even the Assistant DA before thirty, and it was beyond surreal to contemplate actually taking Stephen's place. Most people would say she was too young to be DA, yet that idea excited rather than intimidated her. Lana enjoyed defying expectations. But she still hadn't decided whether she wanted to run.

"I'd like to see how the Hearst case comes out. If I lose, I doubt anyone will want me on the ticket." This case was so prominent in West Oaks that her name would be associated with it, either way. And who would want to vote for the person who'd lost the town's one chance to bring a killer to justice?

"A very wise plan of action, which doesn't surprise me at all coming from you. We'll just have to make them wait for an answer. But I look forward to the day that it's your name outside this office instead of mine."

Chapter Four

*T*hat night, Max spent some time in the gym on the lower level of his building, then decided to check in with Sylvie again.

He strode through their huge open workspace, past desks and computer terminals. When it came to style, the interior of Bennett Security's main floor was as sleek as any premium luxury vehicle. All glass and chrome.

"Sylvie, is there any way you could find out who called a particular number at the district attorney's office at a certain time this morning?"

"Not legally."

"How about hypothetically?"

"Hypothetically? In a make-believe land where I wouldn't be violating multiple state and federal laws? Then yes. Why?"

"No particular reasons."

Lana's "prank call" had been nagging at him all day, the one he'd overhead on his way into her office. She'd sounded extremely upset.

If it had been a simple prank, Lana wouldn't have batted an eyelash. He'd seen her in the courtroom. She was infinitely tougher than that. If someone was bothering her, then Max wanted to know about it. He'd shut that fucker down. And Lana didn't necessarily need to know about it.

Max coughed. "On an unrelated note, I'll send you a phone number and a time window shortly, to do with as you will. And we—"

Sylvie grinned. "Never had this conversation? I've already forgotten it. By the way, I sent you that new batch of resumes."

"Right."

He said good night, promising he'd get through the resumes and choose some candidates for interviews by tomorrow morning.

The elevator dinged, and Max stepped inside, going up.

Bennett Security's headquarters took up most of a three-story brick structure right beside the ocean. Prime real estate, but Max felt proud of the deal he'd gotten on it. His very first big real estate acquisition. He'd outfitted the building carefully, putting in every modern security feature and setting up the whole place to keep evolving with constantly changing technology.

The third floor of this building was his personal retreat. A way for him to stay connected to work at all times, even when he was supposed to be off duty. Max valued his time alone, but he still needed to feel like he was being productive.

He changed into sweats and threw together a vegetable and shrimp stir-fry from the supplies in his refrigerator. He had a service that delivered fresh ingredients every few days, so he always had something healthy to eat. With the kind of hours he kept, he couldn't afford to eat restaurant food or processed junk all the time and expect to stay at his best.

While he ate, he quickly scanned through the resumes, seeing a few potential candidates. But he was starting to think seriously about that idea of cloning Sylvie. He'd push that button in a heartbeat. It wasn't easy to find such reliable, hardworking people.

Lana probably found that difficult, too. Her standards were just as high as his. But she had the additional limitations of working for the government. Max had loved serving his country, but he'd never been a fan of the bureaucracy that inevitably mucked things up. Far better to be in charge of his own operation.

But why did his mind keep going back to Lana?

He rinsed his dishes and walked over to a bank of windows that overlooked the ocean. The waves shimmered with moonlight, and the night sky was clear.

He wished Lana were here. She'd seemed so stressed earlier, and watching the waves crash into shore had a way of calming him. Maybe it would help her, too.

He could picture her standing here at the window, with him behind her. And then he'd slide her blouse down at the shoulder, kissing every inch of exposed skin.

Gah, there he was, doing it again. Thinking of her. He wiped a hand over his face.

Max had achieved everything he'd set out to do in his life. Why wasn't he satisfied? Why did he have this feeling that he had to keep striving for more? That something was *missing*?

There was a hole in his life, and his subconscious seemed to be wondering if Lana could fill it.

He took out his phone and thumbed to her contact. Then he paused, staring down at her name. Max knew what he wanted to do. But he didn't know if he should do it.

"No." Max put his phone away.

He wouldn't succumb to that temptation. When it came to Lana, he couldn't afford to be impulsive. She deserved better. He'd give himself at least another day, and then, if he still felt the urge…maybe.

Chapter Five

*A*ll the next day, Lana prepped for the hearing. She barely came up for air, even for lunch. Then Trevor came into her office, shuffling forward hesitantly, and breaking her concentration.

"Yes, Trevor? Need something?"

"Just checking if you got the list of cases I sent."

"I did. Haven't had a chance to look over them yet."

Trevor had graduated from law school the same year as Lana, yet she'd risen much faster within their office. She knew that she was unusually young to be second in command, but their office had high turnover, and she'd worked her ass off to get here.

Unlike Lana, Trevor came from a family of lawyers. His father was a federal judge, and his mom was a prominent professor of civil procedure in L.A. Trevor talked about vacationing in places like the Maldives, and he drove some kind of limited edition, hand-built Mercedes from the 1990s, a car that Lana found over-the-top. Especially whenever she saw the massive thing parked among the other DAs' Hondas and Toyotas.

Sometimes, she got the sense that Trevor was jealous of

her superior job title and her rapport with Stephen Abrams. But he'd never admitted it aloud. He might not come up with the most creative strategies, but Trevor always worked diligently, putting in long hours by her side, even though he clearly didn't need the salary.

Not everyone on a team had to bring the same strengths. Sometimes, Lana got so focused on her own work that she forgot to express her gratitude.

"Thank you for being quick with it. Anything that stood out to you?"

They chatted for a few minutes. Trevor, along with the other two deputy district attorneys in their small office, had been helping her get ready for tomorrow's hearing. Nobody had said anything yet about its subject matter. She kept waiting for someone to be brave enough to speak up, and she doubted that would be Trevor.

But then he surprised her.

"I can't believe the judge granted this hearing," Trevor said. "Wayfair didn't even make a basic showing of evidence. It's obvious he's speculating about…you know, you and Mr. Bennett to embarrass you. It's ridiculous."

"That's how I feel, too. But it feels even better to hear it from someone else. Thank you."

"Is there…truth to it? Not that you had him plant the evidence. Of course, you didn't. But the relationship part?"

Lana's face heated. "That's irrelevant. But since you asked, no, we're not seeing one another. We're barely even friends outside of work and family connections."

Trevor nodded, staring at his leather shoes. "Okay. Cool. Just curious. Let me know what else you need. I want to do whatever I can to make sure we win this."

"Thanks, Trevor. I will."

She appreciated his help. But in the end, if this went south, the only person she would blame was herself.

~

BY THE END of the day, she was eager to get home. In her kitchen, she poured a glass of wine and dug around in her refrigerator for something to eat. Lana had never been much of a cook. Sometimes, when she had her act together, she did meal prep on the weekends. But when she got busy, she relied on sandwiches, canned soup, and pre-made hummus.

At the moment, her fridge was bare, even by her standards. "Cheese and crackers, it is." At least it went with the wine.

She took her sad excuse for a dinner over to her couch. Tucking her legs beneath her, she switched on the TV, more for the company than to watch anything.

Her phone rang, and Max's name appeared on the screen. She panicked, worried that he couldn't make it to the hearing tomorrow. She'd sent him a reminder earlier in the day, and he hadn't responded.

"Hello? Max?"

"Hey. Is...this a good time?"

"What's wrong?"

"Nothing's wrong. Why does me calling mean there's something wrong?"

He never called her at night. Not unless there was a problem related to a case or a problem with Aurora, his sister.

"You're coming to the hearing tomorrow?"

"Yes. Of course."

She sank onto the couch, closing her eyes. "I can't mess this up, Max. I met with Claire Barnes yesterday, and she's counting on me."

"But you're not on your own. You have a great team behind you."

"Yeah. A small one."

"And you have me."

Oh Max, I've never had you. Not really. Not in the way she wished. "That's kind of you to say."

Though she still didn't know exactly why he'd called.

"What about Stephen Abrams?" he asked. "Why isn't he taking more of a lead on this?"

She explained the DA's situation. His health, his decision not to run again. How he'd chosen Lana to replace him, assuming she could get elected.

"You're running for DA in the next election? Why didn't you tell me before?"

"Let's not get ahead of ourselves. If I don't win this case, then I'll never even be nominated."

"But you'd be incredible at it. Say the word, and I'll start setting up the fundraisers."

"Max, I hate politics. I haven't decided."

"I hate politics, too, but that doesn't mean either of us is bad at it. I'll find you a campaign manager. I have some names I could send over."

"*Max,*" she warned.

"Okay, I'll leave it alone. For now."

He could be overbearing at times. She knew that it came only from good intentions. But there was only so much she could handle now.

Yet she didn't want him to go, either. His deep voice worked at the knots in her shoulders, calming her.

She wandered into her bedroom and lay back against her pillows, staring at the ceiling. "What about you? What's next for your business empire?"

He made a noncommittal sound. "Still looking at options. For a while there, when Aurora had just come back to town, I had her to focus on."

Aurora had left West Oaks for college and only returned a few months ago. Then she'd witnessed a crime, and some very bad people had gone after her. But thankfully, Aurora was safe and happy now. She also had a handsome bodyguard for a boyfriend, Devon Whitestone, who worked for Bennett Security.

"But these days," Max went on, "I guess I feel a little restless. I'm always busy, but it's like I'm spinning my wheels."

She couldn't remember the last time they'd talked like this. Not about work, not about Aurora, but about themselves.

"That's how I always feel," she said. "Like I should be doing more, but I don't even know what that is."

"Then maybe we should be restless together."

She didn't know what he meant. "How so?"

"When I don't know what to do with myself, I'll call you. And you do the same. It might help us focus."

"No offense," she said, tracing the patterns in the ceiling with her eyes. "But you and I don't really have that kind of friendship."

"Maybe we should." He exhaled, and she heard footsteps. Like he was walking around in his apartment in the top floor of the Bennett Security headquarters. "Lana, I know there's been this barrier between us for a long time. We've never talked about it. And I'm not saying we need to. But we can be friends, right? Real friends, the kind who open up to each other."

She was surprised. In all the years they'd known one another, he'd never been the type to be frank about what he was feeling.

"That might be nice."

"Then would you talk to me about that phone call yesterday? The person you were cursing out? It upset you. You should let me help."

Freaking Max Bennett. He had an instinct for reading people. But his talents only went so far. Reading people was one thing; understanding was another.

Max didn't understand her. And he never would.

"I'd better get to bed, Max. The hearing is tomorrow at two. Don't forget. Goodnight."

"Lana, wait—"

She ended the call.

Most of the time, Lana loved her life. Her job was exciting and fulfilling. She felt like she was doing something important. She helped victims find justice, and often helped divert troubled people away from a path that would lead to prison. Plenty of nonviolent offenders deserved another chance, whether it was through a drug treatment program, community service, or some other intervention. She knew that she was making her hometown of West Oaks a better place.

And she had Aurora, friends from college and law school, not to mention some men in her contacts list who she could hit up for a no-nonsense shag.

Then here came Max Bennett, making her question things she'd long thought settled. Making her wonder about what-ifs and could-have-beens.

The man was infuriating. Almost as infuriating as he was attractive.

As she got ready for bed, Lana noticed a new voicemail. It had come from an unknown number. Her heart lodged in her throat.

Her first thought was, *Tell Max.*

But she couldn't do that. She wouldn't just be asking for his help. That, she'd done plenty of times before when it came to her cases. But if she told Max about these stupid calls, she'd be inviting his interference in her personal life.

The absolute truth, the fact they'd never talked about?

She couldn't let him too close because it hurt too much.

Ten years ago, he'd told her not to expect anything more than a few nights of pleasure. He'd made no promises.

But she'd fallen in love with him anyway.

For a very brief period, she'd thought he would at least keep seeing her whenever he was in town, if only because they'd been so good together. Those nights had been the best of her life.

But the next time he came back to California on leave, he'd acted like nothing had happened between them. Just smiled politely and chatted about Aurora, like a wall had gone down behind his eyes.

He'd fucked her. Taken his fill. Three nights had been plenty. Then, he was done.

The heartbreak had nearly crushed her.

Yet her stupid, damaged heart still pined for him. Despite all the time that had passed, all the men she'd hoped would erase him, she only wanted Max.

Max Bennett. Her first love. And quite possibly her last. Wasn't that depressing?

For now, she could handle the mouth-breathing creeper by herself. If things got worse, she'd call her friends in West Oaks P.D.

That was her plan. She already felt calmer.

She couldn't afford to take her mind off the Hearst case. The hearing was tomorrow, and she had to be well-rested and ready.

Lana deleted the voicemail message without listening and went to bed.

Chapter Six

*M*ax sat on witness stand, glaring at the lawyer in front of him.

"When did Ms. Marchetti ask you to help investigate Mr. Hearst?" Wayfair asked.

Max tried to remember the exact chain of events. He'd gone over this with Lana, but he wanted to get it right. "She called me last year, in March. Told me about the case, though I had heard of it. Lana asked if I would have time to take a look and see what I thought. I'd consulted with the DA's office in the past. I said I would see what I could do."

"And what did that mean?" Wayfair his tone was sharp, as if he'd caught Max in some damaging admission. "What did you intend to do?"

"Exactly what I just said. Look at the case. Look at the evidence and see if I had any ideas that might break the log jam and lead to the truth. Which I eventually did, about six months later. After I'd spent a lot of my free time considering the facts."

Wayfair nodded and smiled. He walked back over to the defense table, flipping through some papers.

"How was it you found the locket in my client's bedroom?"

"Objection," Lana said. "We already had a hearing about the defendant's original suppression motion. Your Honor, he's just trying for a second bite at the apple."

The judge tapped her pen against her desk. "I'll allow this line of questioning, so long as it reveals something new."

Max could tell that Lana was furious and holding back her response. But of course, Lana would also know that talking back to the judge wasn't going to get her anywhere.

He'd always enjoyed watching Lana work. Though if he ever told her that, she'd probably call him condescending. Which wasn't his intent at all.

"Could you answer the question please, Mr. Bennett?" Wayfair asked him.

Everyone had known that Ryan Hearst was the prime suspect in the murder of Heather Barnes. So, Max had learned everything that he could about the man. He'd tracked him on social media, read the articles the guy wrote for his college newspaper, spoken to Hearst's former buddies. He'd done everything he could to get inside the guy's head.

Max had realized that Heather's necklace had to be the key: an oversized gold locket with a green glass jewel on the front. Just a piece of costume jewelry, nothing valuable. But Hearst was the kind of cocky S.O.B. who believed he was entitled to anything he wanted. He'd taken Heather's necklace to remind himself of his power over her.

What better way to prove his dominance than to display his trophy in plain sight?

If Max could get into Hearst's inner sanctum, he knew he'd find the necklace. Unfortunately, his hunch wasn't enough for Lana to land a warrant. Max wasn't a law-enforcement officer himself, but because he was working with Lana and the police, he had to observe the constitutional rules for searches.

So Max had investigated the rest of the family. They all lived at the Hearsts' giant mansion in the hills of West Oaks, even though Ryan and his sister were in their late thirties by now. Max had chosen Bethany Hearst, Ryan's sister, as the easiest mark.

He hadn't lied to her, not for a second. Max told the woman exactly why he was there: to investigate Ryan for the murder of Heather Barnes. But had he implied that his visit was perfunctory, and that he had some very different ideas for what might happen once they got upstairs? Perhaps. Bethany had received that message loud and clear, and she had chosen to act on it.

It was never too difficult for him to get women into bed, even when it wasn't in their interest. He'd felt only the slightest pang of conscience for manipulating Bethany, especially given how easy it had been.

But Max had outsmarted the Hearsts, fair and square.

He laced his hands together in his lap. "I approached the Hearst residence. Bethany Hearst was home at the time and gave her consent to a search. I entered the premises. She took me upstairs and pointed out which bedroom belonged to her brother. He wasn't there. That's when I saw the necklace. It was hanging from a board on Mr. Hearst's wall."

He'd spotted the necklace hanging from a corkboard filled with photos and other trinkets from Ryan's high school and college days. Max hadn't touched it. Instead, he'd called the police, who'd collected the evidence and established the chain of custody. When a detective had opened the locket, he'd found a picture of Heather Barnes on one side, Claire on the other.

"But was Bethany Hearst standing there at the moment you supposedly saw this necklace?"

Max glanced at Lana. "No, she was not. She'd stepped away for a moment." Which was exactly what he'd said the last time Wayfair had asked this question at a previous hearing, though he *hadn't* mentioned that Bethany had come back in a far skimpier outfit. Because nobody had asked.

"You really expect a jury to believe that Mr. Hearst left damning evidence lying around, and you happened to spot it? Couldn't you just as easily have planted it?"

"Objection," Lana bit out.

"Sustained. Save your argument, Mr. Wayfair."

The lawyer smirked at Max, as if this was all going according to his plan. "Let's switch gears. How long have you known Ms. Marchetti?"

"Fifteen years. Give or take."

"How exactly did you meet?"

Lana sat up straighter at her table. Max watched her and waited to see if she would object, as she had instructed him to do. But she didn't, so he went ahead and answered.

"She was my younger sister's babysitter."

"And your sister lived with Ms. Marchetti's family for many years, isn't that right? When your parents could no longer care for her?"

"Yes."

Wayfair walked back over to the defense table, flipping through some papers. "Let's go back to you and Ms. Marchetti." He adjusted his glasses, looking up. "You two are close, right?"

"I don't know. What's close?"

"Do you currently have a sexual relationship with her?"

Lana shot to her feet. "Objection. This is irrelevant and inappropriate. He's harassing the witness. And me."

"Overruled." The judge nodded at Max. "Answer the question, please."

"What was the question again?"

Max was stalling, in case Lana had a full set of aces up one of her long sleeves.

Wayfair came closer to the witness stand. He smiled. The

guy had more teeth than a shark. "Do you currently have a sexual relationship with Ms. Marchetti? Yes, or no?"

"No. I don't." *You asshat.*

But he already predicted what question would come next.

"Have you *ever* had a sexual relationship with her? Of any kind whatsoever?"

Again, Max waited for Lana to speak up, but she stared at the table, her hands flat against its surface.

"It was ten years ago."

"That's non-responsive. A yes or no, please." Wayfair gestured at the court reporter. "For the record."

"Then, yes," Max snapped. "The answer is yes."

The lawyer grinned, and his teeth seemed to multiply. "Thank you for that. I don't any have any further questions for you, Mr. Bennett."

Chapter Seven

"I'll hear the People's final comments," Judge Vaughn said. "Ms. Marchetti?"

Lana stood up. "With all due respect, Your Honor, this motion from the defendant is a farce. He's presented no evidence whatsoever of bias or misconduct, either on my part or anyone else's. Max Bennett is a decorated US Army veteran, a licensed investigator, and a respected member of this community. He runs a renowned security company with loyal clients throughout the area."

Max was sitting behind her in the audience. She didn't dare turn around to look at him, even though she felt his eyes on her.

"Any relationship I might or might not have had with Mr. Bennett in the past is irrelevant. Your Honor already determined that he followed the proper procedures when he entered the Hearst home and found the necklace. But the defense won't accept their defeat. They've resorted to speculation and fantastical conspiracy theories, hoping to pressure my office into offering a plea."

Lana glanced over at her opposing counsel. Paxton

Wayfair sat back in his chair, legs crossed at the ankles. The bastard was enjoying this.

"Defense counsel's questions about…" She cleared her throat. "About my personal history with Mr. Bennett are nothing more than a blatant—and sexist—attempt to harass me. His motion has no merit. Let this proceeding go forward as scheduled, with all *appropriate* evidence and testimony provided to the jury. That's all I have to say."

"And Mr. Wayfair? Your response?"

Lana sat back down in her seat. Her opposing counsel stood.

"Your Honor, my client has suffered a terrible injustice. The district attorney's office has concealed the prior relationship between this prosecutor and her key witness. As Ms. Marchetti's former sexual partner, Mr. Bennett is far too biased to be trusted. His testimony, and the necklace itself, are far too prejudicial to be presented before the jury. I urge that you do the right thing and exclude that tainted evidence. In the alternative, we ask that Ms. Marchetti be disqualified and another prosecutor be substituted, one who can objectively and fairly deal with the defendant in this case. That is all."

Lana bit her tongue so hard she tasted blood.

"I'll issue my ruling soon. For now, we are adjourned."

LANA DIDN'T GO BACK to her office. Instead, she went straight to the parking garage and headed for her car. She had to get out of there. Away from Paxton Wayfair's sneers and Judge Vaughn's absurd attempts to be "fair" to both sides.

And more than anything, Max's knowing eyes.

But of course, she heard footsteps dashing after her. Because he just couldn't let her suffer alone.

"Lana, wait. We need to talk."

She spun on her sensible pumps. "Haven't you said enough?"

Max's head jerked back, like she'd thrown a punch. "You wanted me to lie? It would've helped if you'd said so."

"Of course, I'd never tell you to lie under oath. But... Ugh, I'm not mad at you. It's that asshole. He wanted to get under my skin, and he's definitely succeeded." She rubbed her forehead.

Max came closer to her, putting his hand on her elbow. "Let me take you somewhere. You're upset, and I want to be here for you. As your friend."

"What about as my 'former sexual partner?'" she deadpanned.

His Adam's apple moved up and down. "Yeah, that too. All of the above. It's time we talked about it, don't you think?"

She was too drained to argue. She looked across the concrete at the elevators, where lawyers and litigants trailed in and out for their cases. "How do you think Wayfair found out about us?"

Max squinted his eyes. "My best guess? He had us followed. Probably saw how much time we've been spending together lately because of what happened with Aurora. It had nothing at all to do with the Hearst case, and it was totally platonic. But Wayfair was grasping at whatever he could. I can't imagine that he knew about...our past. He just got lucky there."

Got lucky. She snickered at the unfortunate phrasing.

"No pun intended." Max smiled slightly.

"All right. You want to talk about it? Great. Let's talk about our past." She didn't even know what there was to say. But she was definitely curious what Max might come up with.

"Here? In the parking garage?"

"Yep, why not? Right here. Let's do it."

"Okay. Well." He shoved his hands into his pockets,

rocking back on his heels. "I thought that we both…enjoyed what we did. Back then."

"The sex?"

His eyes darted away. Unless she was mistaken, a sheen of sweat had appeared on his brow. "Yes. That. I assumed it was…satisfying for us both."

"I'll say," she said under her breath.

"I've always thought that we were both okay with how it went. Right? I hope."

My god, the man was nervous. She'd never seen Max at such a loss for words. "I felt the same. But I didn't understand exactly why it ended."

He looked at the ground. "Because that's what we agreed beforehand, remember? And it made sense. You were a busy college student, and I had to get back to my unit. Aurora might've been confused or upset if she found out. And—"

Lana put up her hands. "You know what? No. I'm not doing this. There's just no point." She'd thought she wanted to hear his excuses, but she didn't. She really didn't.

"I think there is a point." Max gripped the back of his neck. "Because this is clearly still a sore subject for you. Which I completely understand. I never wanted to hurt you, Lana. That is the last thing I would ever want to do."

"We fucked a few times. It happened a long time ago. So what? Who cares? There, we've talked about it."

Max crossed his arms, and his mouth pressed into a tight line. But he didn't disagree, even though she wished he would. She wanted him to tell her how much it meant to him. How she hadn't just been an easy lay.

But he wouldn't. Because that would be a lie, wouldn't it? And they'd already established today that he had no intention of lying.

"I need to take the rest of today off, and then I'm sure I'll be back to normal. I'll see you later." She made a beeline for her car and got in before the tears started to fall.

Ten Years Ago

*M*ax Bennett was kissing her. His tongue was in her mouth.

This was actually happening.

Lana had never imagined kissing could be such a full-body experience. His tongue licked against hers, and she felt it low in her belly. His teeth nipped at her lower lip, and tingles shot across the skin of her back.

Max's kisses weren't careful and precise, like scenes in movies. But he wasn't sloppy either, thank god, like the few boys she'd made out with before. Max was aggressive. Fierce. Each pull of his mouth took something from her, and then gave it right back.

His hand cupped the back of her neck, controlling the angle of her head. She was happy to let him direct this scene. Lana was just trying to keep up.

Every few minutes he'd stop and ask things like, *Does that make you feel good?* Or, *Lana, do you want me?* As if he couldn't hear it enough. She certainly didn't mind saying yes, over and over again. That was pretty much all her brain was capable of at the moment. With every yes, he smiled and took her mouth again. Max liked hearing yes, so she kept saying it. Moaning it.

"Max. *Yes*."

Slowly, he inched her body across him so that she was straddling his lap. The progress was so gradual she barely noticed at first. One moment, she was balanced across his thighs, and the next, her ass made contact with the bulge in his pants. She inhaled and broke away from his kiss with a small, "Oh."

His dark eyes looked into hers. He panted, catching his breath.

Lana lowered herself onto his lap again. Testing. She felt the hot length of him, straining through all their layers of clothing.

"How's that? Okay?"

She nodded. "Okay."

Which was absurd. Fireworks were okay. Birthdays and Christmas were okay. Straight As in all her freshman classes and a new Mustang convertible would be *okay*.

This? Max and that rocket in his pants, all just for her? This was fucking epic.

He tapped her hip lightly. "Move back a sec?"

Max reached into his waistband and adjusted himself inside his pants. His expression suggested it wasn't very comfortable. But then he pulled her forward, and he groaned lustily when she seated herself onto him, their bodies tight together.

Now, his erection pressed directly between her legs and against her core. "*Oh*," she said again, but this time it was a low sound. Breathy. "Hi."

A grin. "Hi."

She'd understood in somewhat clinical terms why it was called a "hard-on"—she wasn't that clueless—but now she had a highly sensory familiarity with the concept. His dick was like a rock. The ridge of his zipper pressed against her, too, right at her clit, which was both a little too intense and...also intriguing.

Lana tried rocking against him.

Oh.

Max held her hips, his grin growing wider as she moved. "Yes," she said, before he even had to ask.

"Lana. You don't know how sexy this is, watching you."

He thrust up against her, and she had to close her mouth to stay quiet. They couldn't wake Aurora. But this felt so good. It was nothing like touching herself in her bed or in the bathtub. All those times, she'd imagined Max was the one making her cry out, yet she'd had no idea what the reality would be like.

Her body, igniting from the inside out. His size, his smell, his eyes eating her up.

And they were both still fully clothed.

The couch creaked as their bodies rocked against one another. Max's mouth collided into hers again, his tongue battling hers with abandon. He was obviously turned on, maybe almost as much as she was.

Pleasure was building inside her, the pitch moving higher and higher. She gripped his shoulders.

"Are you getting close?" he asked.

"I think so."

"I am, too. You feel amazing. We can stay just like this if you want."

But his statement implied the alternative without saying it. *We can stay like this. Or we can get naked, and you can ride my cock.*

She'd thought she couldn't get any more aroused. She was wrong.

Lana stopped moving. "I want to feel your skin. I want you inside of me."

His eyes squeezed shut. "Fuck, Lana. You're killing me." Then he saw the uncertainty that must've been on her face because he kissed her. Softer this time, sweeter. "I want you, too. So fucking much. You have no idea."

"I have a condom." Lana had planned ahead. She'd stuck it in the bathroom, at the bottom of her box of tampons. Where nobody would find it, including Aurora, who only used pads.

"I have some, too. In my bag."

She swung off his lap, stood, and unbuttoned her pants.

"Whoa, hold on." Max's hand closed over hers. He glanced at the hallway. "We can't let Aurora find us. Fooling around with our clothes on, we can explain that. But if we're getting naked? We need a door with a lock."

Getting naked. She had to pause as a shiver of anticipation threaded through her.

He was right. Aurora and Lana shared a room, and Aurora was sound asleep in there right now. The bathroom was tiny and old and so not sexy.

"My parents' room." She was already so far outside of good-girl territory. Why not be a little badder?

She turned around, but again he stopped her. In fact, he looked nervous.

"Lana. Wait. Before we do this, I need you to understand something. I can't be your boyfriend. You deserve a guy who'll be around for you in every way. That's not me."

"I know," she said automatically. "It's fine." She'd never expected Max to be her boyfriend. She didn't expect to win the lottery, either.

"But you have to be sure. When this is finished, I go back to being just Aurora's brother. Nothing more to you than that. No regrets. No... feelings. Okay?"

"Yeah."

Did she truly consider his words? Did she honestly think she could be objective with him there in front of her, their mouths chapped from kissing, her body wound up like a spring and desperate for release?

Later, she'd realize that she already had feelings for him by then. None of his warnings made the slightest impact. She'd say whatever he liked. It didn't matter. She wanted him. Not just to take her virginity, but to take *her*. One night with Max Bennett was such a monumental idea, she figured it would be enough for her, even if she never got a single night more. Right?

"You're fine with that?" he asked again. Insistent.

"Yes. Of course."

Max grabbed his duffle bag. Lana found a blanket and spread it on her parents' floor. Because using their bed would ick her out. She locked the door, excitement doing funny things to her stomach.

When she turned around, Max had set a gold-wrapper on the dresser. He pulled his shirt over his head in one smooth movement.

Her mouth fell open.

He was flawless. Six-pack abs, golden skin. His dog tags lay in the deep channel between his pecs. Not an ounce of fat.

He smiled, seeing her looking. "Your turn."

Suddenly, she felt self-conscious. Did he expect a sexy striptease? That was so not her. So she decided to be herself. She pretended she was at the front of the class doing a presentation. It was the opposite of the way most people got through public speaking—by imagining everyone else naked. She was going to imagine herself explaining the Supreme Court's decision in *Brown v. Board of Education*.

Nerdy, but at least it gave her confidence.

Lana unbuttoned her top and pushed down her jeans, maintaining eye contact with Max the entire time. His eyes took her in, his focus going soft. But the rest of him was so, so hard.

"You're gorgeous. You're going to ruin me, Lana."

He crossed to her, and finally, his hands were on her skin. Running along her back, squeezing her rear. His mouth followed, kissing her shoulders and her neck. He knelt in front of her and pressed his lips to her stomach. Then between her legs, where her underwear still covered her. Her knees felt weak, and she put her hands on his head to keep from falling over. The short bristles of his hair poked into her palms.

He remained on his knees, looking up at her. "Take off your bra."

She undid the clasp and slid the straps away. Max made a guttural, lust-filled sound. Her breasts were small, and she'd always wished that she was a bit more filled out. But he was looking at her like she was the best thing he'd ever seen. Her nipples stood at attention under his gaze.

Max ran his hands up her legs. When he reached the juncture of her thighs, he pushed the crotch of her panties aside and stroked her with one finger. She cried out.

"Can I take them off?" he rasped.

Lana did it herself, kicking off the scrap of fabric. She widened her stance to give him better access.

He grinned up at her. "Eager. I like that."

With agonizing slowness, his face a mask of rapt concentration, he worked his expert fingers against her clit. He slid one of them inside of her. He removed it and sucked the digit, moaning at what he tasted.

Then his fingers were back, stroking her again. She didn't even know how she was still standing. She felt unformed, like a pliable piece of clay in his hands. She'd never known pleasure could be unbearable, the opposite of pain and yet, its twin.

Her orgasm took her over completely, forcing her to lean against him, gripping his shoulders for purchase.

When she was about to collapse into a puddle on the floor, he stood, shucking off his cargo pants and briefs. She wanted to stare at him, not to miss a single second of this incredible experience. But honestly, it was all just too much.

Lana was in a bliss-drunk daze as Max scooped her up, lowered her onto the blanket, and put on the condom. He covered her body with his, plying her with even more deep, intoxicating kisses.

"Lana," he whispered. "You know what I need to hear."

"Want you, Max. Yes. Please."

When he pushed himself inside, the sting of pain and the sudden, unfamiliar pressure forced her back awake. The sight of Max on top of her, naked, thrusting. She tried to imprint the memory onto her brain. So she'd never forget this single, perfect night.

Chapter Eight

"*I*'m still upset?" she said to the empty car as she drove home. "Damn right, I'm still upset."

Sex with Max had been the most erotic, satisfying experience of her life. No one else had come close. But that wasn't his fault.

It *was* his fault he'd dropped her afterwards faster than she'd dropped her panties in the first place. That had just been cruel.

"Oh, but we agreed to that beforehand. Remember?" she repeated in a mocking tone. He'd reminded her of that fact in the parking garage.

Yes, she remembered. But Max's excuses were bullshit. He hadn't wanted to keep seeing her because he hadn't believed she was worth the effort. Lana was pissed off at him for never admitting it. Even though she'd probably clock him if he said it out loud. She could be unreasonable like that.

She honked at someone changing lanes.

The thing was, even if she and Max had tried to date—and even though she loved him—she knew they would've broken up eventually. They were way too much alike. She and Max had an equal workaholic streak. They were both fiercely individualistic. There was a reason she'd never had a relationship longer than a month, and it wasn't just the long-lingering shadow of Max Bennett over her love life.

With the sole exception of Aurora, Lana didn't like sharing her space or answering to anyone. She got annoyed quickly at a man's ticks or quirks. She wasn't an easy-going girlfriend, and she didn't hold back during arguments, either. Lana refused to dumb herself down to soothe any man's ego.

But she couldn't help thinking that, just maybe, Max could've handled her brains *and* her body. Meeting her as an equal in every way.

Stop, she told herself. *You're going to get sad. And you don't have time for that.*

Lana parked in front of her townhome and stormed inside. She poured an extra-generous glass of Pinot Grigio, then flopped onto her couch and checked her messages on her phone.

Trevor had called and texted, wanting an update on what happened at the hearing. But Lana couldn't think about that anymore right now.

Instead, she opened her favorites and hit the name at the top of the list.

Aurora answered, and then switched to video. Her smiling face appeared. "Wow, that's some glass of wine. Hard day?"

Lana sighed. "Hard enough that I don't want to talk about it. How is L.A.? Are you ready for the wedding brunch?"

Aurora was an event planner. Like her older brother, she had an entrepreneurial streak. She was still getting her business off the ground, and she'd secured several clients already after a slightly bumpy start. Aurora was spending the night in Los Angeles for a wedding tomorrow morning, which she had planned for sunrise at the Griffith Observatory.

"I'm ready, but I'm having doubts about the bride. Today, she alternated between screaming at everyone and lying down with her head in her mother's lap. But I don't have that much experience with weddings, or even with healthy marriages. Maybe that's normal?"

Lana sipped her wine and giggled. "Beats me."

While Lana's parents were still together, they weren't exactly models of the ideal marriage. They didn't fight, but they still didn't respect each other. Instead, they made snide comments behind one another's backs. By the time Lana was in law school, they lived mostly separate lives. They'd both been great parents individually, for her and for Aurora, once they'd gained legal guardianship over the younger girl. But spending time with Lana's mom and dad together was a pretty miserable experience.

And Aurora's parents hadn't fared well, though in different ways. Once again, they'd stayed married. But probably only because they gave up their daughter to get by.

So, neither she nor Aurora had the best examples growing up. But at least Aurora had Devon now. For Lana, it was reassuring to know that her friend, and younger sister in all but name, had found a soft place to land.

Once Aurora had reached high school, Lana had realized her friend didn't need a mother hen. She didn't even need a big sister, exactly. Instead, she needed a confidante. Someone she could talk to about everything that was really going on in her life.

Despite their age difference, they quickly became best friends. Aurora was hilarious, always coming up with new ways to make Lana laugh. She wore her heart on her sleeve, which Lana admired, because she'd never been able to do that with anyone but Aurora herself.

Lana had missed Aurora when the younger woman went off to college in St. Louis. But Lana understood. Aurora hadn't really left *her*. She'd needed distance from her family's troubles and her brother's intense presence, once he'd left the military.

But now Aurora was back, and Lana's days had become

much brighter. Definitely. She and Aurora had still talked all the time when they'd lived in different states, but now they got together whenever they wanted.

Part of her even considered jumping back into the car and driving to Los Angeles right now, just to share this night with her friend instead of sitting alone with her fishbowl of wine. But surely Aurora would need to go to bed early to prep for her morning. She had her own responsibilities to think about.

My girl's all grown up.

"You're doing some serious brooding over there," Aurora said. "Sure you don't want to tell me what's wrong?"

Lana took a gulp of wine. "Remember that trial I was telling you about? The one that's coming up?"

"That terrible murder from back in the nineties? Yeah, of course. Did something happen in the case?"

Lana lay down on the couch, pulling a pillow under her head. "The defense attorney is at it again. He filed this ridiculous motion, and the judge made me go through an entire hearing about it today. Probably because opposing counsel is this big-shot L.A. lawyer, so of course people automatically take him seriously. Meanwhile, his entire purpose was to humiliate me publicly, not to mention try to slut shame me. And why not? I'm a woman litigator. That's what I should expect, right?"

She couldn't keep the bitterness out of her tone. She hated that Wayfair had rattled her so much.

"Lana, I am so sorry. That's horrible. It's disgusting that he can get away with it."

"And Max was there to witness it all. You can see why my day sucked." She lifted onto her elbow and took another large sip of wine. Her stomach was empty, so the alcohol was going straight to her head.

"Max?" Aurora's nose wrinkled. "Oh, because he investigated the case. I remember. But how on earth was that lawyer slut shaming you? What was this hearing even about?"

Lana blinked her eyes closed, cursing herself for not holding back some of those details. Of course Aurora was asking. It was only natural.

She should probably tell Aurora the rest, anyway. Even though she didn't want to. The hearing was public record, so it might get back to Aurora eventually.

Lana sat up. "So, I guess I've been keeping something from you. It involves Max. And me."

"Okay." Aurora leaned forward toward the camera. "This is getting weird."

You have no idea, Lana thought.

"Way back when Max was in the army and I was in college… We slept together."

Aurora squeezed her eyes shut, then opened them again. "You *what*? You and Max? Was this like a drunken incident or something? You slipped and fell onto his crotch?"

"Nobody was drunk. Or slipped. And it was…more than once."

"*More* than once?" She covered her face. "This is like when I first realized that my parents had sex."

Actually, Aurora could've drawn a worse comparison. Parents were supposed to have sex, after all.

"I mean, did you *like it*?" Aurora cringed, squinting.

"I don't think you want me to answer that question."

"You totally liked it! This is Max we're talking about? My brother Max?"

"That's the one."

"As his sister, I'm horrified at the very idea he's ever had sex. Especially with you. But as your best friend, I guess I'm… vaguely high-fiving you? In a very non-specific, generalized kind of way."

Lana figured she shouldn't add details, like the fact that Max had taken her virginity.

"You're not mad, though?" Lana asked.

Aurora made a face. "Of course not. Unlike my brother,

I understand that some things are not my business. And I definitely get why you didn't tell me this before. Because I didn't want to know. Maybe we can just pretend that I still don't?"

"That, I can do. Happily."

Aurora's expression changed again, as if a new idea had just occurred to her. An idea that frightened her. "Wait, you don't think it'll happen ever again, do you?"

Lana barked out a nervous laugh. "Not a chance."

"Thank god." Aurora shook her head, blonde hair falling across her cheek. "Unbelievable. All those times he scared off my boyfriends senior year of high school, and meanwhile, he'd already screwed my best friend? Talk about a hypocrite." Then Aurora's eyes bulged again. "Max wasn't a jerk to you, was he? Do he and I need to have words?"

"No, not at all. It was ten years ago. It's fine." There was a limit to how much Lana needed to share. No way was she confessing her decade-long flame for Aurora's brother.

"Is it awkward, though? Having a history with him? I thought you guys spent so much time together all these years. You know, for work and stuff."

"It didn't used to be awkward. We just acted like it never happened." At least he did, and she pretended that it didn't hurt. "But this hearing in the Hearst case has brought it all to the surface. Maybe it's for the best. We can put it behind us and be friends now." That's what Max seemed to want.

"But I thought that you *were* friends."

"There are friends who get along well enough to hang out occasionally in groups or work together on a project. And then there are real friends. Like you and me."

"And you're saying that you and Max are the first kind?"

"Exactly."

"Do you *want* to be real friends with him? He's my brother, so I'm kind of stuck with him. But you don't have to be nice to him on my account."

Lana got up, walking aimlessly across for living room. "Honestly? I don't know."

She'd thought that she knew how to handle her feelings for Max. She'd worked out a way to have him around without letting it get to her too much.

But could she finally put the past in its place and have a legitimate friendship with him? Was it even worth a try?

She was so confused.

"You can think about it," Aurora said. "If this fling of yours happened ten years ago, then you don't have to figure it all out tonight."

"You're right. Look how wise and mature you are."

Aurora smiled, her eyes twinkling. "I know, I'm impressive, aren't I? I should have a podcast or something. 'Love Lessons, with Aurora Bennett.'"

They got off the phone so that Aurora could get to bed, and Lana wolfed down some cheese slices to help absorb the alcohol in her stomach. She set her wine glass in the sink and wandered into her bedroom.

Lana unzipped her dress and let it fall to the floor.

And just like that, she was thinking of Max again. Not about her conflicted feelings or their years of awkward, almost-friendship.

No, her mind had gone back to the well-worn memories of their first night together. Regardless of how she felt about him otherwise—infatuated or infuriated—the searing after-image of their naked, tangled bodies had never ceased to turn her on.

Lana put on an oversized T-shirt and slipped beneath her covers. She pushed her underwear aside, pretending that her fingers were Max's. He'd made her come so easily, probably because he'd been with a lot of other women before. And since.

With no warning, her body went dry. Damn it.

She couldn't even have a proper fantasy about him anymore without it getting over-complicated.

Lana rolled over, burying her face in her pillow. "I'm such a mess."

Her home phone rang, breaking the silence of her townhouse. The landline that her mother insisted she keep, though hardly anyone ever called that number except the gas company or telemarketers. And it was way too late for either.

Immediately, acid surged in her belly.

The ringing seemed to go on and on. She stared at the handset on her nightstand.

The caller ID said, *UNKNOWN NUMBER*.

Finally, the ringing stopped. But then it immediately started up again.

Furious, she threw the covers aside and jumped out of bed. She grabbed the cordless handset and lifted it to her ear.

She didn't say a word. But the other person breathed heavily into the phone.

He knew she was there.

And unlike the last time, she couldn't find the words to tell him off. An invisible fist had closed around her throat, her lungs not moving.

Then, a voice spoke in a harsh whisper.

"I know you're in your bedroom. Alone. I'm *always* watching. And when I'm ready, I'm going to make you mine."

She spun around, eyes going to the window. The curtain was closed. But she still had the awful, sick feeling that the man was right outside. Looking in.

"Sleep tight, Lana. I'll be with you soon."

The phone dropped onto the carpet at her feet. She backed away from it like it was a bomb.

Who the hell was he? What did he want?

His voice answered in her memory. *I'm going to make you mine.*

She ran into the living room, desperate to find someplace

to escape. To feel safe. But everywhere she saw windows. Everywhere, she was exposed.

He could be right outside her door, even now. Waiting for her.

Watching.

Chapter Nine

*M*ax gently squeezed the trigger of his vintage Colt .45. A third bullet hole appeared at the center of his target, spaced closely together with the others. It was important to use a subtle touch. The Colt was high maintenance. You couldn't manhandle a gun like this and expect it to do what you wanted.

It was the same kind of touch he used with women. Careful, attentive, until they started shaking. Few things gave him more satisfaction than a job well done.

Max glanced over at Devon Whitestone, who was in the stall beside him. Devon waved to show he was finished, too. Max pulled off his ear protectors and his plastic glasses. They both walked over to the counter to clean their weapons. The Colt especially needed extra care.

"Nice shooting out there, sir," Devon said.

"I know. But you don't have to call me 'sir' anymore."

Devon grinned. "Pretty sure I do."

Devon had been dating Max's sister for several months. At first, Max had not been happy about it. But now, he admitted he'd been unfair to the guy. He'd assumed that Devon would be just as much of a bastard about women as Max was himself.

But Devon was a family man, unlike him. Devon seemed to be made for settling down and making commitments. Most importantly, he was devoted to Aurora, even though Max still thought the two of them had leaped into a relationship too fast. But Aurora was happier than he'd ever seen her, so Max couldn't argue with that.

Devon was also a bodyguard for his company, and he was a great asset to Max's team. The two of them weren't totally comfortable socially just yet, but they were getting there. If Devon kept being good to Aurora, then Max had no doubt that he and the other man would become genuine friends. Max could use a few more of those.

But Devon had the right idea. They weren't on that level just yet.

Tonight, Aurora was spending the night in Los Angeles for work, so Devon had volunteered to take an evening shift. But the office was quiet, so they'd gotten in some time at the practice range on the lower level of the building.

They walked across the parking area to the elevators. Other practical features were down here, too, including a vault with all their weaponry, an infirmary suite with an on-call doctor, and the gym.

They took the elevator to the main floor. The only other person working here so late was Sylvie.

Max walked over to her. "Do you have an update for me on that matter we talked about? The phone call?"

"The phone call that you definitely did not tell me to trace, because we don't have permission? Yep. It was a burner. I got the serial number but haven't been able to follow the trail further. Maybe something will come up. I've put feelers out."

"Thanks. I appreciate it."

Devon came up behind them. "Working on a new case?"

"Nothing important."

Sylvie raised her eyebrows, but she didn't say anything. Max didn't want to tell Devon about Lana's mysterious "prank" call at her office because he didn't want to put Devon in the position of keeping anything from Aurora.

And if Aurora found out, there was absolutely no doubt she would go immediately to Lana. Both because she was concerned, and because Aurora had never held back from picking fights with her older brother. She thought he was nosy, and she was probably right. Yet that wasn't going to stop him from trying to look out for the people he cared about.

He did care about Lana. More than he should.

His cell phone rang in his pocket, and Lana's name appeared on the screen, like he had summoned her.

Maybe she'd heard back from the judge about a ruling on the hearing. He knew better than to think this was a friendly hello. "Hey, what's up?"

"Max, I need help." The panic in her voice sent his heart instantly into his throat.

∼

"I'M PULLING UP NOW," he said to Lana over the phone. "I'll look around, then I'll come to your door, okay? Don't answer till you see me."

Max parked a few houses down from Lana's. He and Devon jumped out, and Max drew his M9 from his shoulder holster.

"You take the east side," he told Devon.

They made a quick perimeter around her block of town-homes. Max's pulse was racing.

There's a man. He said he was watching me. I'm afraid he's outside.

She'd sounded so terrified on the phone, and he wanted to make someone pay for doing that to her. But the place was deserted. The only sign of life was a cat that leaped away when it saw him coming.

He and Devon met up at the front. Max tucked his weapon back into the holster and rang her doorbell. Lana opened it, dressed in just an oversized T-shirt, her legs bare underneath.

"Max." She launched into his arms. He grasped her tightly against him. Her whole body was shaking.

Max realized this was the first time he'd held her like this in over ten years. That long. Yet it felt completely natural. So right.

"Devon," she said, seeing the other man. "You're here, too?"

"I was there when Max got your call."

"What exactly happened?" Max asked. She'd told him in rough terms, but they'd rushed over here without waiting for a full explanation. It hadn't taken more than five minutes for him and Devon to speed their way over to her place. Luckily, there was no traffic this late at night, and she didn't live far.

"There was a phone call. It scared me. But maybe I over-reacted."

Max nodded at his employee. "I'll check things inside, but I think we're good. You can head back to the office."

"No problem, sir. Let me know if you need a ride later."

Max drew Lana inside and shut the door behind them.

She recounted what the voice had said on the phone. Max's blood heated with rage. He wanted to run the bastard down and grab him by the throat.

"Do you have any idea who it was?"

She shook her head. "I didn't recognize the voice, but it was kind of harsh. Like maybe he was trying to disguise it. And then I just had this feeling that he was watching me. That he was close. I freaked."

"Why didn't you call the police?"

"I thought you'd get here faster."

He had to admit, she had a point there.

Lana stepped back from him, restoring the usual distance between them. "But if I'm inconveniencing you, I'll call the police instead next time."

Next time? He didn't like thinking of a next time. "That's not what I meant. It's no inconvenience. I'm happy to be here. But if you're in trouble, I want myself, Devon, West Oaks P.D., *and* the National Guard showing up to help you."

She shrugged, hugging her arms around herself. "I'm grateful that you're here. Thanks."

"You don't have to thank me. I'm just glad you're okay." *Let's make sure you stay that way*, he added silently, though he didn't want to frighten her more right now.

He was thinking of the "prank call" at her office the other day. And now this.

"Shall I take a look around? Just in case?"

They walked through the house, checking doors and windows to make sure everything was secure. Nothing looked like it had been tampered with.

So, this is where Lana lives, he thought. Max had never been here before. There was a casual elegance to the place, though so much of it felt empty. Like maybe she'd had plans to decorate the various rooms but had lacked the time to devote to the project.

Max didn't have time for decorating either, so he'd just hired an interior designer. Another one of his three-time conquests, actually. Though now, walking beside Lana through her house, he felt guilty even remembering that other woman. She couldn't compare to Lana, anyway. No one could.

They approached a bedroom. "Hold on. That's my room. I need to straighten up."

"But shouldn't I check it out first?"

"I'll take my chances." She threw a smirk over her shoulder and went inside, closing the door on his view of the room.

What was she worried about, that he'd see her underwear lying around? Were they really such strangers now?

Then he answered his own question. Of course they were when it came to intimacy. He'd known Lana for fifteen years, but he'd only been close to her for a tiny percentage of that time.

She opened the door again, emerging with a pair of leggings underneath her tee. Max was disappointed to see the extra clothing. He'd been admiring her slender, toned legs.

"Ready for me?" he asked.

A flash of something like heat passed across her face. "Whatever."

Max went into her bedroom. The covers were pulled loosely up on her bed. He glanced around behind the curtains, entered the closet. It was strange, being on the inside of Lana's life this way. This was the space where she slept, where she got dressed. This was where she hid away from the world and kept everything that she didn't want anyone else to see.

But he wanted to see it. He wanted that far more than he should.

They went back into the kitchen. Lana had a wine glass in the sink, which she grabbed and filled from a bottle in the fridge. "Want some?"

"No, thanks. I'm good." Max didn't drink often. He didn't like dulling his senses.

He sat at a stool at the counter, watching her. "Lana, is someone stalking you?"

She was still turned away from him, but he saw the muscles in her shoulders tighten. "I really don't think so. Maybe it was just…"

He could almost see the wheels turning in her head. "A prank call?"

She sighed, turning around. Her hands rested behind her on the counter, her back arching and her breasts pushing forward.

Shit. She wasn't wearing a bra.

He struggled to keep his eyes on her face, and then gave up. He let himself glance quickly at her curves. Now that he was seeing past the usual walls that Lana kept against the world—seeing her unguarded—he didn't want to miss any of it. Because he knew those barriers would soon go right back up.

But when his gaze returned to her face, her eyes were narrowed. "Enjoying the view?"

She was daring him to say yes. Normally, he would've had no problem admitting it. *Yes, I'm a dick. Big surprise.* But that was a distraction, and he wasn't going to let her wiggle out of this conversation.

"Did the same guy call your office the other day? The person you were yelling at?"

She slumped. "Maybe. He only breathed then. But... I'm pretty sure it was him."

Outrage made the hairs on his arms raise. "I'm sorry this happened, L. I swear, I'm going to find the guy who did this to you."

She downed her wine in one gulp. "And do what? Rain down vengeance for a few gross, creepy comments? Maybe I'm too sensitive. I shouldn't have bothered you."

"You didn't overreact. This is serious."

"But I *can't deal with it.*" She covered her eyes with her hand, turning around. Max got up and went over to her. He put a hand on her shoulder. Lana shrugged it away.

"I wish you would go."

That stung. But he knew that she was just upset. Type A

people didn't deal well with feeling vulnerable. Max knew that firsthand. "Then why did you call me?" he asked gently.

"I don't know. I just did. I shouldn't have."

"I think it's because you trust me. And you can, L. You can trust me to keep you safe."

Even if she shouldn't trust him with anything else. Like her heart.

Chapter Ten

*L*ana hadn't been thinking when she'd called Max's number. She'd just known that he would believe her. He would know what to do.

But having him in her house right now was overwhelming. She felt exposed and vulnerable all over again. Lana wanted to curl up and disappear where nobody could find her. Not even Max.

Especially Max.

She'd been surprised to see interest in his eyes while they'd been standing here in the kitchen. Maybe his claim that they were "practically family" wasn't so accurate. But right now, she couldn't deal with navigating their complicated history or her feelings for him.

She *did* trust him to keep her safe. Regardless of anything else, good or bad, that she felt for him.

"I trust you," she murmured.

"Then let's go sit down and talk this through. Make a game plan. We could even create a bullet list if you want."

She almost smiled. "I do love a nice bullet list. With sub-headings."

They settled on the couch, leaving a couple of feet of

space between them. Lana thought of that long ago night they'd sat on a couch, watching a movie…

But then she pushed the memory out of her head. The past was over now. She had to focus on the present.

"Have there been any other incidents like this?" Max asked.

"A few other phone calls. It started about a month ago. Recently, I thought maybe Paxton Wayfair was behind it. Like he was playing some sort of mind game that he thought would benefit him in the Hearst case. But this, tonight? I think that was too far, even for Wayfair."

"But no one has approached you in person? You haven't seen any strange guys or cars driving by your house?"

She shook her head. "Not that I've noticed."

Max's expression was stern. "I don't want to scare you. But here's what concerns me. Tonight was an escalation. That suggests his original phone calls weren't enough for him anymore. Soon, he might try to approach you."

"Okay," she said, her voice shaky. What did that mean? What was she supposed to do?

"I'm going to text Sylvie to see if she can trace the call." He grabbed his phone and started typing.

"She can do that? The caller ID said unknown."

"Sylvie has contacts at the phone company. She's pretty good with this sort of thing." He glanced up, hesitating, like there was something else he wanted to say. "But if it turns out to be a burner phone, that won't help us identify the guy. Unless we can find out where he bought it, or if he's using that phone enough that we can track his location."

"Wouldn't you need a warrant for something like that?" Lana had tried cases using evidence from cell phone towers to prove a defendant's whereabouts during the commission of a crime. She'd also gotten wiretaps on a burner—with a warrant. But that wasn't the kind of information just anyone could access.

"Like I said, Sylvie's pretty good with this kind of thing. Let's just give her a chance to work. The fewer questions you ask about what she's doing, the better."

"Okay. I get it." Lana didn't want to break any laws that could undermine a case against the guy later on, but identifying and stopping him was a higher priority. Just so long as she wasn't directly involved.

Max finished typing and set the phone face down on the coffee table. "I'd also like to install one of my security systems here. Some cameras outside, too, if you're okay with it."

"How much is that going to cost?"

He waved the question away. "Don't worry about cost. I've got it. But there's something else you need to do. Report this to the police. So they can open a file and do their own investigation. Unfortunately, a stalker case like this one, without a clear suspect, isn't going to get a lot of attention from them. But you're a district attorney, so that alone should pull some weight in their eyes. They'll at least give it a look. And if anything else happens, they'll hopefully be quick to respond. Like I said earlier, I want as many different people watching out for you as possible."

She already knew all that he was saying. But this was surreal. Lana had been in the DA's office for five years, ever since graduating law school at just twenty-four. She'd prosecuted some very nasty people. Yet she'd never experienced anything like this before. There'd been a few threatening letters from guys she'd put in prison, but those came to her office and got intercepted by the mail room before she even received them. Those attempts at intimidation had been sloppy, obvious even from the envelopes.

This guy was different. He was…insidious.

"Does that sound like a plan?" Max asked. "I can write it down in bullet list form if you want."

Now, she smiled for real. "No. It's a good plan, thank you. I really appreciate this." It was a relief to know what to do.

Whenever she had a major problem, it always seemed less monumental once she'd decided on her next step.

Max reached for her hand, crossing that gulf of space between them. His fingertips brushed her knuckles.

"Is this okay?" he asked, low and husky.

For just a second, Lana was back in her parents' house ten years ago. That same thrill of eager anticipation flared in her chest.

"Yes." Her eyes were intent on his. His pupils dilated, and she was sure he was remembering the same thing.

Then she blinked, and the impression was gone.

Max held her hand, but there was nothing sexual about the gesture. Just kindness and concern.

She liked this. Having Max here as a friend. He was a good man. The kind of person who gave his time and spent his hard-earned money to help other people. Just like he had tracked down the evidence against Ryan Hearst and was going to be the star witness who would bring that murderer to justice.

She did want Max in her life.

The old hurt was still there, the disappointment. But wasn't it time to let that go?

"You said before that we could be friends. We could talk to one another about more than just work and Aurora. Does that offer still stand?"

His thumb moved absently against the back of her hand. "Of course."

"Then I'd like to accept."

He nodded, his expression softening further. "I'm glad to hear that."

"What should we talk about?"

"Right now?"

Lana lay her head on the top of the couch cushion. Her eyes suddenly felt unbearably heavy. "Give me something else to think about. Tell me…why you started your company."

Max sank down into the couch cushions, getting comfortable. But his hand stayed tight around hers. "Well, I had the idea while I was still in the army. I worked with so many inspiring people, but there were a lot of things that frustrated me. I was always proud to serve, but I got tired of only following orders. Never getting to decide things for myself. And I didn't think a position as general was going to be in my future, nor did I even desire a role like that. I didn't want power. Just a way to prove that I was more than my family history suggested I could be."

He didn't elaborate, but Lana understood. While he'd been overseas, his parents and Aurora had been homeless for a time. Even before that, Lana got the sense that home life had been unstable for them.

"And I wanted to provide more for Aurora than I'd been able to before," Max went on in his even, reassuring tone. "Oops. I forgot we weren't supposed to talk about her right now."

Lana smiled, eyes closing. She was starting to drift. "That's okay. Just keep talking."

His other hand now drew circles on the inside of her wrist.

"A former commanding officer gave me a loan to help me get started. I've always been grateful, so I've tried to help other people when they leave the service. Guys like Devon. They've done well by me, so far."

"But what's the goal?" she said sleepily. "Where do you see yourself in five years?"

He huffed a small laugh. "Very funny. I've been asking that question way too much during job interviews lately. What about you? You must've wanted to be a lawyer since you left the womb."

She was tired, but not too tired to notice that he'd completely avoided her question.

"Almost." When she and Max had met, way back when she was just a fourteen-year-old babysitter, she'd already known that she was heading for law school. "My uncle was a prosecutor."

"I didn't know that."

"There's plenty you don't know about me, Bennett. But my uncle really inspired me with his philosophy about serving his community. I wanted to do the same thing. Help the vulnerable, be strong for the victims. I liked that I could help people by using my smarts."

His fingers had stopped moving on her arm while she spoke. Like he was listening closely. "Mental strength, instead of physical. But still strong."

"Right." She yawned. "Plus, I was obsessed with *Law & Order*. My parents had no idea I watched so much of it."

He was chuckling, his fingers resuming their hypnotic circles on her skin.

"I must've watched every episode by the time…" She trailed off, losing track of her words. She couldn't keep going, couldn't even open her eyes.

A soft touch brushed her hair away from her face.

"You can rest now," he whispered. "I'm right here."

Max was here beside her. She had to be dreaming already. So, she stopped fighting and let sleep take her.

Ten Years Ago

*L*ana woke to someone poking her in the side. She opened her eyes. Aurora's face was a few inches away from hers.

"Finally, you're awake! Do you think Max is up yet? Can we go check?"

Lana groaned, dragging her pillow over her head. "I'm tired. Go check yourself."

"But if he's still asleep and he's annoyed that I wake him, I want him to blame you, instead of me."

Lana nudged the girl away with her foot. Not quite a kick, but almost. "Aurora, go!"

She grumbled. "Fine."

But as soon as Aurora left the bed, the memories of last night flooded into Lana's mind. Max's relentless kisses. How he'd felt on top of her. Inside of her.

Oh my god. That happened.

She shot upright. She was sore between her legs, but it wasn't too bad. Mostly she felt warm and gooey and satisfied. She wasn't a virgin anymore.

I had sex.

I had sex with Max Bennett.

But he was sleeping on the living room couch right now. She'd have to face him. How was she supposed to act now?

She'd only thought about getting him into bed, not about the morning after.

She hurried to get dressed, then snuck into the bathroom to brush her teeth. When Lana came out into the living room, she found Aurora on the couch watching TV.

Max was in the kitchen, standing over the stove.

"You're making breakfast?" Lana asked.

"Trying. I'm making pancakes. But there's a certain someone who is supposed to be helping me, if she could drag her face away from the television for a minute or two." He sent an amused glance toward the couch, where Aurora was pretending not to have heard him. "One minute, Rory's excited to see me. Then it's, 'Max, make me pancakes.' I see how it is."

Lana walked into the kitchen, acting casual. Last night, Max had said he would go back to just being Aurora's brother. Nothing more. She'd accepted that. But what did that mean, exactly? Was she not supposed to stare at his body, while visions of everything they'd done last night danced through her head? Because that was so happening right now.

Max smiled at her. "I guess you'll just have to be my assistant instead. Could you grab the eggs?"

She set the carton on the counter beside him.

"You can come a little closer," he murmured. "Promise I won't bite."

They were out of sight of Aurora in the living room. Lana slid over by a couple inches, till she could feel the warmth radiating from him.

"How are you feeling?" His voice had dipped even lower.

"I'm good. Really good."

"So, you had fun last night?" He almost sounded nervous.

He looked over, and Lana found her confidence.

"*Yes*, Max."

He reached over and put his arm around her waist, pulling her in. Lust immediately lit up Lana's entire body. This was Max going back to normal? Did he not remember how they used to be? He'd always been kind to her. But he'd certainly never touched her. Not like this, so casually. Like his hands belonged on her.

Swiftly, Max leaned over to kiss her neck before going back to stirring the salt into the flour.

They stopped talking and made the pancakes. But she kept feeling his gaze on her. And she watched him, too. Every time one of them caught the other looking, they smiled like they had a secret. Because they did. She didn't quite understand what he expected of her, but she liked whatever they were doing right now.

Aurora finally got off the couch when it was time to eat. She shoved blueberry pancakes into her mouth. "Max promised to take me to the beach. Do you want to come too, Lana?"

"Don't you and your bro need some alone time?" Usually when Max visited, he and Aurora went on their adventures solo. Which made sense. The two siblings almost never got to see one another.

"You should come." Max's toes nudged hers beneath the table.

"Then I will." She nudged back. Max set his heavy, sock-clad foot over hers.

As they got their bathing suits on and packed up to go, Lana tried to analyze everything he'd said, both yesterday and this morning. Max said that he couldn't be her boyfriend. That he'd go back to being just Aurora's brother.

But he'd used the words, "when this is finished."

She'd assumed he meant after *last night* was finished. But those words had been ambiguous. Open to interpretation. That was the reasoning that judges used sometimes, right? Words didn't always have a single clear meaning.

Max was in town for two more days.

And her parents wouldn't be returning until the day that Max was scheduled to leave. That realization made her heart leap and every inch of her come alive with anticipation.

Maybe Max still wanted her. Maybe he wanted them to enjoy each other as much as they could, while they had the chance.

If that was what he had in mind, then she was definitely on board.

～

AT THE BEACH, Max and Aurora horsed around in the surf while Lana stretched out her legs on her beach towel. She liked seeing Max like this, laughing and carefree. So often, he was worrying about his sister and feeling guilty that he couldn't be with her more.

Lana rarely got to witness these moments between brother and sister, when they let go of everything else and just had fun. Aurora deserved that. And so did Max.

Well, Max had seemed to have fun last night, too. Lana's chest swelled with pride that she'd made him feel good. Maybe she'd given him almost as much pleasure as he'd given her.

After a while, Aurora and Max returned to the blanket, water dripping from their skin. Lana tried not to let her gaze linger too much on Max in case Aurora might notice.

"Max and I are going to get ice cream," Aurora said. "Come on."

"Oh, I don't need any. I'll stay here."

Max's eyebrows drew down. "You sure? You okay?"

Lana knew that his question held a deeper meaning than just an interest in dessert. She smiled back at him.

"I'm having a great day. I'm going to keep enjoying the sun."

She wanted to let the siblings have more time to themselves. But she'd been telling the truth. She really was having a great time just *being* today. Just existing. Lana couldn't remember ever feeling so content. She had her memories of last night, and she had more of Max to look forward to. How could she complain?

That contentedness lasted until she heard a voice behind her. "You all alone, baby? Why don't you come and join me."

She sat up, looking back. There was a guy standing there, probably in his forties. Old enough to be her father. And he was staring at her body with undisguised relish. He held up a beer can. "I'm happy to share."

Lana grabbed a towel and wrapped it around her shoulders. "No thanks," she said stiffly.

She heard his feet in the sand, coming closer. "The beer's cold. Don't you want to cool down? You must be all hot from the sun. You sure *look* hot, baby."

She turned and stared straight at him. "I don't want to. You can leave."

The guy traipsed away, muttering about her being a bitch. But he'd taken her good mood with him.

Lana focused on the water, remembering something she'd seen on the news. A teenage girl from West Oaks had been murdered years ago, her body dumped on a beach. Heather Barnes.

Stuff like that didn't happen much in their town. But rarely wasn't the same as never.

And Heather's killer hadn't been caught. The thought made Lana so angry. She couldn't wait until she was older and could prosecute rapists and murderers, anybody who went after people who were weaker. Maybe creeps would still stare at her in her bikini, but Lana wouldn't feel so powerless.

"Was that guy bothering you?"

Max and Aurora had just returned. Aurora was licking her ice cream cone with a confused expression. But Max looked furious. "He was, wasn't he? I'm going to say something." He took a step in the retreating man's direction, going after him.

"No." Lana put on a smile and started gathering her things. "Should we go to the boardwalk next?"

Aurora loved playing the games over there. She shouted yes. But Max was still eyeing Lana with concern.

BACK AT THE HOUSE, Max found Lana doing dishes in the kitchen. Aurora was in the bathroom, taking a shower.

He rested his hip against the counter, his body facing her. "Are you really okay? I'm sorry that jerk at the beach was bugging you."

She felt embarrassed that Max had seen. As if somehow, Lana had invited the guy's attention. "It was nothing, really."

"You obviously handled him well enough yourself. Just wanted to check on you."

"Thanks."

"Hey. Look at me." She did. Max held her chin. "I'd really like to kiss you."

"Yes," she whispered, instantly out of breath.

His lips slowly met hers. He wasn't fast and needy, like last night. This kiss was careful. Intimate. Like she was something special, and he wanted to savor her.

Then he took the scrubber out of her hands. "How about I finish these, and you go relax. Army grunts get antsy without something useful to do."

She knew he wasn't a 'grunt,' that he was just trying to be self-deprecating and make her smile. And it worked.

Lana went to the kitchen table and flipped through a magazine, though her focus remained on the man scrubbing plates at the sink. She reminded herself that he would only be here for a couple more days. Less than that now. If she wasn't careful, she was going to end up having real feelings for him, though she'd promised that she wouldn't.

But even as she had these thoughts, she knew that reasoning with herself was hopeless. Max was the kind of guy who didn't come along very often. Just as sweet as he was sexy. And he was so very sexy.

How could any woman not fall for him?

Chapter Eleven

By the time Lana woke up on her couch, Max had already made himself at home in the kitchen. She padded in, looking groggy.

He nodded at the coffee maker. "Just finished brewing."

"I figured. The smell woke me up. I didn't think you'd still be here."

He hadn't really meant to stay. But he wanted to make sure Lana was all right. Actually, he'd wanted to lift her up and carry her to her bedroom so she'd be more comfortable, but he'd thought that might be too forward, considering their history. And then he'd fallen asleep right beside her on the couch.

They were friends now, and he was glad for that. Her acceptance of his overture made him happier than he'd anticipated. But they were still trying to navigate this new closeness, and he didn't want to mess it up before it even got started.

Not that anything was necessarily "getting started." That wasn't the way people usually talked about friends, right?

And they definitely didn't sneak glances at their friend's ass as she poured her coffee, as he was doing now.

He sprinkled cinnamon into a dish of softened butter. "I

wanted to make pancakes. But you didn't have eggs. Or flour. Or sugar. So, I had to make do."

"Pancakes, Max? Really?"

Okay, so the last time he'd made pancakes for her, they'd fucked the night before. And Lana clearly didn't want any reminders of that.

But who didn't like pancakes?

Max spread cinnamon-butter onto a piece of toast and handed it to her. It was the best he could come up with, given her pathetic supplies. He'd have to send over a grocery delivery later.

"Thank you for staying with me last night," she said.

"You're welcome. Any time. I used your mouthwash, by the way. Hope that's cool."

She bit into the toast. "Is that a veiled request that I brush my teeth?"

He laughed. "I was trying to be subtle about it." Actually, she smelled great. Like lilacs and fresh-cut grass and sunshine. Like *Lana*. His cock stirred, ever hopeful.

Not happening, buddy. You've been there, done that.

The rule of three was there for her protection, more than his. Her friendship would have to be enough. And it would be. He was thrilled to be with her right now, cooking and sharing jokes. He was honored that she'd finally opened up to him again, even though he hated the circumstances that had led to this moment.

"Sylvie's working on that trace. Do you want me to drive you to the police station?"

She set the toast down, dusting off her fingers. "Nah, I've got it. In fact, I should check my messages. Usually, I'm at work by now. I'm surprised how long I slept."

Usually, Max was at the office by now, too. But he was in no hurry to get going. He'd been texting with his team to make sure they were having a productive morning. Though some more texts had come in, and he hadn't had the time—or inclination—to check them yet.

Lana grabbed her phone from her bedroom and rejoined him in the kitchen. "Shit. The judge issued her ruling."

"Is it bad?"

"I'm opening it."

She dropped onto the couch, and he sat beside her. Lana's knee bounced up and down, so he set his hand on top of it.

She exhaled. "Vaughn ruled in our favor. Thank god. I figured she would, but sometimes judges do crazy things, you know?"

"Can I see?"

Lana tipped the screen so he could read the ruling.

Ms. Marchetti's prior relationship with Mr. Bennett does not suggest improper bias alone, and the defense does not present any convincing evidence to the contrary. The court makes no findings as to whether a current intimate relationship between a prosecutor and an investigative witness would be grounds for defendant's requested relief. In any case, the witness disclaimed any such current relationship with Ms. Marchetti.

It was strange to see someone writing about their "prior relationship" in such impersonal terms. Especially when he and Lana hadn't spoken about it in ten years and could barely even discuss the subject now. But here it was in a public court filing.

He wasn't embarrassed. But he never would've made their private business public. He respected her far more than that.

"So, this is a fancy way of saying Wayfair's arguments were bullshit?" Max asked.

"Pretty much. The judge decided to be wishy-washy about it, instead of just outright saying that his motion was frivolous. It's like she doesn't want to make him look bad. Wish she could extend me the same courtesy, instead of suggesting that it was a close call."

Max squeezed her shoulder. Friends touched. It was fine, wasn't it? Basically innocent. "But you won. Congrats."

"Now I need to get back to trial prep. I've lost two days to this nonsense, and I—" Her phone rang in her hands. "It's Wayfair."

She answered, standing up. Max got up with her, wanting to keep her close while she talked to that sleazy asswipe.

"I guess you've won this round," the lawyer said, speaking loudly enough that Max could hear him through Lana's phone. "But rest assured, I'm not going to stay quiet about your connections to Max Bennett. When I'm finished, it won't even matter if you win the case against my client. All of Southern California is going to know that you're a corrupt prosecutor who can't keep her legs closed."

Lana's face was turning crimson. She didn't even seem to be breathing.

Max's fingers twitched. *Don't do it*, he thought. *Leave it be.* But he couldn't stop himself. He snatched the phone out of her hands.

"Wayfair, you piece of shit. Listen closely. If you ever speak to Lana that way again, I'm going to come down to your office, rip out your tongue, and shove it up your ass. I doubt that Judge Vaughn will even notice the difference."

Lana's eyes bulged. She grabbed the phone back and held it to her ear, walking across the room. "Paxton, I apologize. Please disregard that because it didn't come from me. No, I'm not. I'll speak to you later. Yes. About the upcoming trial, nothing else. I need to get back to work. *Fine.*"

She dropped the phone to her side, her eyelids sinking closed. "Max, what the *hell* is wrong with you?"

A lot of things? "I'm sorry, I know you can handle him yourself. But I couldn't stand here and let him talk to you like that."

"I have trouble keeping my temper with Wayfair too, but *threatening* him? And you brought the judge into it? I cannot believe you. We'll be lucky if he doesn't file a new motion. He was probably recording every word!"

Max made a skeptical face. "Even if he did, he's not going to tell anybody. He won't want anyone to know what he said to you. And I'll bet he's ready to piss himself right now, since he knows that I heard him. A coward like that would only say those things to a woman on her own."

Her eyes narrowed, and she slowly turned to face him. "So, you *don't* actually think I can handle it. I called you last night, so I *must* need a big strong man around to scare away every bad guy. Because Lord knows I can't do it myself. Right?"

He rubbed the back of his neck. He'd really done it now. "That's not what I meant. It came out wrong."

"I'm pretty sure you said exactly what you intended, since you usually do. I'd like you to leave now. I have a lot of work to do, plus licking Wayfair's boots so that he'll hopefully forget about this."

"Lana—"

"No. I don't want you here, Max. I don't want your help. Just leave."

She stormed out of the room and slammed her bedroom door. So much for the progress they'd made.

But she'd been completely clear about her wishes, and Max had never forced his presence on a woman when it wasn't welcome. He wasn't about to start now.

He grabbed his things, requested a rideshare on his phone, and left.

～

MAX STALKED across the Bennett Security workroom, ignoring the curious glances of his employees.

"Boss," Sylvie said, hurrying after him. "I need you to—"

"Not now." He couldn't deal with anyone else right now. Otherwise, he was going to yell, and none of his employees deserved that. He was really only mad at himself.

Max went into his office and changed the setting on his glass walls so that they frosted over. He'd worked hard to plan out this office and loved the design. When the walls were clear, he could look out over his team below. Not in an arrogant, controlling way, though plenty of other people probably thought so.

He cared about his team, and he wanted to watch out for them. Do right by them. So that they would work hard for him in exchange because he had earned their loyalty. Maybe even their friendship.

But at this moment, he didn't see why anyone should trust him as far as that.

How could he have been so impulsive? Usually, he limited his bad decisions to jumping into bed with women he hardly knew, and even then, he mitigated the damage by laying down his rules beforehand.

But when it came to Lana, he couldn't think straight.

He paced across his office, trying to force his thoughts to the present. To the work he had to do. He'd already been neglecting his schedule that morning.

But it was no use. His focus was completely shot. He was too riled up and full of chaotic energy.

He grabbed the gym bag that he always had ready and jogged back downstairs to the elevator. He stepped inside and hit the button for the lower level. The doors slid closed.

Nobody else was in the gym, and he was glad. He wrapped his knuckles and hit the punching bag again and again, until his body was aching and his anger was spent.

Max slumped onto a bench, bathed in sweat, sucking down water from a squirt bottle.

Only then did he notice that he was no longer alone. Sylvie stood against the wall, leaning her shoulder into the cinderblock.

"You mind if I ask what that was about?"

"I do mind, actually." He squirted water onto his head. Droplets trickled down over his face.

"I get that you want to be alone right now, boss. But I thought you should know that you missed two interviews this morning. Interviews that you had me schedule yesterday at the last minute. Of course, I couldn't blame it on you. I had to act like I'd screwed up your schedule. It's too bad because I think they were really great candidates. But I came off looking like a dumbass, so I'm not sure if they'll want to come back for a second try. Forget the fact that I'm *not your assistant*, and that's one of the positions we need to fill."

He groaned, closing his eyes. "I'm sorry, Sylvie. I put too much on you because I trust you, but you shouldn't have to cover for me. It was a rough night."

Which wasn't even true. It was a perfectly fine night, setting aside the fact that some sicko was bothering Lana. But he wasn't about to pin this on her.

"I know you were with Lana. Is everything okay with her?"

"She's safe." And royally pissed.

"Thank goodness. I haven't made much progress on that new trace yet."

"Of course, you haven't. Because I've just been making your job harder. I promise, I will call those candidates myself and apologize. I'll make sure they know it wasn't you."

Sylvie came over and sat on the bench beside him. Barrettes pinned back her short hair, and she wore her trademark all-black, her short sleeves showing off her tattoos. She pushed her pink glasses up onto her nose.

"I don't mean to pry. But if I don't, who will? So, I'm just going to put this out there. Maybe you need a day off."

He grimaced. "I don't need a day off. I don't take days off."

"But I gotta be honest, boss. People who don't take days

off get burned out. And you kind of seem, no offense, like a guy who's burned out."

He got up and grabbed a towel to wipe himself off, dismissing her words out of hand. Max had never been burned out in his life. Maybe burned *up*. Over his parents' failings, his own guilt over leaving Aurora in another family's care. Regrets about Lana.

But not burned out when it came to work. Not even when he used to be a special operator, with all the horrible shit that he saw back then.

"Even if I was, we're shorthanded. I can't afford to take a day off."

Sylvie got up, brushing off her jeans. "Max, I don't think the rest of us can afford what might happen if you *don't*."

"That sounds dramatic. I'll get myself in order. Just let me grab a shower, and I'll be back to work."

But Sylvie wasn't having it. Even though the petite woman had to look up to meet his eyes, he felt like she towered over him.

"This place can barely function without you. That's true, and we all know it. But if you don't let us even try, then we won't have the chance to learn. And someday, you won't be here. You'll be sick or injured, god forbid, or out of commission for some other unforeseeable reason. Do I hope it doesn't happen? Of course. But at least give us the chance to get ready. If you don't, it's not because you're devoted, or a workaholic, or because you're a great boss. It's because of your *ego*."

Damn. Her words were harsh. She was exactly right.

But this was who he was. Max didn't know how to be anything different.

Chapter Twelve

*L*ana sank into the seat across from Aurora. They were on a restaurant patio overlooking the water. Lana had finished speaking with Claire Barnes again, doing their final witness prep.

Aurora reached across the table and squeezed her arm. "How are you feeling? Ready for tomorrow?"

The trial would start first thing in the morning. "I think so. It's been really busy, and I've still got more to do. But I really need an hour to decompress. I'm so glad you could meet me."

"If I can help by distracting you for an hour and helping you relax, then I've earned my title as best friend."

"Oh Rory, you earned that a long time ago. Now you can rest on your laurels. Please tell me you're going to order a mimosa so I can live vicariously through you. I'd get one, but it's back to the office for me after this."

The waiter brought over the menus, along with the mimosa that Aurora—of course—had already ordered. She made a show of sipping it, and Lana laughed, happy as always to see Aurora enjoying herself.

Lana opened her menu. This was a seafood place with Mediterranean influences, and she looked for the most indulgent choice on offer: lobster pasta in a champagne-tomato cream sauce with fresh tarragon. Aurora chose the sea bass with risotto.

Once they'd ordered, she sat back in her chair, admiring the beachfront that curved away from them. The restaurant was situated at one of the prettiest vantage points in their entire town.

"Tell me about you and Devon. Catch me up on everything, and don't leave a single detail out."

The last two weeks had been hectic for Lana. But in some ways, they'd also been uneventful. The creepy stalker hadn't contacted her again.

Max had come by her place when she wasn't home to install the new security system. They were speaking again, getting along in a perfectly civil manner. But they hadn't had any more open, friendly conversations like the one when he'd spent the night. They were back to limiting themselves entirely to the subjects of work and Aurora. Which suited Lana just fine, since she needed to be focused on trial prep anyway.

Lana and Max had met several times, both at his office and at her own, to cement every detail of his testimony. She was still seething over what he'd said to Wayfair, and the disrespect Max had shown her by stepping so far out of bounds. But she felt completely confident that Max was ready for his role in the trial.

He wasn't going to let her down. And that meant Lana wasn't going to let Claire Barnes down.

She had to admit though, Max's outburst with Wayfair seemed to have actually made a difference. The lawyer had been nothing but professional with her ever since. Curt and ill-tempered, maybe, but still professional.

Aurora took another sip of her mimosa. "Sure you can't share some?"

"Nope. Not today. Maybe not even until the trial is over, and I hear that guilty verdict."

Aurora played with her napkin. Something was clearly on her mind, and Lana was surprised she hadn't brought it up already. Usually, Aurora didn't hesitate to share her opinions.

"How are things with Max?" Aurora asked.

So that was it.

Lana hadn't told Aurora anything about Max spending the night because she hadn't mentioned the stalker. Aurora had been through some difficult times several months ago herself. She'd even needed a bodyguard detail for a while, but that danger was behind them. Lana didn't want to bring up any traumatic memories.

"Everything is fine. Pretty much the same as it always has been. We're both busy as ever."

"But have you given any more thought to you two trying to be friends? Real friends, like you said? I know I acted all weird when you told me what happened between you two a long time ago. I just wanted you to know that I'm fine whatever you decide. I don't need you and my brother to be besties for my sake. But if you do want to…you know, spend more quality time with him, I'm fine with that too. It's all good."

Lana choked on her ice water. "What kind of 'quality time' are we talking about?"

Heat filled her belly as she pictured Max naked. Even when she was annoyed with him, that image had a way of popping into her head at inconvenient moments.

"Nothing that I want to spell out," Aurora said. "I just realized that I might've given the impression that I was judging you for getting your freak on. Please know I would never do that."

"I know you wouldn't." Aurora was the most sex-positive person that Lana knew. But she didn't need Aurora's blessing because nothing was *ever* going to happen again with Max. That ship had sailed right off the edge of the earth ten years ago, and they'd already proven that a friendship would be difficult. But Lana was glad that Aurora's initial horror at the idea of her and Max sleeping together had worn off.

"If he had what you needed, that's nothing to be ashamed of." Aurora took another pull of her mimosa, looking thoughtful. "Max was single and on leave and probably super horny —ew, by the way. Sorry. And you were always working so hard in school. You deserved to let loose. When you see a dick you want to ride, and you're both free, consenting adults, why not jump on that thing? I certainly have. In the past, anyway. These days, Devon's got the only joy stick I want to sit on. My poor vibrator is getting lonely."

The server arrived at that moment with their plates. He was working very hard to keep a straight face.

"Anyway," Lana blurted, "we'll be choosing the jury tomorrow, so it'll be a long day."

"So smooth," Aurora said, once the server had left. "I'm sure he had *no idea* what we were really talking about."

Lana shrugged. She had few sexual hang-ups, but she'd never delighted in talking about it as much as Aurora did.

They dug into their food. It was delicious, and a cool breeze blew in from the water. It was hard to imagine a better way to spend the afternoon. She could almost feel her energy recharging, like a solar battery. She rarely treated herself to a meal this nice, but the expense was worth it today.

They were nearly finished eating when the server returned, holding two wine flutes.

"Two glasses of champagne. Enjoy, ladies."

"We didn't order these," Lana said.

"I know. They were sent over from the guy at the end of the bar. I'm guessing you know him? Or maybe he's just an admirer." The server winked and moved on.

Lana glanced through the open doors of the restaurant. The bar was clearly visible inside. But there was no man at the end of the bar. Just a woman and an older couple, who were deep in conversation.

Her blood turned to ice. Lana stood up and dropped her napkin onto the table. "Don't drink that."

"Why? What's wrong?"

Lana ran over to the bartender. "Excuse me, was there a man who ordered two champagnes for my table?"

"Oh, sure." He looked around. "I guess he left. You don't want the wine?" He didn't seem surprised or concerned. Perhaps he'd seen women reject drinks from men all the time.

"What did he look like?"

The bartender grabbed a towel and started wiping off his workspace. "Ball cap, dark sunglasses. Average, I guess."

Which was so incredibly helpful. "Please tell me you guys have security cameras here."

The guy shook his head. "Nah, but we need them. Some money went missing from the till last month, and I got blamed. It was ridiculous."

Lana pushed away from the bar and walked back out onto the patio. She spun in a circle, her eyes scanning everywhere. The other diners, the people out on the beach and in the parking lot. She was starting to attract stares.

Was he out there, watching her? Was she looking at him right now, and didn't even know it?

Their server came over. "Are you all right, ma'am? Do you need something?"

"The check. I need to leave."

He frowned, but he moved quickly toward the computer. Lana returned to the table, where Aurora sat twisting her hands together. "Please tell me what's going on. Why do you look so scared?"

Lana grabbed her purse from the back of the chair. "For the past month and a half, I've been getting weird phone calls. The guy threatened me a couple of weeks ago. I thought he'd given up, had decided to leave me alone. But I'm worried that he was here. I think he sent those drinks."

Aurora cursed, her large eyes growing even wider. "Then we need to get you out of here."

The waiter returned with a check. Lana had enough cash, so she dug the bills out of her wallet and tossed them down.

Aurora grabbed her hand, and together they rushed out into the parking lot. Lana had parked her own car in a different lot farther down the beach, where she'd been meeting with Claire Barnes.

"We'll take my car," Aurora said. "But you drive. I'll call Devon on the way."

"On the way where?"

Aurora looked at her like she was dense. "To the Bennett Security office. Isn't that where we're going?"

Lana knew that was probably the best choice. She remembered what Max had said two weeks ago. Her stalker wasn't satisfied with phone calls anymore. He was escalating. And she had no idea what he looked like or what he might do next.

Aurora tossed Lana the car keys, holding her phone to her ear. They both got in and slammed the doors. Lana reversed and sped out of the parking lot. She had to slam on the brakes when a pedestrian walked past with his dog. The guy had sunglasses on. Could it be him?

He's making me paranoid.

She pressed the accelerator and shot down the street.

When she'd gone half a block, a dark car pulled out behind her. She glanced into the rearview mirror. The driver had on a ball cap and sunglasses. Her pulse jumped.

It's not him, she told herself. *It's just a coincidence.*

But just in case, she took an abrupt right turn and went down to take a parallel street.

The guy followed.

"Yes, we're on our way." Aurora lowered her phone. "Devon's going to drive out and meet us. He said he'll let Max know. Hopefully we're being too cautious and this isn't necessary, but I'd rather be on the safe side."

Lana's eyes kept darting to the rearview mirror. The man in sunglasses was keeping pace with her, turn for turn. Fear was starting to spiral in her head. Someone honked when she swerved out of her lane.

"Hey, watch the road, okay?" Aurora said. "We're going to be fine. It's only few more miles."

Lana's throat unclenched enough for her to get words out. "I think he's behind us, Rory."

Aurora turned around in her seat. "Are you sure?"

"No." But she felt it. It was him. He'd told her that he was always watching. Maybe he'd been with her for the past two weeks, waiting for his moment.

Lana drove on. The car behind her was getting closer. Too close.

He was going to hit them.

Oh, shit.

His front fender smacked into her bumper, making Lana and Aurora both whip forward against their seatbelts.

"Oh my god!" Aurora cried. "What does he want?"

Whether he was just trying to terrify them, or if he had some other intention—if he was going to do something to hurt her and Aurora both—Lana didn't know. But if fear had paralyzed her at the thought of this man targeting her, the realization that he might harm Aurora filled her with adrenaline.

She slammed on the gas, roaring through the next red light. Cars honked. Aurora screamed.

The sunglasses guy had to stop to avoid hitting other cars. But she saw him take an immediate left. He was going to try to cut them off. Did he somehow know where they were going? It was possible that he'd guessed, given her connection to Max.

But the guy wasn't omniscient. He might want her to think he was everywhere, but that was impossible.

Lana turned the wheel, cutting to the right.

"Where are we going? This is the wrong way."

They were driving away from the ocean instead of parallel to it. But Lana didn't slow down. She went through a yellow light. At the next intersection, there were already cars going the opposite way. She had to stop and wait at the red.

Aurora was gripping her seat.

"I think I lost him," Lana said.

Aurora was nodding, her chest moving as she breathed. "Okay, I've got it, those were evasive maneuvers. Right. I'll give Devon an update on where we are."

The light turned green, and Lana drove on, resuming their course toward Bennett Security. Each moment seemed to last an hour. Her senses were heightened as she kept watching for the reappearance of the man in sunglasses and his dark car.

But she didn't see him. Soon, Aurora waved at a Jeep waiting at the curb. Devon pulled away and into position behind them. He escorted them to the Bennett Security building, and they drove through the gate into the parking garage.

Lana parked and shut down the engine. Aurora jumped out right away, running toward Devon.

Then, finally, Lana let go of the steering wheel. Her hands were cramped from gripping so hard.

The driver's side door opened. Max stood there.

"Lana? Jesus, are you hurt?"

She shook her head. "Max, he could've... Aurora..."

He leaned over, slid his broad hands beneath her, and lifted her straight out of the car. Lana let herself fold into Max's arms.

Chapter Thirteen

*M*ax carried Lana into the infirmary and closed the door.

"What do you need? How can I help?"

He knew that Devon was seeing to Aurora. They had to figure out what the hell had happened, and who this bastard was who'd gone after them.

But all of that would wait. First, he had to make sure that Lana was all right. He didn't know exactly what had gone down, just that someone—he assumed Lana's stalker—had been following the two women in their car.

It had probably been a frightening experience, and Lana was no doubt jacked up on adrenaline right now. Any moment she would crash, and he wanted to be there to catch her.

Suddenly, Lana lurched away from him and into the bathroom. Vomit splashed into the toilet.

He started to follow, but she held up her hand, palm out. "Just wait."

He backed up, leaving the bathroom.

The water ran. Finally, she emerged. Max sat down on the infirmary bed, and Lana crawled into his arms. Her eyelids were heavy, her lashes damp.

"I'm okay. I just need a minute."

"Anything."

"Don't go anywhere? Stay here with me?"

"You've got it. Wild horses... You know how the saying goes."

She put her face against his chest, muttering something. But he didn't catch it. "What was that?"

She didn't repeat it.

Max rubbed circles into her back. Soon, she was sitting up and extricating herself from his grip. "Thanks. I'm better. Where's Aurora?"

"Devon's got her."

She covered her eyes with her hand. "I was so scared, Max. If she'd gotten hurt because of me..."

His heart was swelling painfully in his chest. "Aurora is just fine. You brought our girl back safe, L. You did great."

She nodded wearily.

He tried to hug her again, but she shook her head.

They went upstairs to the main level. Sylvie ushered them into a conference room, where Devon sat with his arm around Aurora. She got up and rushed over to Lana. They hugged.

Lana was fighting tears and sniffling. Max thought about reaching for her again, but he figured that she wouldn't want him to do that.

"Who needs what?" Max asked. "Tea? Soda? Water?"

He called their orders down to the reception desk. Then they all sat down. Lana took a seat on the opposite side from Max.

Aurora had her face hidden against Devon's shoulder. This had to be rough for her, considering what she'd been through in the past.

Max wanted to know who'd done this to Lana and his sister. Who was he going to have to destroy?

"I already contacted my friend Chase Collins in the police department," Devon said. "He's going to send a detective over so that Lana and Aurora can make a statement."

Max nodded his approval. It was exactly what he would've told Devon to do, and he felt gratified that the man had anticipated him. "Lana, if you'd rather, we can wait until the detective gets here so you only have to say this once. But if you feel up to it, we'd like to hear what happened."

Lana sipped her mint tea, which had just arrived. Her gaze remained downcast on the wooden surface of the table.

"We were having lunch, and the waiter brought over a couple of drinks that we hadn't ordered. He said they came from some guy at the bar. But when I went to check, the guy had disappeared. I knew something wasn't right." She took a breath. "So, we went to leave, but when we were driving out of the parking lot, I saw this car pull in behind us. And I just knew it was him. The guy who's been calling me."

Devon leaned forward. "How did you know? Did you recognize him?"

She shook her head. "The bartender said he was wearing a hat and sunglasses, and so was this guy driving the car behind us. But I guess I didn't really know for sure until he rear-ended us."

"Fuck," Max muttered. He hadn't even noticed the damage on the car. Not that a car mattered, of course. Only Lana and Aurora.

"I drove as fast as I could and took some turns, hoping to lose him. And I'm pretty sure I did. We headed straight here. That was Aurora's idea. She really thought fast."

"But you maneuvered like a race car driver to get us out of there."

Lana had gone pale while she was talking. She hardly seemed to register Aurora's statement.

"Lana already knows this," Max said, "but just so Aurora and Devon are aware, we tried to trace the call that Lana received at her house a couple of weeks ago, as well as calls she previously received at her office. They all lead to the same burner phone. So far, we haven't had luck trying to locate the signal or tie the serial number to any known individuals."

"I'm still working on that," Sylvie added. "Lana, do you have any ideas about who this man could be? A disgruntled defendant, maybe?"

"Not really. He didn't look like Paxton Wayfair, the lawyer who's against me in the trial that starts tomorrow. Paxton has a beard, and this guy didn't. But aside from that, he looked really generic. He had on a jacket, which I guess concealed his frame. And he was driving, so I couldn't see most of his body." She gave them a description of the car. Sedan, domestic manufacturer, dark in color.

Max rubbed a hand over his chin. It was natural to think that someone related to one of Lana's cases would be doing this. Any prosecutor would make some enemies.

"We need a list of potential suspects. People you think were particularly angry at how their trials or their plea deals came out. Lawyers who might hold a grudge. Do you think you could do that, L?"

"Sure. I'll go over my old notes and calendar when I can. My trial prep comes first. But it's hard to imagine who would want to go to these lengths. I don't know if he wanted to scare us to death, or if he intended to make us crash."

She closed her eyes and stilled, like she was trying not to cry.

Aurora exchanged a glance with Devon, who tightened his arm around her. It was a relief, knowing that someone with training like Devon had his sister's back.

"Lana, I just thought of something." Aurora was biting her lip. "You prosecuted people from the Silverlake Syndicate recently."

The Syndicate was a criminal organization from Los Angeles that had been making inroads into West Oaks. Aurora had gotten mixed up, by no fault of her own, in an internal dispute within the Syndicate. She was out of danger now, but a few people associated with the Syndicate had been prosecuted by Lana's office. But neither Lana nor any other law enforcement agency had been able to take down the entire organization.

The Syndicate was ruthless and well-funded enough to send someone after Lana like this.

Max nodded at Sylvie. "Can you look into it?"

She agreed, already typing on her phone.

"It's worth a shot," Lana said. "But I finished those cases before any of these phone calls started."

"They could want payback," Aurora pointed out.

"Maybe. But it must be connected with the Hearst case, somehow. It can't be a coincidence that the trial starts tomorrow, and somebody nearly runs me off the road."

Max stood, unable to contain his surge of anxious energy. "You're absolutely right. That's the most logical explanation, given the timing. So, it seems to me that you have no choice but to ask Judge Vaughn for a continuance. It's just too dangerous for you to proceed right now, given what's happened."

Lana shot up like someone had zapped her with a taser. "Delay the trial? You have got to be kidding. That is absolutely out of the question."

Max circled the table, walking toward her. "Why not? The case has waited this long. The murder took place over two decades ago. We're talking about your safety here. That has to be the priority."

"But I just spoke to Claire Barnes this morning. The victim's sister. I promised her, yet again, that we would do everything possible to nail Ryan Hearst to the wall. This is not an easy case, Max. Gathering the evidence, finding the necessary witnesses after so much time has passed... I've been working my ass off to get it ready. And there is no way in *hell* I'm going to ask Claire to keep waiting, as if every single day isn't agony for her. As if twenty long years isn't fucking *enough*."

Max and Lana had squared off against one another, each of them holding their fists at their sides. Everyone else in the room was staring.

"All right, here's what we're going to do." Max put steel into his voice because he wasn't going to back down. Not if it meant her safety. "The trial can go forward. But an escort, either Devon or I, will drive you to the courthouse and back every day."

"Oh, the trial can go forward? You'll allow that? How generous of you."

"*And* you're going to stay upstairs in my apartment, with me, where I can be sure you're safe." He didn't trust anyone else to watch over her.

Lana's eyes flared with indignation. "Do you know how arrogant you sound?"

Max shrugged, digging his hands in his pockets. "You're just now figuring that out? I thought we'd known each other long enough that my character was obvious."

Sylvie cleared her throat. "Awkward," she said quietly.

"No kidding," Aurora whispered back.

Max didn't take his eyes off Lana's. He waited for her to keep arguing. After all, that was what she did best. She'd built her career on it.

But miraculously, she didn't.

"Fine. I'll stay here, but only because that man today not only terrorized me, but someone I love. If I'd reported those phone calls from the beginning—taken it all more seriously—then maybe we'd have caught him by now." She pressed her lips together. "I'm not too proud to admit I need help. But I'm only staying for as long as the trial lasts, or until we figure out who this asshole stalker is. Because I don't intend to be trapped here with *you* for a second longer than I have to be."

Chapter Fourteen

_L_ ana got through the first few days of trial without much incident. They selected a jury and empaneled them. Then came the first witness: a retired detective who was one of the first to respond when some surfer kids found Heather's body.

Next was the current coroner, who could testify as an expert witness about the 1998 autopsy report, since the previous coroner had died.

Wayfair had been behaving himself, so far. Lana had mentioned to him that she'd gotten into a fender bender, and the lawyer had seemed completely unfazed. If he'd had something to do with the man following them, then he had the best poker face Lana had ever seen.

Wayfair was a prominent lawyer, but he got by mostly with bullying and throwing obscene amounts of money at a case. There was no way he was that unflappable. So, she had to assume that Wayfair hadn't been behind the harassment.

The last she'd heard from Sylvie, they still hadn't found any new leads as to her stalker's identity. Reviews of surveillance cameras around West Oaks had turned up images of the man and the car. The vehicle, however, bore stolen plates from Oregon.

Her stalker was out there, somewhere. And she had no clues as to whom he might be.

Yet as Lana arrived back at Max's building on Friday, after the fourth day of the trial, she felt optimistic. The testimony had been going well. She thought she was developing a rapport with the jury, and Wayfair's attempts to rattle her or make her look stupid had made several of the jurors frown.

Four days of the trial down, about two weeks to go. It might end earlier, but then, the jury would need to deliberate.

Devon had been driving her back and forth to the courthouse. In fact, she'd hardly seen Max at all since their argument in the conference room.

"Anybody home?" Lana asked as she exited the elevator and walked into Max's apartment.

Nobody answered. Max wasn't here, and that was just fine with her.

First, she went to her makeshift office. The space had become an unofficial war room for her trial team. Max had sent someone to gather her things, and Trevor had been coming back-and-forth whenever they weren't able to accomplish everything by email or phone.

Lana had already conferenced with Trevor that day at the courthouse, but she'd thought of some new legal research she needed over the weekend. Lana sent off an email, making the request.

Then she changed out of her suit and into a soft knitted top and leggings. After washing her face and brushing her teeth, Lana felt like she was emerging from a stupor.

She walked into Max's spacious living room. Through the windows, the sun was setting over the ocean.

Max's apartment was quite a contrast to hers. Where her place was simple and homey, awash in beige and gray, Max's looked like the lobby of a fancy downtown L.A. building.

Metal and leather chairs that came straight out of some vintage designer collection, and abstract artwork that could've been in a museum.

He had a massive kitchen filled with every appliance and convenience, from the commercial-style refrigerator to the Italian cappuccino maker. She ran her fingers over the quartz countertops, breathing in the citrusy scent that some house-keeper had left here during the day.

Lana was in the mood to take a break. Maybe even cele-brate. Nothing that would jinx the presentation of her case, but just enough to reinforce her confidence over the small wins she'd made, despite all her difficulties.

She opened Max's wine fridge. Lana rarely saw him drink, so she assumed it was for his guests. She found a bottle of rosé and poured herself a glass. Then she went back over to the bank of windows overlooking the water and watched the sun set. The sky was turning orange, and the clouds were like tufts of pink cotton candy.

"Nice view."

Max was behind her. She hadn't heard him come in. But she didn't turn around.

"It is."

"It's even better up on the roof. Can I show you?"

She figured it wouldn't hurt. Lana took her glass of wine and followed Max up to the rooftop.

Lana stepped out into the open air. "I didn't know this was up here." The sun was nearly down. The roof had a panorama of water, city, hills. All of West Oaks lay before them. The sun looked like it was sinking into the ocean.

Max was wearing a suit. She tried not to notice how good he looked. He loosened his tie and took off his coat, tossing it onto one of the outdoor couches.

"This view is a big reason I bought the building. I should've given you the full tour at the start of your visit. Sorry I neglected that."

"I doubt I would've gone on your tour anyway. I was too angry."

"What about now?"

She shrugged, sinking onto one of the upholstered chairs, and raised her wine glass to her lips. "Now, I've got four days finished on the trial and a bit of a buzz going. I'm feeling slightly more reasonable."

He sat on the next chair over. Not close enough that they could touch, but close enough that she could study his features. He had more stubble on his cheeks than usual. His eyes looked more bloodshot, with dark half-moons beneath. She worried that he wasn't sleeping. Hopefully, it wasn't because of her presence in his space.

"I appreciate you making room for me here. It took a big weight off my mind not to have to worry these past few days about anything except the trial. And…I'm sorry I yelled."

He smiled, though it wasn't his usual vibrant expression. "And I'm sorry I came across as an arrogant ass. I am one, but I try not to let it show quite that much."

She lifted her glass to show that he was forgiven. "You've been busy the past few days, too. Anything exciting?"

He sighed and pulled off his tie, then started rolling up each sleeve. "Trying to hire some new people, since we've been growing here a little faster than we can keep up with. Meetings… Nothing that's the least bit exciting, now that I think of it." His gaze drifted into the distance, like this admission disappointed him. "What about the trial?"

"I'm feeling really good about it. The jury likes me, I think, and there haven't been any surprises or problems. You're still on schedule for Tuesday."

"Do you want to go over my testimony again?"

She shook her head, taking another sip. "Nope. You're ready. I think we may have to talk about something other than work. I'd bring up Aurora, but I haven't seen her, either."

Out of an abundance of caution, Aurora was staying with

Devon's family while he was busy being Lana's driver this week. None of them actually thought Lana's stalker was after her. But Lana felt better knowing Aurora was surrounded by people who cared.

Max leaned back and stared up into the darkening sky.

"Maybe you could share whatever's bothering you?"

He turned his head to look at her. "That obvious?"

"You seem tired. You aren't your usual energetic self." Lana got up and sat on the edge of his chair. It was an over-sized piece of furniture, plenty of room for her, even with his large frame. But she was significantly closer. Close enough that he could've touched her with a flick of his wrist if he'd wanted.

She offered him her wine glass. He took it. Max drank the pale pink liquid, his eyes locked on her the whole time. She felt her nipples hardening against her bra.

What the hell am I doing? she wondered.

But she knew. She'd always been drawn to him. That was exactly the reason she'd stayed away and put up walls between them for so long. She was still in love with the man.

Right now, the simple fact was that she hated to see him looking sad.

"It's like I'm going through the motions lately. And I don't know why."

"You don't know why you're expanding the business and hiring new people? Or…"

"Why I work so much. Why I can't slow down. Why I… fight some things so hard."

"That *is* a lot of questions."

"You can see why I can't sleep."

"Oh, Max." She gripped his shoulder, massaging the tense muscles there. "I didn't know you weren't sleeping. I've heard you coming and going, but I guess I've been hiding away in my room."

"You were busy. So was I. It's okay." He drained the glass. "And now I drank all your wine. Let's go get you some more."

As they descended the stairs, she felt his fingers brush the small of her back. But it was so quick she couldn't be sure it was intentional.

Max refreshed her glass. "Have you had dinner yet?"

"No, your kitchen scares me."

"Then what have you been eating since you got here?"

Lana tried to remember. "Trevor's been bringing me take-out. Aside from that, tortillas with cheese warmed up in the microwave. That's one of my go-tos."

He gaped at her, horrified. "Haven't you ever heard of a vegetable, woman?"

"Isn't salsa a vegetable?"

Shaking his head, Max opened the fridge. "My last grocery delivery was a couple of days ago. I should have all the ingredients I need..."

"So that's how this stuff keeps magically appearing inside your fridge." Delivery was an efficient choice, but usually Lana couldn't even spare the brain power to place an order ahead of time.

He started pulling out bags and containers. "I'm going to make you a spinach lasagna."

She set the wine glass on the counter with a clink. "You wanted to make pancakes for breakfast a couple weeks ago, and now it's lasagna for dinner? Really?"

The morning after they first had sex, he'd made blueberry pancakes. And that same evening for dinner, he'd made lasagna. Right before their second night of lovemaking.

She clenched her thighs together at the desire those memories elicited.

"Maybe that's all I know how to make."

He hadn't learned any new tricks in ten years? She doubted it.

His eyes were both perceptive and mischievous. He knew exactly what he was doing. Trying to force her to acknowledge the reference. Talk about their past. Why? She couldn't say. But Max wasn't the type to toy with her emotions on purpose, so clearly, he didn't realize the effect those memories still had on her.

"Then lasagna it is," she said.

"Here, you chop the spinach. I get the kind that's pre-washed, so it's ready to go." He handed her the bag, a knife, and a cutting board. She chose a space at his massive island and got to work.

"I wouldn't have thought you'd be making a vegetarian dish," she said as she chopped. "Aren't men all about the protein?" At least, a man as muscular as he was.

"I'm adding meat, but only half as much as most recipes call for. And I cut back somewhat on the cheese and sub in cauliflower instead. Sounds weird, but I promise it's good."

"Who knew Max Bennett was a health nut."

He smirked. "I'm not in my twenties anymore. I have to watch my figure."

I can watch your figure for you. Lana checked out the way his ass filled out those tailored pants. How his biceps tested the seams of his dressy shirt. Maybe he wasn't twenty-something, but he still looked pretty damn good to her.

"Fishing for compliments?" she asked.

"The real question is, how do you still look the same as you did back in college? You could probably fit into the same jeans. Those ones with the ripped knees you used to wear. I liked those."

The knife dropped to the cutting board. "Max, are you flirting with me?"

He stopped peeling an onion to look at her. "Is that okay?"

Yes, Max, she thought automatically. "If you find it entertaining, then I'm not going to stop you."

He was in a strange, unsettled mood tonight. That had to explain his behavior.

Max heated a skillet to brown some ground beef, along with the onions and minced cauliflower. He told her to add the spinach.

Next, he dumped a pile of flour onto the counter, made a divot in the middle, and broke eggs into the center.

"What on earth are you doing?"

"Making the pasta. Can't have lasagna without it."

"You're making lasagna noodles by hand? That's a thing?"

He laughed, mixing the dough with his long fingers. She leaned her elbows on the quartz, fascinated as she watched him roll out the pasta into sheets with a metal pasta maker.

"I knew you could cook, but I didn't realize you were so into it."

"Most of the time, I'm too busy to do anything this elaborate. But cooking and working out are the two things I do to relax."

And probably having sex. Because he was pretty good at that too, so why wouldn't he? How many other women had stood at this counter?

"It's nice to have someone else to cook for, though. I cook for Aurora when she lets me. But a lot of the time she's annoyed with me, or I'm busy, so it doesn't happen too often."

Aurora had been back in West Oaks for less than a year, and she and her brother were still getting used to living in such close proximity again.

Lana had watched the two siblings go through many stages, from closeness when Aurora was younger, to near estrangement, and now this careful dance of learning to relate to one another as adults.

After Lana headed off to law school, he'd heard second-hand about all the drama when Max had realized that his high-school-aged sister was sexually active. Aurora used to call her up, seething about his latest affront. He'd chased away more than one guy that Aurora liked.

One of the few times the three of them had all been

together was Aurora's high school graduation day. First time
Lana had ever seen him in a suit, his hair military short. That
day, she'd wondered if he had his dog tags underneath his
dress shirt. If he still left the tags on when he stripped everything else off.

"What are you smiling at?" Max was cutting long strips of
the dough and setting them aside.

Lana grabbed her wine glass and took a sip. "I was just
thinking of when Aurora graduated high school. What a great
day that was. We were all so proud."

Max nodded, his wistful expression matching hers. "Yeah,
and relieved too. Even my parents were there, as if they
deserved any of the credit. It was all your family. I don't know
what would've happened to Aurora without you."

"Or you. She lived for her brother. We did it together."

Something like pain passed across his face. But then it was
gone.

A laugh bubbled out of Lana's chest. "Do you remember
after the ceremony, though? When we were all supposed to go
out for an early dinner? You and I couldn't find Aurora
anywhere in the school building, and finally we opened a
random janitor's closet, and there she was. Tumbling out with
the mops and some poor kid with his pants around his
ankles."

Lana's head tipped back as she laughed. She'd never forget
the terror on the poor boy's face when Max had snarled at
him. Aurora had just shrugged. *Is it dinner already? I lost track of
time.*

"That had to be your influence," Max grumbled, though
his eyes were laughing along with her.

"Me? No way. I was too uptight to have so much fun."
Then she realized that wasn't entirely true. "Okay, I did
misbehave that one weekend, but my parents didn't catch us,
thank god. Otherwise, they never would've let *you* back into
the house."

As the words spilled out of her, she realized she'd broken her embargo on talking about their past. But it hadn't killed her. Instead, she was laughing about it. Go figure.

But Max's smile had vanished. He was quiet as he constructed the layers of the lasagna.

After he'd put it in the oven, he picked up her wine glass and took a drink. He hadn't bothered to pour his own, which should've annoyed her. Lana didn't usually like it when men picked off her plate or shared her beverages. She liked her space.

But with Max, she didn't mind. To be fair, she was the one who'd offered him her glass on the rooftop. So she'd started it.

"Do you ever think about it?" he asked.

"About what?"

"The nights we made love."

His statement made her chest contract. It was impossible to breathe. "Do you?" Her voice was low.

"I think about it. About *us*. All the damn time."

"Why?" she choked out.

"How could I not? You were beautiful. You *are* beautiful. I wouldn't want to forget a single thing about those nights."

Her body was overheating. Lana took the wine glass, but her throat was too tight to swallow. "I think about it, too. But I shouldn't. We were good together, but it was over a long time ago."

"Does it have to be?"

Chapter Fifteen

*M*ax turned to face her, seeking out her eye contact. Lana didn't shy away. Not that she ever would. When it came to confrontation, she could talk circles around him.

He'd meant to leave the past alone. She hadn't wanted to talk about this. But he couldn't hold this inside any longer. Max needed her, even though he shouldn't, and he just didn't have the mental wherewithal to keep denying it.

According to his rule, he wasn't supposed to touch Lana again. Three nights... Yeah, he could count. He knew the score. But his rule had failed him. And he'd be an idiot if he kept doubling down on a failing strategy.

But Lana didn't seem to be taking him seriously. She scoffed, rolling her eyes.

"I can't understand you, Max. Back then, I knew you weren't looking for a relationship, and I was fine with that. But the next time you visited Aurora, it was like none of it ever happened. That really *hurt*." She shrugged. "I thought you'd had your fill of me."

The thought of Lana hurting caused him physical pain. "I've always wanted you."

She ran her fingertip around the rim of the wine glass. Lana had that deliberative look, the one she got when she was in the courtroom. "But not enough to show me. Instead, you made me assume those nights meant nothing to you."

She had no idea what a struggle it had been to see her and pretend to feel nothing. How many times he'd jacked himself off to the memory of her body, her taste, her moans, even though he'd lied to himself, pretending it wasn't Lana he was picturing.

He was getting hard just thinking about it.

"Our time together meant a lot."

Her calm broke. "But if you wanted me, then why end things in the first place? Don't give me those same tired excuses."

A natural question. But a hard one to answer. "It's complicated."

"Then explain it to me. You were afraid I'd fall for you, and my poor little heart would break?"

Maybe. As arrogant as that sounded.

"I have a rule."

God, was he really about to tell her this?

Max braced his hands against the countertop. "When I'm with a woman, I never let it go past three nights. That's my limit. A rule of three."

Her eyebrows slowly arched. "Are you for real right now? 'Rule of three?' Seriously?"

"It works for me," he said defensively. "After that, things get messy and awkward."

"And that's why we never slept together again? Because we'd done it three times?"

"I think it was four times, actually. If memory serves. I said three *nights*. Obviously, I can go more than once a session."

She burst out laughing.

"What? You know it's true."

"I can vouch for that, yes." She was smiling, shaking her

head at him. "But three is so arbitrary. I don't see why three nights is okay, but four is too much. Or seven. Or ten."

Why did I tell her about the rule? He always made sure his partners had no expectations. But he'd never told anyone in such explicit terms. With other women, he'd always gotten his point across without spelling it all out. "No-strings attached" was usually all they needed to hear.

Lana seemed to sense his discomfort and pounced. "Why is it three, Bennett? Why three? You must've thought about this. You picked three for a reason."

"It's three because of *you*."

She went silent.

"We had three nights. So…that's what I picked. No more than three. It seemed to make sense."

"I don't know whether to be offended or flattered."

Lana turned away and crossed the room, stopping in front of the windows. Probably plotting her next volley of questions.

Max unbuttoned his dress shirt and stripped it off, leaving his undershirt. Getting himself ready for the next round. Her interrogation only made him want her more. Because this was Lana in her element. Whip-smart, formidable in an argument. Sparring with her was more excitement than he'd had in ages. He couldn't make himself look like a dumbass, though. He wanted to win her over. That meant being honest, while making her see his side of things.

But he definitely wasn't feeling tired anymore. His blood was pumping. He felt awake and alive.

Lana spun around, her hands clasped behind her back. "You say you decided on this rule after me. But before we'd ever slept together, you made clear to me that we couldn't last. You already planned that we'd have an expiration date."

"Yes. I know."

"Why is that?"

"Because I'm shitty at relationships."

"Did something specific happen to make you think that?"

Something specific *had* happened, but he wasn't going so far as to share it. She didn't need to know every crappy thing he'd ever done.

"I just *knew*. I wouldn't be good for you in the long run."

She made a circuit of the living room. Max remained in the kitchen, like he was on the witness stand.

"I'm shitty at relationships, too," Lana said. "I've still tried. I've never made it past the one-month mark with any of the men I've slept with, but at least I've made the effort."

His face went hot. "I don't need to hear about you and other men."

"Thinking of me with other men bothers you?"

"It does."

She lifted one shoulder. "Half the time I was imagining you while I fucked them, anyway."

"Lana," he warned, his jaw tight. He'd never had a jealous streak, and he had no right to be possessive of her. Yet he hated to think of another man kissing her. Moving inside of her. It made his head pound.

She smiled, obviously glad she was getting to him. "You took my virginity. If that makes you feel better."

"I know, and it doesn't." The admission filled him with shame all over again.

There'd been plenty of clues. And even if he'd somehow failed to guess, he'd seen the blood on the condom.

Her lips pressed together. "Why didn't you say anything?"

"Because you didn't. And because I didn't want to think about it, I guess. What it really meant for you. I'm an asshole like that."

She snickered, even though he'd been completely serious. "An asshole for showing me a good time?"

"No, for taking your virginity when I didn't deserve it. You should've had your first time with a guy who'd stick around for you. But I didn't care about that. I just…wanted to have you."

She bit into her lower lip, and Max wished those were his teeth marking her. His tongue, licking at the same spot afterward.

"I know my reasoning doesn't exactly hold up in hindsight. But I thought I could have you and still not hurt you if it was only one night."

"*One* night?"

"I told you, the rule of three came after."

The night he took her virginity, he'd sworn to himself it would just be the one time. She'd clearly wanted *someone* to bed her. She'd been so eager, and he was sure that she felt only passing lust for him. They'd go back to being acquaintances the next day, brushing off the night before as a fun diversion. Nothing more. Thanks for the roll in the hay.

But the next morning, his own longing hadn't been sated. And she'd seemed raring to go for more. So he'd talked himself into it.

"Every time I asked, you said yes, and I was fucking glad for it. But I also hated myself for being so selfish. For disregarding the fact that I knew you were better off saying no."

One night became two.

Then two became three.

Every night increased the likelihood that Lana would get attached.

And the following morning, he had to leave. If he hadn't, he probably would've kept it going, like the self-centered bastard that he was. Even though he knew that he couldn't be the kind of boyfriend a girl like Lana needed.

He would never have cheated, but he would've resented the other demands that a girlfriend had every right to make. His attention, his emotions, his time. He would've gotten restless and done something impulsive and stupid, and she would've been disappointed or worse.

"Who are you to decide what's ever been best for me?"

He threw up his hands. "Then I suck for being presumptuous, too. Take your pick." *Great job, Bennett. Way to convince her to jump into bed with you again.*

"I'm just trying to explain what was in my head ten years ago," he said. "Once I'd left West Oaks, and my dick had stopped making my decisions, I felt bad about what I'd done to you. What I *thought* I'd done. That's why, the next time I saw you, I acted like it never happened. Because I was afraid that I'd let myself get carried away again."

"Yes, that would've been *so* unforgivable. Couldn't let anyone think that Max Bennett was unsure of himself. Or that he had actual *feelings*. What a disaster."

"I told you, I'm bad at this." He pinched the skin between his eyes. He didn't want to fight with Lana. Maybe some vigorous banter, but fighting was the exact opposite of what he wanted.

He wanted…more. Just *more*. What that meant—if he wanted more from Lana than just another night of incredible sex—he didn't know.

It would've been easier if she hated him for taking her virginity and then leaving. Easier if he didn't know her so well and respect her so much.

Lana was exactly right. She'd always been able to make her own decisions, and he should never have imagined that he knew better.

So, he was going to put it all on the line and let *her* decide.

She'd returned to the window. He pushed off the counter and walked toward her, a single slow step at a time.

"I'm sorry I was stupid back then. I'm so sorry that I made you believe you didn't matter to me. But I can't stop thinking about you."

Max was just inches away from her. Lana looked up at him. But he didn't stop there. He kept closing that distance until their foreheads met, their noses touched. He cupped the back of her neck, holding her in place. Her hair was soft between his fingers. The scent of her, lilac and grass, added to the wine already in his stomach. Intoxicating him.

"I need to touch you. Taste you. I think I'll lose my mind if I don't."

"What about your 'rule of three?'"

"Fuck my rule."

He didn't ask permission this time. He just tilted her head back and took her mouth. After a brief pause to let her stop him—she didn't—his tongue pushed past her lips. Lana's answering moan went straight to his cock. His free hand went around her hips, drawing her against him.

Max walked backward until they reached the couch. They tumbled onto the cushions, legs tangling, yet their mouths didn't break contact. Too much time had passed since the last time he'd tasted her. He wasn't letting her go.

Lana was halfway on top of him. Max sat upright, hitching her up by the thighs, and spreading her legs to either side of him. She straddled his lap, just like the first night they were together.

His teeth nipped at her lips. He gave her hair a tug, checking her reaction, and the sound she made was pure sex.

"*Yes*, Max, like that."

His erection was trying to burst straight through the expensive wool of his pants. She ground herself against his hard-on. Such delicious friction. Hell, this woman was so fucking sexy. Lither than she'd been at nineteen, with a few more curves for him to hold onto. She moved with the confidence gained from years of experience. But Max had a secret thrill that he'd given her that first taste of lovemaking. Her first orgasms from another person's body, tongue, hands.

He didn't want to think of her with other men. But he was still eager to find out how much she'd learned. He'd learned a thing or two himself.

Her next words, though, were a cold splash of reality.

"Wait. Wait, stop."

He froze. She scrambled off him and stood. Her lips looked bruised, her eyes unfocused. She stepped back and looked at him, blinking like she'd just woken from sleep.

"I don't know...I didn't..."

"It's okay." He tried to adjust himself, so his dick wasn't the most prominent thing in the room. "Is something wrong? Or..."

"Um." Lana put her hands over her mouth. "It's just really sudden. I'm trying to give my brain a chance to catch up."

Really? He thought. *That's the last thing I want my brain to do.*

"There's no rush. Do you want to talk about it?"

"Not yet."

"I moved too fast, didn't I?"

She managed a weak laugh. "Yes. And no. In a way, it took ten years. But I think that's why I feel a little...over-whelmed."

Lana walked toward her bedroom. Max got up and followed her, but not too close. Giving her space.

When she reached her doorway, she turned to face him. "I don't know what you expect from me. Is this another one-night thing? Or three? Are we just restarting the clock on that expiration date?"

He tucked his hands into his back pockets. "I don't know. I just want you. In my bed, in my life." That part wasn't easy for him to say. "I wish I could be clearer. But I'm kind of in uncharted territory here. For me."

Her eyes lifted to his. So uncertain.

"Can that be enough?" he asked.

This time, it was Lana who bridged the gap. She came toward him and put a hand in the center of his chest. Kissed his jawline. The corner of his mouth.

"Lana," he murmured, "do you want me?"

She searched his eyes. Then her expression hardened.

"No, Max. I'm sorry. I don't."

She swept into her room, and the door closed in his face.

Then the oven timer went off. The lasagna was done.

Chapter Sixteen

In the morning, Lana waited until Max had left the apartment. Then she snuck out of her room and into the kitchen. She felt bad about avoiding him. But she wasn't ready to face him yet after last night.

She'd skipped dinner, and she was starving. She opened the fridge, happy to see the lasagna pan there with foil over the top.

Then she noticed the half-full coffee pot, still heated. And the note.

L,

I hope you slept well. There's coffee, plus chocolate muffins in the pantry, which I think Aurora said once were your favorite? I'll be in the gym if you need to find me.

M

Well, that was perfectly friendly. If she didn't remember every agonizing detail of their conversation last night—and that explosive kiss—she might've thought everything was normal between them.

She was still shocked she'd said it. That she didn't want him. Because obviously, that was an out-and-out lie. She wanted Max more than ever. Her whole body ached with wanting. But her confusion had only grown.

Everything she'd thought was true about their "fling" had gotten flipped on its head. All this time, he'd wanted more. He hadn't been able to forget about those nights any more than she had.

Max felt something for her. It was a huge relief to know that, the kind of relief that could've made her younger self cry tears of joy. And at first, that small glimmer of emotion from him had seemed like enough. He'd kissed her, and she'd melted right into his arms. The chemistry between them hadn't abated one bit.

How many times had she fantasized about that exact scene playing out? Max saying he still wanted her, essentially throwing himself at her feet?

But then she'd stopped herself just in time, before potentially making a far bigger mistake than losing her virginity to a guy who didn't care.

For one, Wayfair was going to ask Max about their relationship again during his cross-examination at trial. She didn't need that awkwardness or the distraction from her case.

But far worse? She'd been about to have sex with a man she was *in love with*. She had no clue if his feelings for her were anywhere near that deep. She didn't even know if he wanted a relationship.

And when she'd tried to get clarity, he'd offered her nothing of the kind. Because Max didn't know how he really felt.

He was willing to go against his made-up "rule" about three nights. Yeah. She hadn't quite unpacked *that* baggage. But setting aside the absurdity of his "rule" in the first place, it was clearly a big step for him to break free of it.

As his friend, she admired that he was taking a chance. Going after something he'd been afraid of before.

But as a grown woman who might get her heart broken in

the process? She wasn't a teenager, blinded by lust anymore. She had to be more careful. She wasn't willing to be his test case.

Max had said, over and over, that she deserved better than him. Well, she was listening. And maybe he was right.

She cut a piece of lasagna and ate it cold. She closed her eyes and moaned at the flavor. A perfect balance of acid, creaminess, and richness. Damn, the man was a good cook. So perhaps that was one stroke in his favor.

After breakfast, she changed into some gym clothes, determined to at least go talk to him. If not to sort out all their issues, then at least to show there were no hard feelings. His note had been a gesture, a peace offering. The least she could do was extend her hand right back.

But she didn't know where the gym was.

Lana took the elevator downstairs to the main floor. She stepped out into a bustling space. She said hello to the people she knew, making a beeline for the far corner, where Sylvie had set up her alcove of computer screens.

"Hey, how's it going?" Sylvie gave her a hug. "How's the trial? It must be intense. I haven't even seen you since it started."

"A first-degree murder trial is always demanding. And a cold case can be really tough, since a lot of the witnesses are no longer around. But I'm feeling good about it. Fingers crossed." She held them up, making the gesture.

"That's great news. And speaking of news, I may have a lead on that burner phone the calls to you came from. I put out feelers on the serial number and got a hit. The phone is tied to a big seizure of property made by federal agents in downtown Los Angeles. I'm hoping to get more information on that soon. With luck, we might be able to put together some kind of chain of ownership for the phone. Or at least, get us a few degrees closer to the guy who's using it now."

"Excellent. Let me know."

Lana was so grateful for the effort Sylvie was making on her behalf. But between the Hearst case and Max, she'd been too busy to devote much brain power to the stalker. Thank goodness for that. If the guy fell off the face of the earth and she never heard from him again, so much the better.

"Have you seen Max this morning?" Lana asked. "I think he said he was going to the gym."

Sylvie nodded. "That would make sense. He's been spending a lot of time in there lately. I always know when he's stressed because he starts training like an Olympic athlete. He's got a computer down there so he can keep up with work and run at the same time. He used to have a treadmill desk up in his office, but it drove us all crazy with the pounding on the ceiling."

Lana smiled at Sylvie's description. "What's he like to work for, anyway?"

"Max? He's a great boss, usually. When he can keep things balanced. He's always reminding us of the importance of our work, and he takes care of his employees. I've had plenty of bosses who didn't do that."

"Same here, during summers in law school. It stinks."

"That's an understatement. But Max isn't always the best at taking care of himself." Sylvie had lowered her voice to a murmur, glancing around to make sure none of her coworkers were close enough to hear. "I'm only saying that because I know you're close to him. For heaven's sake, convince the man to take a vacation. If only for *my* sanity."

"I don't think I have that much pull with him. But I'll see what I can do."

Sylvie told her how to find the gym, and Lana headed down to the lower level.

Max was working on the punching bag when she walked into the room. He didn't notice her at first. She just watched his back muscles moving beneath his T-shirt. The prominent shape of his triceps.

She was struck with longing. If anything, the man was even more gorgeous than he'd been in his twenties. Why did he have to be so enticing?

He noticed her and turned. The bag kept swinging. But he didn't say a word. Max's tongue darted out, licking a bead of sweat as it trickled past his chin. His shirt had patches of dark wetness under the arms and at his chest.

He lifted the thin fabric of his shirt to wipe his face, and oh holy—his stomach was a broad expanse of smooth skin, a thin trail of dark hair, and flexed muscle. Not quite as lean as his army days, but somehow even sexier. Manlier.

When his tee dropped back down, he met her gaze with undisguised desire in his eyes. She struggled not to react.

"Hey," she said.

"Hey."

He walked over to a bench, unwrapping the fabric from his knuckles. "You got some breakfast?"

"I did. And coffee, thank you."

"Sleep well?"

"Yep. You?"

"Better than I have in a long time."

"You do look less tired."

He grinned, wiping his neck with a small towel. "Maybe rejection suits me."

She closed her eyes, dropping her head. "Max, I'm…"

"No, it's good. My ego needed a check."

She searched his tone for sarcasm, but there wasn't any. He was being sincere.

"What's your agenda for the day?" he asked.

"Not much. I checked in with Trevor this morning about some research, and he'd found the cases I needed. I spoke to Sylvie on my way down here. She might have a lead on the stalker."

"Indeed? She hadn't mentioned that to me yet."

"She's still working on it." Lana crossed her arms, looking at the rubber matting on the floor.

"We haven't talked about the stalker in a while. How are you feeling about that subject?"

He'd asked the question gently. He claimed to be an asshole, but he didn't know the meaning of the word.

"Afraid," she admitted. "When I really think about it. I hate that he's out there somewhere."

"Do you know how to throw a punch?"

She lifted her eyes. "What?"

He was striding toward her. "I'm talking about self-defense. Have you taken any classes?"

"Um, a time or two, through work. I didn't get that much out of it. Why?"

"Then let's have a lesson. Right now."

"Do you think it'll help me feel less afraid?"

Max stood in front of her and dropped his chin. "Fear can be a very powerful thing. The first thing it tells you is to run, like you and Aurora did a few days ago. That was exactly the right call. But let's say you can't run."

She blinked, thinking of the voice on the phone. The driver in the car behind her.

I'm going to make you mine.

Lana shuddered. "I'd be terrified. I don't know what I would do. If I'd freeze up, or be able to fight back, or what."

"Lana, fear is natural. It's a given. You can't fight it. The key is to transform that fear into action."

Of course Max could do that. But Lana wasn't sure if she was up to the task. "How?"

"Some practice. It takes less training than you'd think to throw a well-aimed blow. But the key is to move explosively. He'll probably think you're weaker than him, so he won't expect that. You have to lash out before your attacker knows what's hit him."

He took her hand and pulled her into an open space,

where mats lined the floor. Max circled her until he was behind her back. Close, but not touching. Lana felt his body there, as if his presence alone had a physical weight. A gravity. She tried to glance over her shoulder.

"Keep looking forward."

She kept her head straight, facing the wall.

"Imagine someone comes up behind you. Grabs you."

He suddenly clamped his arms around her, holding her arms to her sides. Lana gasped. She could feel his breath on the back of her neck, and then the sweaty dampness of his chin against her ear. Max's arms tightened against her ribs. It didn't really hurt, but it was getting to be a challenge to fill her lungs.

She tried to ignore the surge of arousal that sped through her center and went straight to her clit.

"First thing you'll want to do is shift your shoulder into me. It'll feel strange. You're actually going *closer* to your attacker. But you'll use that space you've created to pull up your arm. Like this."

He held her wrist and demonstrated the movement a few times in slow motion.

"Then, jam your elbow as hard as you can into my ribs and stomach."

He clamped his arms down again. Lana wiggled, trying to find the gap he'd mentioned. But Max was holding her so tight she couldn't move an inch. His heart beat against her back, and his fingers dug into her skin.

"I can't. This is impossible."

"Remember, be explosive. Be *angry*."

The harshness of his tone made her jump. Lana remembered the car accelerating behind her. Hitting her bumper. Her pulse leaped, her rage growing.

Max's arms tightened again, a vise around her, in anticipation of her movement. She took a deep breath, then threw her shoulder back toward his chest and pulled her elbow up at the same time, driving the point into his side. He barely budged.

"That's better," Max said. "Try again."

She did. It was surreal, fighting off Max like he wanted to hurt her. A couple of times, when he pinned her arms, she felt his lips brush the top of her ear. It both infuriated her and excited her so much she thought she'd burst with frustration.

After a while, she could feel the force of her elbow driving into his torso. His body was like hardened steel. Her arm was starting to ache. But she did feel slightly more confident. Energy surged through her, like she was ready to run or fight.

Or fuck, a naughty voice whispered in her head.

God, so many mixed-up feelings were going through her right now. Wanting Max to pull her close and wanting to push him away at the same time. Wanting him to bend her over and have his way with her.

Max let her go, moving so that he was in front of her. "Now, what if he's coming at you head-on? You have to stop his progress. And you want to stop him from taking you down. Because when you're on the ground, his strength will be harder to overcome."

He showed her how to brace her forearm against his collarbone to keep him at bay. "Hold me here and grab my sleeve with your other hand. Feel that stability? Even if he's stronger, he'll struggle to get any closer to you in this position."

She placed her arms as he instructed. Lana was staring straight into his dark eyes, their mouths just inches apart. She was finding it difficult to concentrate.

But they kept practicing. He tried to tackle her, take her down, while she held him back with her forearms. She was surprised at her own strength. Max's lesson had been going for forty-five minutes at least, and Lana was panting and sticky with sweat. But this felt *good*. The fear was still there underneath when she thought of the stalker. But she could channel it. Make it useful.

"Now, knee me in the crotch."

"*What?*"

"I'm attacking you. Knee me in the balls. Make me suffer."

"Max, I—"

"Do it," he roared.

Her knee jerked up between his legs, slamming into something solid. He flinched.

"Oh, I'm sorry! Are you okay?"

"I'm fine. I'm wearing a cup." His voice was slightly strained.

"Why did you make me do that? You were yelling!"

"I wanted you to practice. I just didn't think you'd get so…into it."

"Do you need ice?"

"No. Just to sit. For a sec."

He sat on the bench, scratching his head sheepishly. And she just couldn't help it. Lana started to giggle.

"I kneed you in the balls. That happened."

"It happened."

"And you *told me* to do it."

"I know. I didn't think that through."

"Is this a predatory sex thing? You offer self-defense lessons to trick women into sadomasochistic role play?"

"*That* is not funny."

"But I'm laughing."

He stood. Was he walking weird?

"We should probably call it there," he said. "Do you feel like you've made progress?"

"I do."

"Ready to head up?"

"Um, yeah. Sure."

Upstairs, they showered and stayed in their separate rooms

through the afternoon, emerging only to grab sandwiches for lunch. Lana looked at model jury instructions and reviewed her lists of questions for the upcoming witnesses.

For dinner, they had leftover lasagna, still joking about his unusual methods for teaching self-defense. He didn't make any further romantic overtures to her, nor did he talk about the past, the way he had last night. But he didn't make any secret of his desire, either. His eyes did all the talking for him, his yearning plain in those dark brown irises.

Her mind kept going back to the feeling of his arms cinched around her. His lips brushing her ear while she pretended to fight him off, though she'd really wanted to invite him closer.

By the end of the evening, Lana felt torn in two—between her fear of getting her heart broken, and her overpowering physical need for him. She hadn't felt this way since she was a teenager. Such blatant, undeniable lust.

"I should turn in." She got up from the table.

"Goodnight, Lana." Those eyes again. Undressing her, devouring her. "You know where I'll be."

A clear invitation. One that she shouldn't accept.

Lana tried to distract herself with work, and then with a book. But it was no use. She tossed and turned in bed, her body like a live wire. Her panties were soaking. It was past midnight, and she was lying awake, more turned on than she'd ever been in her life.

If I don't come, I'm going to lose my ever-loving mind.

She could try touching herself. But the man she wanted more than any other was in the room right next door.

Waiting for her.

*M*ax spent all day at war with himself. He'd taken his little sister's babysitter to bed. Lana, who should've been off-limits.

But last night wasn't enough. He still wanted her.

He'd noticed before how much she'd matured in the last few years. Any man would. How she'd grown into a stunning, confident young woman. The kind who might even be out of his league in another year or two.

Lana wasn't just attractive; she was smart. Really smart. Driven, too. Max hadn't gone to college, but he could recognize and respect Lana's ambitions as a mirror to his own. Her sharp mind sometimes intimidated him, when he normally didn't let anything, or anyone, rattle him. Not because he thought he wasn't capable compared to her, but because she made him want to prove his worth all the more.

But while she was probably smarter academically, Max had the advantage when it came to experience.

Last night, he'd known immediately that she was a virgin. He might've guessed before, based on her seriousness about school and family and the lack of guys in her orbit. But her body language last night told the story, too. The way she sat so rigidly beside him, the hesitant way she spoke. Everything about her broadcast loud and clear that she'd never done this before. And he knew in his gut that he should gently but firmly point her elsewhere. Give her some advice but discourage her from thinking anything would happen between them.

But then she'd touched him, kissed him, and all that logic went straight out the window. He'd wanted her so badly. She was so soft and yielding under his hands. And he'd asked her, again and again, if she really wanted this. Wanted *him*. Almost begging every time for her to come to her senses. Just tell him no. That would've been the end of it. He would've done the right thing and let this amazing, gorgeous girl find some other guy who would give her everything, his entire heart and soul. Everything that Max could never give.

It wasn't just Lana's heart at risk. It was Aurora's stability, too. He was sure that, no matter what happened between them, Lana would never take it out on Aurora. But Lana's parents? If they found out he'd fucked their nineteen-year-old daughter in their house? They were wonderful, generous people, but everyone had their limits.

He should've known better. He *did* know better.

But Lana said yes. Yes, and yes, and yes. *Max, yes*. So, he let his body make the decision for him. Because his mind was too weak to hold back that surge of insatiable craving.

Then again, he'd had the presence of mind to first tell her not to expect a relationship. So maybe blaming lust was just another excuse. Maybe he'd been keenly aware, at every single moment, of just what he was doing. But he wasn't a good enough man to choose the honorable course.

He'd touched every part of her, entered her, gotten off inside of her.

Then, this morning and all day, he had the chance to set her free. Make sure she knew how wonderful she was, how incredible last night had been, but that they shouldn't repeat it.

And once again, he'd failed. He'd taken one look at her standing in the kitchen and known he had to have her again. As long as Lana was saying yes, he would take whatever he could get.

Take everything she had to give, even though he had no right to any of it.

Max lay on the couch, pillow under his head, a blanket stretched out over him. Aurora and Lana had already gone to bed. He'd read Aurora more of the third Harry Potter book, since they were working through the series together for a second time. It was their special thing.

He'd been hoping that Aurora would go right to sleep, like she had last night. But instead, she'd protested that she wanted Lana there beside her. Because she was scared that someone was going to break into the house.

Max was sure that Aurora had seen that guy bothering Lana on the beach. Aurora had gotten quiet and skittish afterward. That probably explained her sudden fear tonight of sleeping alone. At thirteen, Aurora was both a teenager and a little girl, wrapped up into one attitude-filled hormonal package. But she was old enough to understand the implied threat that the man on the beach had represented.

Aurora needed to assure herself that Lana would be there to protect her, and that Lana was safe from the unknown, too. The two of them, united against all the threats that could be waiting out there.

The threatening *men*.

Max wasn't really his sister's protector. Lana was.

Yet another reason that he was selfish. Because he could've sought a discharge from the army if he really wanted to, even though it was a difficult process since he hadn't finished his current obligation yet. He could've chosen his sister over everything else.

But he didn't. Fucking selfish. He'd already proved that about himself, time and again. Tonight was no exception. Here he was, in typical form, hoping that Lana would leave Aurora's side tonight and come to *him*.

Instead of feeling all the self-loathing that he'd earned, his cock was stiff, and his balls were full and heavy. If Lana didn't join him soon, he'd have to go into the bathroom and beat himself off.

He was imagining all the things he wanted to do to her body. All the ways he wanted to make her come. That tight, sweet channel that he'd claimed before any other man. Max reached into his pajama pants, fisted his shaft, and squeezed, trying to calm himself down.

He heard a door open, and his nerves went right back to high alert. He'd stopped breathing.

Lana appeared at the mouth of the hallway, a dark silhouette.

"Max?"

"Come here."

Lana walked over beside the couch. He lifted his blanket and she crawled onto him, stretching out over his prone form. He knew that she felt his arousal pressing into her stomach. Lana kissed him before he could say anything, her tongue darting into his mouth as she writhed against his hard length.

She was wearing a long T-shirt. He touched her leg, trailing his hand along her inner thigh toward where her legs connected. There, his fingers met exposed skin and slick, warm wetness. She wasn't wearing any panties.

He cursed. This girl. She was going to be the end of him.

It wasn't too late to stop this. He had to give her a way out.

He broke their kiss. "Are you sure you're not too sore?"

"I'm fine. I've been wanting you all day. I can't think about anything else."

"Tell me what you want."

"Everything."

"What first?"

"Your…" He heard her swallow. "Your tongue. Between my legs."

His vision clouded over. There was no fucking way he'd turn down that request. Somebody would have to tear him away from her, kicking and screaming, because he sure as hell couldn't do it himself.

Max sat up, holding her around the hips. He kept going, standing all the way upright with her in his arms, her weight cradled against him. The blanket fell to the floor.

He carried her into her parents' bedroom and shut and locked the door.

Chapter Seventeen

*M*ax gasped and sat up. He was in his bed, sheets tangled all around him. His body was bathed in cold sweat. Moonlight shone into his bedroom, painting the space with pale blue and gray.

His mind grasped for clarity. What had just happened? Where had he been?

Oh—he'd been dreaming of Lana. Of their second night together ten years ago at her parents' house.

And he had a giant hard-on, his cock so swollen it was painful.

"Fuck me," he muttered to himself. "I'm a masochist now, apparently." Because all of this was just an agonizing reminder of Lana's rejection of him. Not once, but two nights in a row. First, when he came out and told her that he wanted her in his life. He'd never said that to a woman. Ever. And he'd crashed and burned. Pretty much the same thing had happened tonight. He'd put himself out there; she'd walked way.

Ouch.

Of course, he couldn't blame her for not trusting him. In her shoes, he wouldn't have trusted him, either.

But he'd faced obstacles before. He wouldn't have been able to build this business or any significant wealth if he gave up so easy. He wanted Lana, and he knew that she was worth all the time and work it would take to win her.

He was going to be patient. But he wasn't going to hide his desire for her, not anymore. He wanted to make sure that she had no doubt where he stood, at least about the fact that he found her irresistible. Maybe he couldn't say yet where this would go in the future, but he definitely wanted something real. And exclusive.

He'd also resolved to focus more on her needs. That was where the self-defense lesson came in. Lana was afraid, and he wanted to give her the skills she needed to fight back on her own. He had every intention of being there to keep her out of harm's way if he could. Yet he also realized how important it was to her to feel prepared. The woman had made it through college and three years of professional school. She clearly liked to learn.

Plus, it was an excuse to get close to her. So, maybe it wasn't *just* for her. Could anyone really blame him?

The tension between them had skyrocketed in the gym. He'd noticed her elevated heart rate when he locked her in his grip, the way her nipples poked at her sports bra. She'd been just as turned on by their wrestling as he was. Except for the unfortunate knee-to-the-junk interlude, which had been entirely his fault and provided some much-needed levity. He loved to see her laugh, though hopefully next time, it wouldn't be at his expense.

Afterward, Max had no expectations whatsoever that she would fall into his arms. But...he'd hoped. Of course he had. Because he was predictable.

And she'd gone, once again, into her bedroom and stayed there. While his overeager unconscious mind dreamed of her and delivered him an epic case of blue balls.

"Max?"

Jeez, he was hallucinating her voice now, too. When would his brain stop torturing him?

"Max?" she said louder. "Is everything all right?"

His head whipped toward the sound.

Lana stood in the doorway, like a vision straight out of his dreams. "I thought I heard you yell."

Max grabbed his blanket to cover the tent in his pajama pants. Then he switched on his bedside lamp. Lana's face appeared, hair pulled up into a loose ponytail. She was wearing a gauzy sleeveless top. Sleep shorts, which showed off her smooth legs. It was another glimpse of the secret side of her, an intimacy he hadn't been privy to for so long.

"Just a dream," he said.

"A bad one?"

Ha. Not even close. A dream so good that it hurt. "Not really. Did I wake you?"

She stepped further into the room. "I was up." Lana crossed her arms beneath her chest. He could see the outline of her breasts beneath the thin white fabric. The darker blush of her nipples against soft skin.

"I was feeling restless." Her eyes darted over his bare torso. "What about you?"

He really couldn't take any more banter right now. "I should get back to sleep."

"What was your dream about?"

"I'm not in the mood to talk," he ground out. "Try me tomorrow."

Her eyes were wide, pupils dilated. "Maybe I'm not in the mood to talk, either." She took another step toward him. Another.

God, what she was doing to him. His pulse thrummed at his neck. He would wait for her to be ready, but he didn't want to be teased. "If you don't mean that, please go. I don't have a lot of patience at this exact moment." Not after that dream.

"Who says *I* do?"

"Enough with the questions. Don't cross-examine me." He couldn't keep the anger out of his voice. She was playing games with him. "Lana, what are you doing here? Just tell me."

He could see her debating.

"I lied when I said I don't want you. I do."

His cock jumped. But the rest of him was still making a valiant effort to hold back. "You want me to *what?*"

"Now who's being difficult?" She sat on the edge of his bed.

He reached for her. The movement was involuntary at this point. There were cracks forming in his willpower, and that dam was ready to break.

Definitely not a masochist. He'd had just about all he could take.

Max wound his fingers into her hair. Inhaled her scent. "If you don't want this, you'd better tell me right now." He pulled her head toward him, his mouth meeting her ear. "Because I'm not as gentle as I used to be."

"Then be rough with me. I won't break."

Fuck. His eyelids closed, his breath seizing in his lungs. His teeth closed onto her earlobe. He made a fist in her hair, tugging hard at the strands.

"Oh, Max. I like you bad."

He slammed his mouth onto hers. His tongue forced its way past her lips. His kiss was punishing. Demanding. Lana opened to him instantly, then answered his intensity with her own. She sucked at his tongue, and he felt it all the way in his sac. He kicked the blankets away, and they fell to the floor.

Max swung his leg past her, turning his body. He pushed her onto the mattress. He was on his hands and knees, his body like a cage above her. Holy shit, this woman was beautiful. His eyes were greedy for her, marveling that he finally had her beneath him again. He'd wanted this for far too long, even if he hadn't admitted it until recently.

His lips moved to her neck, her collarbones. Kissing, tasting. The scent of lilacs was heady in his nose.

"Arms up."

Lana complied. He shimmied her loose top past her head and tossed it across the room.

His mouth came down on her breast, tongue swirling around her nipple. He nipped at the pink nub of flesh, gratified by Lana's moan in response. For several moments he lost himself in her round, perfect curves, until he felt Lana's hand slide past the waistband of his pants.

He grabbed her wrists and extended them over her head. "I'm not ready for you to touch me yet. When I am, you'll know."

So far, Max had been letting his desperate need for her drive him. But at this pace, he was going to blow his load as soon as she got ahold of him and gave him one firm stroke. This moment had been ten years in the making. He forced himself to slow down and pay attention.

Lana was giving him a chance, and he had to make it count. He was going to make tonight last as long as possible. By the end of it, he was going to have her panting and begging and screaming his name. He had to make her feel him so deeply that she would never be satisfied with anyone else. And only then would he allow himself to finish.

He'd hit the brakes on their momentum. Max brought his mouth down on hers again, more deliberate this time, taking slow pulls from her lips.

He resumed his path down her body, running his nose along the skin between her breasts. He tried to notice all the little details of her. The freckles and the tiny hairs that were nearly invisible. The lines of her ribs and the indentation of her belly button. His hands traced down her arms, then along her sides, fitting into the notches of her waist. His feet lowered to the floor as he moved down her body.

When he got to the elastic of her shorts, he hooked his

fingers into the fabric and pulled. They slowly slid downward, past inch after inch of toned, elegant leg. He left her underwear in place. As he nudged the shorts over her feet, he paused to kiss each ankle. The sole of each foot.

Then Max lowered his knees onto the floor, sitting back against his heels.

"How do you want me?" Lana asked.

"Stand up."

She did. Max remained on the floor, staring up at her. "I've seen this view before. Just as beautiful as I remember."

She smiled and tucked her fingers into his hair, then cupped his face. But he had other plans. Max held her hands and returned them to her sides.

"Turn around."

Again, Lana did as he asked. Her back was long and smooth, her ass curving outward enticingly.

"Bend over."

She glanced back at him. "What are you going to do?"

"What I want. Unless you say no."

She bit her lip, turning back around. Lana bent over, resting her forearms on the mattress. Her panties still covered her core, but he could see how wet she was. He pushed his nose into the damp fabric. Her smell was pure sex. His cock pulsed in his pajama pants, leaking in response to the stimulus.

"Oh, god," she moaned.

"Do you remember the first time my tongue was inside you?"

Her voice was strained. "How could I ever forget?"

Max remembered that night in vivid detail. Their second night, the one he'd just been dreaming about. He'd laid her down on the floor, marveling at his luck. This girl had chosen *him* to share herself with. He'd spread her legs wide, and with his mouth, showed her just how much he appreciated her.

But in some ways, his task that night ten years ago had

been so much easier. Because then, he was her first, and she had no one else to compare him to.

This Lana was older and wiser. More discerning. She'd had other partners.

Possessiveness made his chest tighten.

He'd never gotten jealous over his past lovers because they were temporary diversions, nothing more. But thinking of Lana with other guys made his competitive side wake up and take notice.

Max intended to erase every other man from her memory.

He yanked her panties over her hips. He wasn't asking permission. Lana had a voice, and she could tell him to stop if she wanted to. Until then, he was going to do anything and everything to please her.

But first, he had to sit back and admire this view. Fuck yes. Miles of leg, the globes of Lana's ass, and the heaven between her thighs. Right here on display, just for him.

She widened her stance, like she could feel his eyes. "Like what you see?" She wiggled her hips. He smacked playfully at one of her cheeks.

She started to laugh, and he dove forward, tonguing her slit. Lana cried out.

There we go, he thought. *Got you exactly where I want you.*

With his tongue and his lips and his teeth, Max worshipped her. Lana angled her hips to improve his access, pushing her core against his mouth. Fucking herself on his tongue. He loved the taste of her, the sounds she made. If she'd let him, he'd do this all night.

He switched the pressure to her clit, flicking over that sensitive bud again and again.

"Harder. Yes. Max, I need to come."

He sucked on her clit, smacking her ass again with the flat of his palm. Lana nearly screamed as she orgasmed. She bucked against his face. Max grabbed her hips and gave her several more good laps of his tongue, until she stopped shuddering.

Then he kissed and caressed the cheek he'd spanked.

"Stay right there. Don't move." Wiping his mouth, Max got up. He shucked off his pajama pants. He'd left a spot of dampness on them from his precum. His cock bobbed, still leaking. The drawer of his nightstand slid out, and he found a condom inside. His fingers deftly rolled the latex into place.

"I'm going to fuck you now, Lana."

She made an incoherent sound, but it was unmistakably an assent.

Her sex was still plenty wet from his efforts. Max lined himself up with her opening and buried his shaft inside.

Chapter Eighteen

*L*ana closed her eyes, basking in the sensations. Her orgasm had finished, yet every time Max pumped inside of her, she felt another delicious aftershock.

His hand was drawing circles over the spot on her ass that he'd spanked. Wow, that had worked for her. The contact hadn't been painful, but it got right to the edge. And her resulting release had been just as intense.

She'd never asked a guy to be rough with her before. Not because she was shy. She wasn't. She hadn't been shy in bed pretty much since Max. It was more that she didn't think the usual guys she dated would be into it. They were mostly fellow attorneys, or sometimes the experts and accountants who worked on civil cases for the county. Nice men that she met at the office yet didn't work with directly. Because that would've been too complicated.

Distantly, she thought of the Hearst trial. Of Max's cross-examination and Wayfair's questions. But she didn't want to ruin this moment with reality.

For too much of her life, she'd been avoiding personal "complications" to focus on her career. Either work or Aurora came first. She guessed that Max could tell her a similar story.

But this moment, with him… She was finally just letting go. She'd almost forgotten how to do that.

Max felt so good inside of her. That fullness, the friction of each movement in and out. He moved so smoothly and gracefully, like an athlete. His balls swung against her with each thrust, hitting her clit with a delightful little tap.

She felt lost when he pulled out and stepped away. "Wha—"

Max stood her up and spun her around, yanking her immediately into a kiss. Like he needed some part of him inside of her again, even just his tongue. His latex-covered erection was slick between them.

"Did you like all of that?" he asked.

"You know I did."

"I didn't hurt you?"

"Not more than I could take."

Max's head leaned back, studying her. As if he knew she was talking about more than a light spank and some mild hair pulling. The lust burning in his expression softened to something more tender.

He kissed her forehead, her nose, while his arms remained snug around her. Almost too tight, yet not crossing that line.

"Lana." Her name rumbled out of his chest.

She needed to get back to the sex. Because her heart was starting to do an excited dance, and it was way too soon for that. Max had still promised her absolutely nothing beyond the present. She wanted to just focus on this moment and worry about the future later.

She was in so deep with him. Walking away wasn't going to happen, so what other choice did she have?

"Do you want me on my knees?" she asked. "On my back?"

Instead of answering, Max swept her off her feet and into his strong grip. He knelt on the mattress, walking her to the center of the bed on his knees. There, he lay her face up, touching a gentle hand to her cheek.

That same hand trailed down lower, and a finger pressed inside her. "Good. Still wet for me."

He held himself above her, looking down at her naked body. She parted her knees and put her arms over her head, stretching her back. Enjoying his gaze.

With infuriating slowness, he eased his tip into her entrance.

"Still so tight."

Then the rest of him slid in.

She wrapped her legs around his waist. Max fucked her just like that, his upper body propped upright, eyes fixed on hers, until his movements grew fevered. He came with a roar and collapsed against her.

∼

THEY LAY on their sides in Max's bed, facing one another. He'd discarded the condom and brought them a glass of water to share. Now, they were both fighting back sleep. Lana didn't want this night to end, and she sensed he didn't either.

"I worried I'd lost any chance I had with you," Max said. "Why did you change your mind?"

"It was your little self-defense class. I knew exactly what you were doing, by the way. But it worked."

He grinned sleepily. "Mostly that was just for you. I want you to feel safe, L."

"I do. With you."

"Safe without me, too. I know that's important to you."

She put her hand to Max's, palm to palm. Their fingers folded together.

"I told Aurora that we slept together," she said.

"Just now? Do you two have a telepathic connection I don't know about?"

Lana kicked his leg beneath the covers. "No, I told her that we slept together when we were younger. I kind of had to, after the hearing. Since the entire world could theoretically know if anybody cared to read Judge Vaughn's opinion. And we both know what a small town West Oaks can be."

"How did she react?"

"Completely disgusted, at first. But when we talked about it again, she seemed okay with it. About the idea of…you and me."

Whatever that might mean. She let her words hang there, not sure if he'd volunteer to clarify things. But he didn't.

Max looked up at the ceiling. "I was a hypocrite with her. All those lectures about personal responsibility and self-control. As if I ever showed any."

"Of course, you did. When we were together, you made absolutely sure I was all-in at every moment. I don't think a girl could ask for a better way to lose her virginity."

She could tell he wanted to disagree, but he kept his mouth shut. Which was progress.

"You were so sweet to me. And you were as good as a father to Aurora, which doesn't mean you were perfect. It means you made sure she had what she needed, including your love."

"Do you think she'll forgive me for the things I screwed up?"

"I'm pretty sure she already has. But I know she'd appreciate hearing all of this from you." She didn't mention that Aurora had called him a hypocrite, too. And would probably do it again. Max would go a long way toward building an easier relationship with his sister if he was more upfront about everything he was feeling. Especially about his mistakes.

Max pulled her into his arms. She nestled her head against his chest.

"I'm still worried I don't deserve you," he said. "But if you think I do, I guess that's something."

Neither of them said anything else. Lana closed her eyes and listened to his heartbeat as she drifted toward sleep.

IN THE MORNING, Lana woke up before Max. She let herself stare at the unconscious man beside her. A shadow of whiskers darkened his chin, and his hair stuck out in every direction. His lashes splayed beneath his eyes. She didn't think she'd ever seen him this peaceful, or this vulnerable. She'd never had the chance to wake up next to Max before, and she liked it.

Last night had been...mind-blowing? Earth-shattering? There were no words. The nights she and Max shared ten years ago had been good, but Max in his thirties was dangerous in so many ways. More handsome, more uninhibited, even better with his hands, which she hadn't thought possible. Yet he was somehow more observant, too. Attentive to every aspect of her pleasure, not just what she said aloud, but what she communicated between the lines.

She could almost imagine forgetting everything else—her career ambitions, her obligations to the DA's office—and just losing herself in him. She wouldn't, of course. She wasn't that kind of woman.

But Lana was even more infatuated with him now than ever. It was a heady feeling. Wild and frightening and exhilarating. Sex with Max was more intoxicating than any wine, and she'd find herself an addict if she wasn't careful.

Infatuation? her heart scoffed. *Really?*

Okay, in love. She was so in love with him. She could be headed for more pain and disappointment if this ended badly. But she'd survived heartbreak over Max Bennett before.

She could survive it again. If she had to.

He inhaled sharply, opening his eyes. "Good morning. I had quite a dream last night."

Lana rested her elbow on the mattress and propped up her head with her hand. "So did I. I ended up in bed with a very sexy man."

"Was I any good?"

"Oh, you weren't the guy in my dream. It was someone else."

With a growl, Max rolled on top of her, capturing her hands above her head. "And who was this man? Who do I need to get rid of?"

"He was tall, good looking. Military bearing. A self-defense instructor, I think. So you'd better watch your back."

"Hope you kissed him goodbye, because if I see him, he's history." Max lowered his head to brush his cheek against hers. "I'm not letting anyone else have you."

She felt him getting harder. Lana tilted her hips to improve the angle, so he'd rub against her in just the right place. They were both already naked, and she was so tempted to let him slip inside of her. She was wet and ready to go.

Yep, this man was dangerous all right.

"Condom?" she said.

Max grabbed one from his nightstand and put it on, lightning fast. She tried not to think about why he was so skilled at that. All the women who might've been in this bed.

"Turn toward me," he said.

They were both lying on their sides, facing one another. His arm hooked beneath her top knee, raising her leg. Max worked his cock into her, taking his time. Lana pinned her leg over his behind, enjoying the way his glute muscles flexed with every thrust.

He held her close against his chest, making love to her with sweet, deep strokes. Their heads were bent together, lips just grazing, sharing one another's air. If Max had morning breath, she didn't notice. Everything about him turned her on.

It didn't take long for them to start panting, their bodies slapping together with more desperate movements. Max rolled her so she was flat on her back. He pounded her into the mattress with abandon, his mouth in a sexy snarl. He knew she was strong enough to take it, and she loved that. Lana's orgasm began an instant before his. Max's cock pulsed as her body tightened around him.

Afterward, she felt about as energetic as a puddle of goo. But Max jumped out of bed, throwing on his pajama pants. Wasn't the guy supposed to be exhausted after sex, not the girl? He was actually humming an upbeat tune.

"Where are you going?" She couldn't lift her head from the pillow.

"We both need coffee. And food. Then I was thinking we could go for a walk on the beach? Or I could hit the gym if you have work to do."

Lana pushed herself into a sitting position. She tried to smooth down her hair, which was a wild halo around her head. "You don't have your own work?"

"It's Sunday." He opened his hands, all casual, like he actually believed in weekends.

"Max, you literally live at your office. I've called you about cases on plenty of Sundays before. Remember that fraud case you consulted on, and we read through a thousand pages of documents on New Year's Day?"

"But I'm taking the day off."

Her mouth opened in shock. No sound came out.

"I want to spend it with you," he added. "If you're free."

Lana didn't think much of weekends, either. She loved going to the office on Sundays because it was so quiet.

But she was ahead on her trial work. She didn't have any appointments. She could give herself a single, glorious day to be with Max, even if it was the only one she got.

"I'm free."

He grinned, leaning his forearm against the open door-frame. "Then get that hot ass out of bed, before you tempt me to get back into it. I need to eat some actual food, not just you."

Chapter Nineteen

*W*hen was the last day Max had taken off work? Sylvie could probably tell him. But he didn't want to see or hear from anyone today but Lana. As if Bennett Security didn't even exist, and she was the only other being in their tiny, perfect universe.

They had coffee and breakfast. Lana insisted on eating leftover lasagna, which Max thought was both hilarious and ridiculous. He made himself an omelet and would've made her one, too. But she claimed that his spinach lasagna was great cold. So, he left her to it.

They were more than a little sweaty and sticky, overdue for a shower. They got each other off again under the hot water. Her hands were like magic on his dick. He hadn't given and received this many orgasms in close succession since… God, he had no clue. Since his twenties? With a soldier he'd met on base. She'd been a fan of no-strings sex, too, and she'd had some major stamina.

But Lana was proving she could hold her own in the bedroom. Or the shower. And later, every other room in his apartment, if Max got his way.

One night down, he found himself thinking as they toweled

off. *Two more to go.* Then he cursed himself. His rule of three was dead. He didn't have an arbitrary limit with Lana, not anymore. But that habitual thinking was proving harder to break than he'd expected.

They both had to go back to work tomorrow, and he had no idea where this—whatever it was—would go, anyway. But he vowed to have the same philosophy he'd had last night: he would get as much out of this time with Lana as he could and make their happiness last as long as possible. Even if it couldn't last forever.

"Were you serious about walking on the beach?" Lana asked after they were dressed.

"Absolutely." Max didn't usually spend time taking beachside strolls, but it seemed like the kind of thing people did to relax. It was romantic, wasn't it? There had to be a reason that he saw so many couples walking hand in hand from his rooftop.

Jeez, he was becoming a softy. He'd never spent time picturing romantic dates before. But Lana was bringing out new sides of him.

"We should put on bathing suits," he said. "We'll go swimming. Grab some lunch later." Max doubted the stalker would be on their trail, but in any case, he would be near Lana the whole time. There was absolutely no danger.

She was nodding, though she still looked skeptical. "Okay, that sounds nice. But I don't have a bathing suit here. All I've got are work clothes and pajamas."

"Then we'll go shopping."

Max went to his closet to find his own swim trunks, which had to be around here somewhere. He had a membership at a fancy athletic club with a pool, and sometimes went there when he was bored with his usual workout.

"Who are you? What did you do with the real Max Bennett?"

He looked back over his shoulder, grinning at her. "It's all your fault. You must've cast some sort of spell over me, making me break my rules and shirk my responsibilities. You should be enjoying this."

Lana had stopped at the entrance to his closet, watching him as he dug around through his various shelves and drawers. He had an elaborate closet organizing system, but usually couldn't figure out where the housekeeper had stowed things.

"But *you're* enjoying it, right?" she asked. "This isn't some guilt trip you're on. Like you feel you owe me?"

He slammed a drawer shut and went over to her. Max put his hands on Lana's hips, looking deep into her eyes. "Today, there is no place in the world that I'd rather be than next to you. So, grab your stuff, and let's get out there and make the most of it."

"TRY THIS ONE." Max handed Lana one bikini after another. "Oh, and this."

"I am not wearing this in public. This is all strings and no bikini." She held up the offending item in question, squinting at it.

"I know. But who said you have to wear it in public? You could wear it in my bedroom later."

The little old lady who owned the boutique appeared at his elbow, smiling angelically up at him. "Shall I get a fitting room started?"

"Yes, please." He took the pile of swimsuits from Lana's arms and gave them to the shopkeeper.

They were in a boutique that Max had passed any number of times on Ocean Lane, though he'd never been inside. The mannequins all wore sexy swimwear, and the place had chandeliers and soft lighting. It had seemed like just the sort of shop to take Lana because Max doubted that she'd come to a place like this on her own. She always looked well dressed, but he doubted she spent a lot of money on herself. DAs didn't get paid what they were worth.

Lana sighed, though she was smiling. "All right. Anything for you, Bennett."

She went into the dressing room to change. The boutique owner sidled up to him. She looked to be about ninety years old, with tight white curls forming a helmet around her head. She adjusted her glasses, which had a thin chain running around her neck.

"We have some lovely coverups as well. Would your wife be interested in anything like that?"

His chest seized at the word *wife*. But just as quickly, the shock passed. He didn't bother to correct her. He'd never cared what anybody thought. Why start now? "I'm sure she would. Why don't you grab a few for her to choose from?"

She bustled away.

Lana came out in a black two piece. The top was a push-up, which lifted her breasts nearly to her chin.

"I feel like one of those billboards for a gentleman's club." Lana turned to the side, giving him a view of the back. The bottoms covered far too much of her ass.

"You're right, this isn't the one. Less padding on the top would be better. You don't need that. You're perfect as-is, no need for enhancement."

Lana rolled her eyes, as if he wasn't being perfectly sincere.

The next suit was midnight blue, the top just two triangular pieces of gathered fabric that let her natural beauty speak for itself. The bottom could've been skimpier, but it had sexy bows at the hips. Some cheeky action in the back. He could see her underwear peeking through underneath.

"What do you think?" he asked.

She studied herself in a three-way mirror. Max enjoyed the view, as well. It was Lana in stereo. What he wouldn't do to be alone with her in here, with that mirror at their disposal. He was imagining all sorts of creative choreography.

"I like it." She spoke decisively, and she didn't ask for his opinion. But then she looked at the tag attached to the bottom half of the suit.

"Max," she hissed. "This thing costs $300! That's robbery. I'm not buying this."

"Whoever said you were buying? It's my treat."

He'd never bought her a gift before, at least not something this intimate. Back when they were younger, Lana's family didn't blink an eye at spending money to take care of Aurora, and even him, when he was visiting.

Now that he was the one with the funds, three-hundred dollars was an embarrassingly small amount of money to spend on her compared to what he owed this woman. Not in the sense that Lana had used earlier, like he was doing her a favor that he didn't otherwise enjoy. This was a gift that he wanted her to have because she deserved something special, and it would bring him joy to provide it.

"I can't accept this. It's too much."

Max slid his arms around her. "Then consider it a gift for me since I'm the one who's gets to see you in it. I'm just thinking of myself here."

She harrumphed, but she didn't issue a comeback. "Just for that… I'd like something for myself, after all."

She walked across the shop and grabbed a different bathing suit from the rack. She held it up. "I want you to buy this, too."

It was a men's suit. A tiny set of swim shorts.

"I think you'd look good in it."

She had to be kidding. "I am not wearing that." He doubted he could even fit his various parts into that miniature rectangle of shiny black fabric. It was made for some European swimwear model, not a real human.

"At least try it on. For me." She smirked because she knew

she had him there. She'd been indulging him, so he figured that this was fair turnabout. Even though there was no way in hell he was going to step out of the shop with that thing.

He'd let her have her fun. Max had an ego, but he was finding that he didn't mind when Lana laughed at him. Just so long as he could keep her smiling.

Max went into another dressing room, while Lana went back into hers. He'd thought briefly about sharing a single room, but there was no way they'd both fit, and they'd probably give the poor shop owner a heart attack.

He quickly stripped off his T-shirt and his set of swim trunks, laying both carefully on the little seat inside the dressing room. He unhooked the black suit from its wooden hanger, stretching the fabric in his hands. He couldn't believe he was actually doing this. How was this thing even going to fit? It said one-size-fits-all, which seemed to him the height of absurdity.

But when he slid the fabric over his legs and tucked his package inside, he had to admit that it was pretty comfortable. The stretchy fabric hugged him, but it wasn't too tight. Instead, it melded to his body like a second skin.

He glanced at the price tag. Four hundred bucks. No wonder. He checked the small mirror and confirmed that he did look pretty damn good in it.

Max pushed aside the curtain and stepped out into the shop, just as the boutique owner emerge from the back holding an armful of coverups. The woman's eyes went round.

"Oh, *my*."

He tilted his head at Lana, who was dressed back in her street clothes. He held out his hands, slowly spinning around.

"What do you ladies think?"

The shopkeeper made a small, strangled sound. Max glanced at himself in the huge three-way mirror. Yep, not bad. He didn't work out for vanity, but it certainly hadn't done him any harm. The suit left very little to the imagination, and he found he didn't actually mind it so much. And he definitely liked the look on Lana's face.

Her smile was absolutely devious. "I think we're ready to go swimming."

A few minutes later, they both wore their new swimsuits, sans tags. Max had put his regular clothes back on top, but Lana had consented to adding one of the coverups that the shopkeeper recommended. It was a long dress of almost transparent material. You could just make out the shape of her bikini underneath.

At the register, Max grabbed a summer-weight scarf on a whim and added it to their purchase. After they stepped out of the shop and onto the street, he pulled the scarf out of the bag and circled it around Lana's neck.

"What's this?"

"Just another part of that gift for me. I thought you'd look good in it." And she did. The perfect touch of elegance for an elegant woman.

She touched the silky fabric, pleasure clear in her expression. "Who am I to deny you?"

Max kissed her, took her hand, and they crossed the street toward the ocean. When they reached the sand, Lana pulled off her sandals and walked barefoot. For a while, they strolled hand-in-hand along the damp shore, waves lapping at their feet.

They stopped at a stand for fish tacos, eating at a counter. They didn't talk about anything important, yet the conversation wasn't slow or awkward, either. They kept coming up with new topics to discuss, the pauses easy and their banter effortless.

Max couldn't believe they'd wasted so many years holding back from one another. He couldn't remember a time when he'd felt so relaxed. So happy.

After lunch, they found a secluded spot way down the beach, far from the boardwalk and the most popular tourist swimming areas. They shed their outer clothes, piling their belongings onto the sand with Lana's sandals placed upside down to keep anything from blowing away.

Then they ran down to the water, splashing and laughing like teenagers. Like they had nothing else to worry about except this beautiful summer day. Max wished he could stop the clock and make it last forever.

Chapter Twenty

*L*ana swam head-on at the waves, ignoring the chill of the water. Usually, the Pacific was too cold for her. She preferred lying in the sun to braving the chilly currents. But today, every one of Max's glances turned up her temperature to feverish levels. She needed to cool off.

And my god, he looked unbelievable in those swim shorts. The poor woman in that boutique had barely survived the experience of seeing so much man at one time. Max's muscles weren't bunched up and blocky, like some strong guys. Instead, he was all swooping angles and long, steep curves, one muscle flowing into the next like some kind of Greek statue.

She liked the few pounds of fat he'd put onto his form in the last ten years. It softened the lines of him and made him that much more inviting, that much easier to wrap herself up in.

Max swam over to her and hooked his arms around her. Their bodies pressed together, slippery and hot compared to the icy cold of the water. He lifted her up, resting his hands underneath her to hold her weight. She put her arms around his neck. They kissed lazily, not getting too worked up. Like they had an endless stretch of time before them, and there was no rush at all.

Lana had a fleeting concern that someone would see them. Max had testified under oath just two weeks ago that they had no current relationship. But he hadn't lied. This was new and unexpected, and…not even a relationship. Not yet. Just something they were both exploring.

And who would notice them out here, anyway? This spot wasn't crowded, and most people looking for either Max Bennett or Lana Marchetti would check the courthouse or a conference room before they'd check the beach.

They splashed each other and wrestled in the water, Max alternating between tender kisses and aggressive play. At one point, he tossed her over his shoulder and pretended he was carrying her out to sea. Lana reached down to grab his ass cheek in those sexy little swim shorts, and Max retaliated by grabbing hers, letting his thumb graze a bit too close to the crotch of her bathing suit for public display.

But soon, she felt her skin tightening under the sun. She'd put on sunblock that morning, but it would've washed off by now. And despite the illusion that they had all the time in the world, the day was clearly passing. The sun was already beginning the downward portion of its journey across the sky.

"We should probably head back in," she said. "I can't believe you've gone so long without touching your phone."

"I can't either. But you know what? I don't actually care." Then his nose wrinkled. "I guess I care a little. I probably should check my messages."

"It's okay. So should I."

They waded hand-in-hand back to shore. When they reached their clothes, Lana took her cover-up out of the bag and put it on. She found their phones at the bottom of the pile, handing Max his. He unlocked the screen and started swiping his thumbs.

"Sylvie wrote. She's got news about that burner phone. A possible lead."

"Oh, that's good." Even though she wasn't happy about the intrusion of reality into their fairytale afternoon. The reference to her stalker quashed her mood.

Lana pushed her hair back, squeezing out the excess water over the sand. Max put on his clothes. Lana picked up their shopping bag, ready to go. Then she noticed that her new scarf wasn't here. It wasn't in the bag, or in the sand.

"My scarf is gone."

They both looked around, thinking that it might have somehow blown away. Yet Lana was sure she'd put it beneath their phones. She'd been worried about the wind because it was so lightweight.

The scarf wasn't anywhere.

An eerie feeling was creeping over her, the knowledge that this was no accident. Someone had been here, going through their things. Someone had taken it.

But she was afraid to voice that suspicion aloud. She had no reason to think that anybody had been here. And she didn't want to spoil this perfect day by making another reference, even tangentially, to her stalker.

Besides, even if someone had taken it, it had probably been some kid looking for something to sell.

But even as she had that thought, she knew it was ridiculous. Max had left his wallet here, too. But it hadn't been touched.

"I'm sorry," Max said. "Let's go back to the store. I'll buy you a new one."

"Maybe another time."

Even though she knew there very likely wouldn't be another day with Max like this one. But she didn't want to think about that, or the scarf, anymore.

She grabbed his hand and pulled him along the beach. "I'm salty. Let's go back and have another shower." She smiled suggestively, knowing that Max would be all too eager. "Then we can talk to Sylvie afterward."

But as they walked back, she couldn't help scanning every face on the street. Wondering if someone here could be him. Her stalker.

If he'd been following them, watching, this whole time.

BACK AT THE Bennett Security building, they didn't have time for a leisurely visit to Max's five-piece master bath.

Instead, Sylvie pounced the minute they walked into the entrance. "Max! Where have you been? You've got to take a look at this."

Sylvie slowed down, getting a better look at them. "Wait, where *have* you been?"

Max stuck his hands into the pockets of his swim trunks. The ones he'd brought from home, not his new tiny shorts. Lana guessed that those would've made a much bigger impression on the workroom.

"We were at the beach. I took the morning off."

Lana could see many things passing through Sylvie's mind. But the woman seemed to decide that no comment would be a wiser course, so she continued with her previous subject.

"I figured out who may have owned that burner phone."

They followed Sylvie across the workroom to her computer. "As I mentioned to Lana earlier, I found out from the FBI office over in L.A. that our serial number was tied to a bunch of burner phones seized from a downtown warehouse."

She leaned a hand on her desk, smiling with satisfaction. "And that warehouse belongs to the Silverlake Syndicate."

Sylvie explained what else she'd found out. The FBI seizure had been related to a drug bust. They'd found a cache of weapons, cocaine, and unmarked bills. The burner phones were probably their supply to use as needed, since various people throughout the levels of the drug operation would need new phones on a regular basis as they tried to stay a step ahead of the authorities.

Lana knew far more about the Syndicate than she wanted to. She'd spent the last few months prosecuting several senior members, including Dominic Crane himself, the organization's former leader.

"Dominic Crane is no longer the head of the Syndicate, right?" Max asked. "Lana, do you know who's heading them up now?"

"That's a complicated question without a clear answer."

Previously, Dominic's older brother Warren had led the criminal organization, but Warren was now in San Quentin serving a sentence for tax evasion. Many within the Syndicate hadn't approved of the choice of Dominic as his successor. They saw Dominic Crane as weak because he wanted to limit the Syndicate's activities to the slightly less-unsavory spectrum of the criminal underworld. Crane didn't like to engage in things like human trafficking, underage prostitution, or selling fentanyl.

A civil war had erupted within the Syndicate between those loyal to Crane and those who wanted a more brutal style of leader. Someone who had no qualms about exploiting every potential source of profit.

A few months ago, Crane had gotten caught up in a murder conspiracy, and there were still charges pending against him. His lawyer had opted to delay his trial, and Lana had already had enough to deal with.

While in jail, Crane had narrowly survived an assassination attempt by his former friends. Now that he was out on bail, Crane was stuck in his house wearing an ankle monitor.

"From what I've learned from talking to the L.A. gang unit," Lana said, "the civil war within the Syndicate has been ongoing. Several different factions have been trying to take power, but no one has come out ahead yet."

Sylvie folded her arms. "That's pretty much what the Feds were telling me, too. One of the particular factions was tied to this warehouse where the drug bust took place. So even though the Feds have made some arrests, it's nowhere near a death blow. This thing with the burner phones, though, shows that Lana's stalker is probably a member of the Syndicate, or someone low-level who works for them. They're coming after her for revenge."

"It could be one of Dominic Crane's few remaining allies," Max suggested, "trying to put pressure on her to drop the case against him."

"But I haven't heard a peep from Crane's lawyer in months."

"That doesn't surprise me at all." Max glared at Sylvie's computer screen, which displayed the info about the FBI seizure. "He's probably waiting until just the right moment. Exert pressure first, create fear. Spread chaos in the target's mind. Then claim credit and make demands. It's textbook."

That made sense to Lana. Yet she had trouble imagining that Dominic Crane was behind this. The last she'd seen him, his pompous demeanor had been diminished. He'd seemed more like a monarch who'd been dethroned, stripped of all his titles and trappings.

Yet she could also imagine that a man like him, though not as ruthless as some, would stoop to new lows when faced with such humiliation and defeat. Maybe Crane was having second thoughts about his kinder, gentler methods for running the Syndicate.

This could be his first step toward making a play to regain his rightful place.

And what better way to prove his cruelty than to go after the West Oaks prosecutor who'd dared to charge him?

"Your point is well taken," Lana said. "I'll get Crane's lawyer on the phone. I want to hear what he has to say."

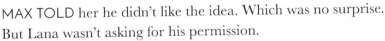

MAX TOLD her he didn't like the idea. Which was no surprise. But Lana wasn't asking for his permission.

She did, however, need his facilities to make the phone call. Either that, or she'd have to go upstairs to her makeshift office, and neither of them suggested that. His apartment was their private space, and Lana didn't want to invite Crane inside, even through technology.

Max agreed to set her up in his glass-walled office above the main workroom.

Lana dashed upstairs for a quick shower and a change into more work-like attire. Then she got Crane's lawyer, Aaron Sandford, on the phone. She couldn't contact Crane directly because he had representation.

Sandford didn't appreciate the interruption of his Sunday afternoon, but Lana was insistent. "I've discovered evidence that your client hired someone to stalk and harass me. So, if you don't want me to start adding new charges, then you'd better get him on the phone to explain himself. *Now.*"

Within an hour, the massive screen in Max's office showed a video feed of Dominic Crane's living room. He sat in a chair upholstered in expensive-looking fabric, legs crossed casually, while Sandford stood beside him wearing a golf polo and khakis. Crane's ankle monitor was just visible below his pant cuff.

"Always a pleasure to see you, Lana," Crane said brightly, as if they were great friends. "What can I do for you?"

She sat against Max's desk, trying to match Crane's easy demeanor. Max lounged on his couch, off-camera, drumming his fingers against the jeans he'd changed into.

She laid out some of what she knew so far. How someone had been stalking and threatening her, though she kept the details vague. How the phone used to make the harassing calls had been tied to the Syndicate.

"You have no evidence of my client's involvement in anything," Sandford barked.

Crane acted like his lawyer hadn't spoken. "And you think I'm behind it?"

"Your name came to mind."

Crane glanced to the side, inclining his head. The man had no right to be so attractive. His features were classical, downright beautiful, like old medieval paintings Lana had seen in museums. Like Lucifer contemplating the Garden of Eden, perhaps.

"I'm sorry someone's been bothering you. But I don't regret being on your mind. I never talk to anyone as pretty as you these days, being trapped in this house." His head tilted back the other way. "Though pretty isn't the right word for you. Stunning? Captivating? Maybe we should ask Max Bennett what he thinks, since no doubt he's off camera scowling at me."

Lana held up a hand at Max, who was indeed scowling. "Mr. Crane, you're talking to me right now. The only reason I'm here at Bennett Security, instead of at my own office, is that this stalker tried to run me off the road. That's an attempted murder charge to add to your Murder One, once we prove he was working under your orders."

Sandford was apoplectic. But once again, Crane seemed to be pretending his attorney didn't exist. A wrinkle creased his otherwise flawless face. "Why would I want to harm you? The first-degree murder charge is weak, and you know it. That's why you've been more than happy to delay my trial, as have I, though for different reasons, obviously. I don't want to be out in the open while people are trying to kill me. And you've already gotten guilty verdicts against two other individuals for the murder I'm charged with."

"Those are your accomplices. All of you are equally guilty."

"But the jury won't see it that way. I didn't pull any triggers, and I didn't issue any orders. I'm innocent. You must know that."

She had to admit, Crane's reasoning wasn't too far off. Lana knew the weaknesses of her case against him.

But innocent? No way. Dominic Crane was far from innocent.

He was definitely guilty of other crimes, so she wasn't eager to simply turn him loose and dismiss all charges. For now, Crane still had a motive to get rid of her, or to put pressure on her.

"But how do you explain the connection between my stalker and the Syndicate? You expect me to believe that's a coincidence?"

"I can't explain it. But I'm happy to look into it. As a favor to you. A personal favor."

Lana heard Max grumbling. She didn't look over.

"What do you want in exchange?" Because there had to be something.

Crane smiled like the wolf meeting Red Riding Hood. "Your promise that next time, you'll come see me in person. I never have visitors. I'm lonely."

Max's eyes bugged. But he managed to keep himself seated, to Lana's relief.

"That's not going to happen. But if you provide me with useful information, I'll entertain other suggestions. Mr. Sandford can let me know."

Lana pressed a key on Max's computer and cut off the call.

Chapter Twenty-One

*M*ax held his tongue for Lana's entire call with Crane. He was quite proud of his self-control, actually, because what he'd really wanted to do was leap through that screen and bloody Crane's perfectly shaped nose. Max hadn't struck out in violence against anyone since the army, but he had no patience for reprobates like Crane. He knew Lana wanted him to behave, though, so he was trying to act civilized.

"Please don't tell me you believe his denials," Max said, once Lana had ended the call.

"Not really. But I have to at least entertain the possibility that he's telling the truth."

"Why is that?"

"Because if it's not Crane, then I'll have left myself blind to whoever's really behind it."

Max stood up from his office couch. "You're right. Can't cover one flank while leaving the other open to attack."

"Exactly. Thank you for repeating what I just said."

She was sitting in his chair, typing on his computer. Max leaned over and kissed the back of her neck. He was glad he had his walls frosted over, so nobody could see inside. Max was having some ideas about that couch he'd just been sitting on.

"Have I told you how sexy you look in a tailored suit?"

"Have I told you how sexy you look out of one?" She didn't look away from the screen until she'd finished her email. "I wrote to Trevor asking him to pull the files we have on defendants from the Silverlake Syndicate. I'm going to send Crane the names and see what he can tell me about them. Whether he's truthful or not, his answers will be revealing."

"Am I allowed to say that's a good idea? Or will I get in trouble?" He smiled to show he was teasing. She gave him a heated look.

Definitely in trouble, he thought. *I'm way out past the shallows right now, but I'm loving every second of it.*

"Are you up for another self-defense class?"

Her eyebrows shot up. "Max, are you trying to seduce me? Or are you trying to get a workout in?"

"Can't I do both? But this class won't be in the gym, and it's not a workout. I had something else in mind."

Lana went up to change out of her work clothes. While he waited for her, Max updated Sylvie on the developments with Dominic Crane. She agreed to keep investigating on her end.

"I don't trust Crane," Sylvie said. "His story's a little too easy for my taste. He claims no knowledge, then dangles out the possibility of information? I'm sure he'll come up with something and end up looking like the hero. That could've been his plan all along."

Which were Max's thoughts exactly. That was why he trusted Sylvie so much. He didn't have to explain things. "Keep after him."

Lana stepped out of the elevator in ripped jeans, not unlike the ones she used to wear as a teenager. Max tried to hide his reaction, but when he looked back at Sylvie, his employee was smirking.

"Took the morning off, huh, boss?"

"Watch it. I know your bank account and your social security number."

Sylvie winked. "You think I don't know yours?"

Chuckling, Max went over to meet Lana by the elevator. "Where are we going?" Lana asked.

"Lower level. The gun range."

Downstairs, Max held open the door, gesturing Lana inside. The range wasn't occupied right now. As always, his employees had left the place tidy. Max hated to see spent cartridges or messy target paper hanging around.

He strode over to a wall cabinet and unlocked it. Inside were an array of handguns: a Sig Sauer P226, a Ruger LC9, reliable Glock 22s, and the easier-to-conceal Glock 19, among others.

Max chose the Ruger, since it was nice and compact. "When's the last time you practiced?" He figured Lana had at least a basic knowledge of how to shoot, given her profession. But she surprised him.

"Never have. I don't like guns."

"No? They're necessary."

"I accept that. Some of the other DAs carry. But they're not necessary for *me*."

"Nobody's saying you have to walk around Ocean Lane packing heat. But you should know how to use a weapon. In case you're in a situation and that's the only way out."

"Is this because of Dominic Crane? You're trying to prove something?"

"No, it's about keeping you safe, whether I'm with you or not. Humor me, all right? If you want to chalk it up to my insecurities or my ego, go right ahead."

He got them both protective glasses and ear covers. Max checked that the Ruger was in good shape and unlocked the separate cabinet where they kept the ammo. He showed Lana how to load the gun. As he did so, he pointed out the different parts of the weapon, explaining the basics that she would need to know in order to use it safely.

He ushered her over to a stall and put a fresh target up about ten feet away.

Max held out the gun, keeping the muzzle carefully pointed away from either of them. "Go ahead. Point and shoot."

He saw her throat work as she swallowed. Lana held the gun awkwardly in her hands. He stepped over behind her, stretching his arms around her, and covering her hands with his.

"Like this," he said loudly against her ear, so she'd hear over the covers. He helped her position her fingers properly. "Grip it gently, but firmly. Not too tight."

"Like my hands on your dick?"

Actually, he liked a tight grip. But he played along. "You got it."

Lana spent almost a full minute shifting her weight and moving her fingers around on and off the trigger. He could almost see the gears moving in her mind, trying to apply everything he'd said. She'd made it clear that she didn't want to be doing this, yet she was taking everything he'd taught so far to heart.

Finally, she squeezed off a shot. It hit the very edge of the target.

"Not bad."

Max stepped in close behind her again, stretching his body over hers. "See if you can feel how this is different." He held her arms, telling her how to sight the gun. Then he told her to squeeze the trigger.

This shot came much closer to the center of the target.

"That did feel better. Thanks."

Max stepped back again, and Lana kept working on the target. She was a quick study, as Max had known she would be. Before long, she was getting most of her shots onto the figure outlined on the target.

She set down the gun and took off her ear covers. Max did as well.

"Always aim for a body shot. Not the head. You'd probably miss. It takes a whole lot more practice than this to have any real accuracy. And remember, never point your weapon at someone unless you're prepared to pull that trigger. Prepared both physically and mentally. Because you're right. That gun could be used against you if the other person can get it away from you. If he senses that you're not willing to do what's necessary, he'll take every advantage."

A serious look came over Lana's face. She stared at the target with its array of bullet holes. "If that stalker comes after me, and I can't run or talk my way out, then I *will* do whatever is necessary. I'm not going to let anybody stop me from protecting the people—or the ideals—that I love."

"I know you wouldn't."

Max doubted so much in this world, including himself. But in Lana, he had absolute faith.

Chapter Twenty-Two

While Max cleaned the handgun she'd used for practice, Lana went out into the hallway to get some air. The range was stuffy to her, the smell of gunpowder and cleaning chemicals too strong despite the ventilation.

She dealt with law-enforcement every day, and she respected what a difficult job they had to do. Part of that job required using guns. But she also spent her days talking to victims of gun violence. So, she had mixed feelings about using a deadly weapon herself.

She knew Max had a point, though, and she appreciated the effort he was making to teach her how to protect herself. She didn't feel comfortable carrying a gun on a regular basis, but at least she would know how to handle one if the need arose.

She was excited about the new lead in their investigation to find her stalker. That made her feel more secure as well. Whether Crane was involved or not, at least she had another puzzle piece that might lead her to the answer.

And as for the scarf going missing from the beach, any number of things could've happened to it. She had no real reason to suspect that the stalker was involved. So, there was also no reason to tell Max about her suspicions.

It was almost the end of their day together, and tomorrow they would both have to go back to work. The Hearst trial would resume. With these last few hours, Lana just wanted to concentrate on Max. She had no idea what the next few days would bring for them, whether they could maintain the closeness they'd been sharing all day. No matter what, she was going to cherish every memory she'd made with him today. Even if those memories turned bittersweet.

The elevator opened, and Devon came out. He stopped when he saw Lana standing there in the hall.

"Hey," she said, "Max is in the range. If you were looking for him."

"Actually, I was looking for you. I wanted to check on the schedule for tomorrow. Since I'll be your chauffeur again."

She told him when she planned to leave in the morning, and how long she expected tomorrow's trial proceedings to go. It would be another long day.

He nodded along, entering the information into the schedule on his phone. "I'm about to head out for Sunday dinner with my family. Did you want to come? I know Aurora would love to see you."

Normally, Lana would have said yes without a thought. She loved Sunday dinners at the Whitestone residence. Devon had an adorable baby niece, and his mom and sister were always fun to be around. She wanted to see Aurora, too, and find out how her friend was doing after their scare a few days ago.

"Max is invited," Devon added. "In case you were worried about not including him. Or anything like that."

Lana hid her smile. Devon clearly had questions about what was going on between her and Max. The Bennett Security office was small, and rumors seemed to fly pretty fast. Everyone had to have noticed their beach attire when they returned in the afternoon, and Max's decision to take most of the day off had no doubt caused a buzz.

She considered whether Max would want to come along with her. They had both gone to Sunday dinners at the Whitestones' before, but they hadn't been...whatever they were now. A couple? That seemed like a stretch.

Her uncertainty answered her question. She and Max definitely weren't ready to make any appearances at family dinners. They needed to know what the heck they were doing first.

"I'll stay here. Max and I wanted to spend some time together before work starts up again tomorrow. But I'd love to come for Sunday dinner next week."

Devon twisted his lips, his hesitation obvious. She almost put him out of his misery. But she was really curious how he was going to handle this.

"I'm not trying to get into your business, but... You and Max? Does Aurora know?"

"She knows it's a possibility. I haven't spoken to her about recent developments."

"I just don't want to keep anything from her, and I definitely don't want to lie. Because I love her, but also because she'll be able to tell."

"You can tell her whatever you think you should. But don't ask me what's going on between me and Max because I honestly don't know."

Aurora wasn't a kid anymore. She wasn't going to get hurt or confused if Lana and Max didn't work out. The most likely possibility was that Aurora would insist on taking Lana's side and get angry with her brother. Even if Lana wasn't upset, and Max wasn't to blame.

Devon was hesitating again. "Lana, you can tell me to butt out if you want, but I just want to make sure you're doing well. You're happy? A few days ago, you were pretty pissed off to be staying here. I didn't want to say anything, but..."

"You're looking out for me? That's sweet Devon, thank you. But I promise I'm good. You can tell Aurora that, too."

Max came out into the hall. "Evening, Whitestone. Heading home?"

"Yes, sir." Devon nodded at Lana. "You have a nice night. I'll see you in the morning." He pushed the button and got into the elevator.

"What was that about?" Max asked. "He seemed tense."

"Oh, we were talking about you."

"What *about* me?"

"You don't need to know everything, Max." Lana pushed the button for the elevator again. When it returned, she stepped inside, smiling. "Going up?"

"YOU'VE BEEN GIVING me some lessons, which I've appreciated," Lana said. "But now it's my turn. I'm going to teach you my favorite recipe."

They were in Max's kitchen. After coming back upstairs, the two of them had both stopped by their rooms to check their messages. Neither of them could go too many hours without plugging back in. Lana was glad they had that in common. At least she knew that this, whatever "this" was and wherever it might lead, wouldn't end badly because of a mismatched commitment to their work.

Max arched a skeptical brow. "You're going to teach me to cook something? I thought you didn't cook. And, no offense, but I already know how."

"Oh, but you don't know how to make my grandma's famous mac and cheese." She opened the fridge and started grabbing ingredients. Milk, a block of cheddar, eggs. "I know it's not fancy but give it a chance. It was my favorite as a kid."

He scoffed. "I don't need things to be fancy. I'm not fancy."

"Are you kidding? Have you seen this apartment? Or this entire building? You are *so* fancy."

"I like nice stuff and spending the money that I've made, but I don't really *need* any of this. It's not really *me*."

She snorted a laugh. "Sure. Says the guy who wore a four-hundred-dollar bathing suit the size of a deck of cards today."

"That was for you, and you know it." He grabbed her and swung her around. When he set her down, Max buried his face against her neck. "L, you knew me before any of this stuff. You know the *real* me."

"Do I?"

"I think so." He lifted his head, eyes intense. "I want you to."

She stretched up to kiss him. "I want that, too."

Lana found dried macaroni in his pantry and told him to boil it. While Max's water was heating, she pulled out a heavy saucepan and started melting butter. Next, she mixed flour with the butter, then whisked in the milk.

"My grandma was from the South, so she always added egg to her milk mixture, which makes it custardy."

"Please tell me there's an onion in there somewhere. Celery?"

She smacked him with an oven mitt. "You and your vegetables."

Lana told him the rest of the steps, but she couldn't tell if he was listening. He was too busy watching her, his eyes as melty as the cheese. Once the pasta was finished, Lana mixed everything together in a baking dish and stuck it into the heated oven.

"See? I can cook something. I used to make that for Aurora, whenever she felt down. It's the ultimate comfort food."

They ate sitting on bar stools at the kitchen counter. Max opened a bottle of French white wine to go with it, which

Lana argued was the very definition of fancy. But she couldn't deny that the pairing was phenomenal.

They did the dishes together, and Lana could almost imagine doing this every day.

"Did you have a good time today?" he asked.

"I did. I haven't spent all day with you like this since... well, you know. Ten years ago."

"You wore the jeans." He touched the denim at her hip.

"Not the same ones as back then. But, yeah. You still like them?"

He answered by slanting his mouth onto hers. Lana remembered their first kiss, how aggressive he was. But younger Max had still needed reassurance that she wanted the same things he did.

Now, Lana felt like they were perfectly in tune without any need for second-guessing. Max's hands and lips were more confident, yet he also showed her even more tenderness. As if he knew exactly how much strength he had and knew just when to use it.

I love you, she wanted to say.

Max, I'm in love with you.

But those words stayed firmly inside.

They were still standing in the kitchen. She reached for the button of his fly and popped it open. "There's something I wanted to do back then. But I was too nervous."

She pushed his tee up over his ridged stomach. He helped her take it off. Then she nudged his zipper down the rest of the way and yanked down both his jeans and his briefs in one go. Max stepped out of them, his cock jutting out, already glistening. He smirked, bracing his hands back against the countertop, like he knew she wanted to look at him.

She took her time, letting her eyes move over him inch by inch. Her breath quickened in her nostrils, the scent of him stronger every second. Lana lowered herself down to her knees.

Her tongue darted out, flicking over the pearl of precum at his tip. The salty taste of him spread through her mouth.

"Oh, fuck yes, Lana…"

She took more of him, suctioning her lips against his shaft. Max's fingers dropped into her hair and guided the rhythm. Her hand reached up to squeeze his ass cheek. He growled, growing more uninhibited. She was happy to keep on taking all he had to give.

But he pulled her off him. "That's amazing, but it's not how I want to come."

Max peeled off her clothes. Once she was naked, he slung her body over his shoulder, just as he had in the ocean. His fingers teased her from behind. But he didn't carry her to his bed.

He went to the couch instead.

He set her down on the sectional, then sat beside her. "Come here." His palm tapped his thigh. Lana rotated herself so she was straddling him. She surged forward to kiss him, rubbing herself against his shaft.

Early that morning, she'd felt the urge to go without the condom, to feel all of him, and now that craving was even stronger.

"Max," she murmured between kisses, "I have an I.U.D. And I've been tested since my last partner."

He stopped to look at her. "I tested clean, too. You want to?"

She nodded, not bothering with more words. Her lungs were already tight from desire.

Yes.

Chapter Twenty-Three

*L*ana's opening met his the tip of his cock and she slid down. They both gasped at the sensations. She was so tight around him.

Max felt his orgasm already imminent, so he held her hips to slow her down. Her talented mouth had already gotten him close, but the feeling of being inside her with no barriers? It was over the top.

"I've never gone bare before." With his rule of three, he'd never developed that level of trust with anyone. But he got tested on a regular basis, and he wasn't worried about pregnancy for certain…reasons. That was something he might need to mention if this thing between them kept going.

But not now. Jesus, he could hardly concentrate. Lana's lush naked body was perched on his dick. How the fuck had he lucked into this?

"I've never gone bare, either," Lana told him.

He couldn't help grinning. Once again, he was having her in a way no other man had before. That gave him a private, possessive thrill.

"Okay, we can move now. I won't lose my shit like a teenager."

She rocked her hips, and he pumped into her. He loved how wet she was, how slickly their bodies moved. Max brushed her hair back from her shoulders and face. He had this inexplicable swelling feeling in his chest, nothing he'd experienced with any other woman. Like he wanted to do more for her, be more, and he had no idea how he'd ever be enough. But damn, he was going to try.

Lana braced her hands on his shoulders, chasing her own pleasure against his cock. Her tits bounced hypnotically. *Yes, more*, he thought. With Lana, he always wanted more.

He felt her start to come even before she cried out, her channel tightening around him. That was all he needed to set him off. His hips bucked and he shouted, his balls emptying everything they had into her.

Lana slumped into him. His dick was still pulsing inside of her. With his eyes drifting closed, Max kissed her head and her shoulder, rubbing her back.

I love you, he thought.

He'd been drowsing, but now his eyes popped open. Where the hell had that come from?

She raised her head, smiling. "I might consider getting off of your lap, but I'm afraid to make a mess on your *fancy* couch."

"Oh." Max grabbed hold of her and stood. Lana yelped, arms reaching for his neck. He was still inside of her. He walked them both to the bathroom to clean up. Not that he cared so much about the mess, but he wanted an excuse to take care of her.

The faucet splashed warm water into the sink. He ran a washcloth under it and wiped it gently over Lana's legs, then himself. They both brushed teeth, got ready for bed, kissing in between.

After that, he picked her up again, cradling her slender form against his chest.

"Max, I do know how to walk."

"But why should you have to?"

He took her to bed, switching off lights along the way. They snuggled beneath the covers. In the dark, he stared at the ceiling.

I love her.

Oh my god. I love her.

Could that really be right? Max loved Aurora, even certain friends, especially from the army. But that "love" was nothing like what he was feeling now.

The longer he lay there, the more intense the feeling grew. A throat-squeezing, chest-collapsing anguish that was also, somehow, the most potent and exhilarating thing he'd ever experienced.

The more he thought about it, the more he knew it was true. He'd felt a weaker form of this same sensation around Lana countless times before. Excitement to be near her, which he'd chalked up to residual lust from their past fling. Restlessness when they were apart.

Maybe he'd been in love with her for a long time.

Max wasn't afraid of many things. He wasn't afraid to tell her. But there were other important things he had to tell her first.

He didn't really want to do this. But Lana was worth every risk. Including the truth.

And if Lana was going to be with him, then she needed to know exactly what she was getting.

He turned onto his side. He could see her in the dim light, sleepy but still awake.

"Hi," she said.

"Thinking about the trial tomorrow?"

"Yep. Going over my questioning of Claire Barnes in my head. It's going to be a big day. But you look like you have something on your mind, too. What is it?"

He brushed her cheek. "It's okay. It can wait." *That's a cop out*, he thought. But he didn't want to distract her from tomorrow.

"Tell me."

Shit. Here goes.

He licked his lips. "You asked a few days ago if there was some reason that I think I'm shitty at relationships. Some specific reason. There is, and I need to tell you." He pushed a breath out of his lungs. He really did need to do this, though it wouldn't be easy.

"Okay." She sat up, tugging the covers around her to keep warm.

He propped his arm against the mattress, resting his head on his hand.

"I have had a girlfriend before. But not since high school. Tori. We dated for two years."

"Wait. Two *years?*"

"Yeah, I know. Hard to believe. It started out casual. For me, anyway. I liked her, but I didn't take it too seriously. I was busy with my friends, stuff that I wanted to do. My teachers said I was driven, that I should plan for college, but I knew that wasn't right for me. I wanted to get out of West Oaks. Get away from my parents. But I wanted to do something that mattered to me, and that wasn't ever going to be academics."

He ran a finger down Lana's arm, needing that sense of connection with her. "I saw how my mom and dad lived paycheck to paycheck, often falling short. I wanted to believe I could be more than that. It wasn't that I didn't respect their jobs in the service industry. I'll respect anybody who works hard, no matter where they came from, or what job title they have. But my parents were so irresponsible. They shirked off work when they felt like it, spent more than they had. Expected me to get a job at fifteen to help them make up the difference. Aurora has this rosy idea of who our parents were, like they were doing the best they could. But I don't agree. I've forgiven them, but... They could've done a lot more to prevent what happened later, having to send Aurora away to keep themselves afloat."

Max sat up and put his arm around Lana. He couldn't keep still. This next part was harder.

"Never once did I think about where Tori, my girlfriend, would fit into my life after graduation. I thought we were just having fun, passing the time. She said she loved me, and I probably said it back, just because that was easier. And I thought maybe I did love her. Even though I had no idea what that really meant.

"But near the end of senior year, she invited me to dinner at her house. Her father pulled me aside and said he was happy to welcome me into the family, and that he'd help me pay for a ring. He just wanted to know when I'd hurry up and pop the question, because he knew I was fucking her, and it was about time."

"Wow," Lana breathed. "That's a lot of pressure at eighteen."

No kidding. "I was in shock, pretty much. I talked to Tori after, and she was on the exact same page as her dad. Two years was plenty of time to know we loved each other, and since neither of us was headed to college, it made sense to settle down. I told her I needed to think."

Max's stomach churned as he thought of what happened after.

"What did you do?"

"The next day, I went to a recruitment office and joined the army."

"Really? The next day? Had you been planning to enlist?"

"No. Never. I just walked past it, saw the sign, went in. On impulse. No real thought."

It had been pure instinct to walk into that office. He hadn't known what to do about Tori. He'd liked her a lot. Hadn't even wanted to break up. Tori was a good, sweet girl who was worthy of real love.

But the thought of getting married, having kids, playing out his parents' lives? He'd felt himself shriveling up on the inside. It was like thinking about *dying*.

He'd needed to escape. That was the only thing that mattered. *Run.*

"It's not like they shipped me out that afternoon, like it was World War II, or something. The recruiter asked me all kinds of questions about why I wanted to join. At first, maybe I was bullshitting, but the more I talked to him, the more it made sense. Like somehow, I'd known all along, deep down? And of course, it was a great fit for me in the end. But that was just it. I wasn't thinking of anybody but myself."

"What happened to Tori?"

"She was confused, and shocked, but willing to consider life as an army wife. Then I told her I didn't want her with me. She was devastated. Heartbroken. Of course, she was. I mean, who does that? My girlfriend basically asked me to marry her, and I joined the army to get away from her?"

"That's obviously not the only reason. You said it was the right place for you."

He rubbed his temples. "I wasn't thinking of Aurora, either. How I'd be leaving her with my parents to fend for herself."

Lana stayed quiet for a minute or two. Max's thoughts were spinning out, the way they always did when he remembered that time in his life.

"But I didn't just join the army, L. There's more."

"Yeah?"

"I got a vasectomy."

She didn't say a word.

"It took a while to find a doctor willing to do it, since I was so young. But I kept thinking that if Tori had been pregnant,

I'd have been stuck. Trapped inside a life that, for me, was as good as death. Or maybe even *worse* than death. That's why I'm shit at relationships. Because I've never been good at giving up my freedom for someone else. That's why…you need to understand what I have to offer. It might not be everything you want."

And nowhere near everything you deserve.

"Okay," she said slowly. "You don't want kids?"

Just the word made his anxiety ratchet upward. "I'm not sure." If he could want a family with anyone, it would be her.

"I mean, if we're talking about this… Vasectomies can get reversed, theoretically. But I'm focused on my career. I'm nowhere near ready to think about those kinds of decisions."

"Neither am I. Believe me."

"So, let's set that aside. Are you telling me you don't want marriage? Or that you don't want *any* long-term relationship? Ever?"

"I don't know." His voice sounded so small.

He hadn't been able to give up his own wants for a woman before. But maybe he could for Lana… Maybe. He liked to think so.

I just know that I love you, he thought.

Yet, after what he'd just told her, those words felt like a demand. *Love me back, even though I'm offering you no commitment whatsoever.*

"Can we take this one day at a time?" Max asked. That wasn't even truly what he wanted. But he thought that was the safest course for them both. So that her expectations wouldn't be too high.

"Of course. We can do that." She kissed his forehead. "If you're offering more days like today, it won't be too hard to convince me."

Relief crashed over him, but somehow it still didn't feel right. Like he'd gotten away with something.

They settled back under the covers, arms wrapped around

one another. He wanted to make her happy. He didn't want to lose her. Taking this day by day could be enough for them both. For now.

Until he was ready to tell her how he really felt, and she was ready to hear it.

Chapter Twenty-Four

"The People call Claire Barnes," Lana said.

To her right, the jurors and alternates fidgeted in their seats. Trevor, Lana's second chair on the trial, ushered Claire into the courtroom from the hallway. The woman stepped into the witness stand, taking the waiting chair. The bailiff swore her in.

Lana went through her preliminary questions, establishing Claire's identity as the older sister of the victim, Heather. It was both to introduce Claire to the jury and to get her comfortable. They'd gone over her testimony so many times, but it was always different doing the real thing.

Claire wasn't nervous, though. Lana knew this woman was more than ready. She had a hard glint in her eye that said nothing would stop her from telling her story. After all this time, she finally had her chance.

"When was the last time you saw your sister Heather?"

"September 17, 1998. It was a Thursday."

"Could you tell me what happened that day?"

Claire shifted in her seat. "I went to the beach to look for her. Heather spent a lot of time there, sometimes sleeping there with some other kids who were runaways. I went to check on her as much as I could, to bring her food and try to convince her to come home for a shower or a hot meal."

"Why wasn't Heather living at home?"

"She didn't get along with my parents. They were very strict, and they came down really hard on her after they caught her sneaking out one too many times. But it backfired. She took off altogether."

Lana had to ask each question carefully, not leading Claire's testimony and not jumping too far ahead. It took patience, but it was the best way to lay the groundwork and make sure the jury observed every important detail.

"And how old was Heather at this time?"

"Seventeen."

"How old were you?"

"Eighteen. I had just graduated from high school, and I was starting at West Oaks Community College."

"What happened when you got to the beach on September 17, 1998?"

"I started looking for her. There were different spots that she liked to hang out. There are a couple beaches with good surfing, and she'd go there in the mornings. She could usually borrow someone's surfboard and get out on the waves. In the afternoons, she and her friends stayed closer to the tourist areas, hoping that someone would buy them a meal, or that they could find leftovers from a picnic. That day, in September, I checked all those places, plus some others where I'd seen Heather before. But I couldn't find her."

"What time of day was this?"

"Around lunchtime."

"Did you return home?"

"Yes."

"Did you go back to look for Heather again that day?"

"I did. At night."

Now, Lana needed to set up the rest of Claire's testimony. "Did Heather have a means of making money at that time?"

Lana had practiced this answer with Claire so many times, and yet the witness still hesitated. "She told me that she was giving blow jobs or sleeping with men for money."

Wayfair stood up, his hands face down on the defense table. "Objection. Hearsay."

"Statement against interest," Lana countered.

"Overruled."

Lana said a silent thanks. Back in 1998, Ryan had claimed to police that he just gave Heather a ride, that she'd only been in his car for five minutes. But if he'd picked her up for sex, Heather would've gone willingly with him to a secluded location. So the fact that she'd been turning tricks was important to undermine Ryan's version of events.

Lana flipped through her notes again, returning her focus to her primary line of questioning. "Did you find Heather on the night of September 17?"

"When I got to the beach that night, where people sometimes set up sleeping bags, I didn't see her right away. Someone had a fire going on the sand, and it was hard to make out the different faces in the dark. I walked around for a while, hoping that I would spot her. I was going to give up and head back home again when I turned back to look at the street. That's when I saw Heather. She was standing on the curb of Ocean Lane, on the opposite side of the road, so she was facing toward me."

"You're sure it was her?"

"Absolutely. It was Heather. Then a car pulled up, and a male got out of the driver's seat. He walked toward Heather and started talking to her. She smiled at him, like they knew each other."

"What did the male look like?"

"Nice leather coat. Around my age then, eighteen or nineteen. I recognized him. It was Ryan Hearst."

Claire testified that Ryan was well known around West Oaks. He went to a private academy but dated a lot of the girls at the local public high school. He had a reputation of providing drugs or alcohol or even money for dates.

"Then Heather got into the car with Ryan," Claire said. "And that was the last time I ever saw her alive."

AFTER THEY FINISHED for the day, Lana met Claire out in the hallway. They found a quiet spot to talk. Trevor was still inside the courtroom, gathering their materials, and getting things ready for the next day.

"How do you feel about your testimony?" Lana asked.

"I think it went well. Do you?"

Lana could hardly contain her smile. "Yeah. Yeah, I do."

She was trying not to get overconfident, but Claire's testimony had been a huge success. Trevor had watched the jury. The entire time, they'd been rapt, nodding their heads as Claire spoke. Even Wayfair's cross-examination couldn't make her waiver from her testimony.

Claire had told them all about Heather, creating a picture of a real—if troubled—person. Not just a name or a picture. A real girl who'd been vulnerable, but who'd been loved.

She had also testified about Heather's locket, which the girl always wore and never took off, not even when she went swimming. Tomorrow, Lana would drive home the most damning evidence in the case: Max's discovery of that locket in Ryan Hearst's bedroom.

Claire exhaled, closing her eyes. "You don't know how good it feels to have that over with. It's like I can feel Heather here, cheering me on. That's the only way I made it through. Just remembering her, thinking of how much she deserved this day. This entire trial." She blinked away tears. "It's really going to happen, isn't it? He's going to pay for what he did."

Lana squeezed the woman's hand. "We're almost there."

"And it never would've happened without you. Thank you,

Lana. This means so much to my family. To me. And I will forever be grateful."

～

DEVON DROVE her back to Bennett Security. Lana had rarely felt such elation during a case. She'd known from the start that proving Ryan Hearst's guilt would be difficult. But everything had been lining up just as she needed. Her witnesses, the jury, even her own level of focus. She knew she could thank Max for that. The stress of having a stalker hadn't affected her one bit.

As they walked inside the building, a receptionist stopped Lana. "Miss Marchetti? There's a package for you. Just got dropped off by a courier. I think it might be something related to your trial?"

Everyone in the building knew all about her stay here and the trial that was going on.

"Thank you." She took the box. It was stamped with the label of a local shipping company, though she didn't recognize the name on the return address.

"Need anything else?" Devon asked.

"No, not tonight. Max is driving me tomorrow, so I'll see you in a couple of days."

She spotted Max upstairs in his office. The glass walls were turned to transparent, and he was pacing around, talking into a Bluetooth headset. She couldn't wait to see him and tell him everything that had happened at the trial today. But that could wait until he was ready to end his own workday.

She went upstairs to change her clothes and relax. She could get used to this, coming home to Max. Of course, it wasn't going to last very long. Even if they continued keeping things "one day at a time," as Max had suggested, she would go back to living at her own townhouse soon. Assuming they identified the stalker, or the guy left her alone.

Yet, she still could imagine it so easily. Seeing him for dinner, discussing their day. Making love before bed and getting up early to go together to the gym.

She hadn't had much time to think about what he'd shared with her the night before.

His high school girlfriend. His vasectomy.

Lana had always assumed she'd have children someday, though it wasn't on her agenda for the near future. She wasn't bothered by the possibility that Max couldn't give her biological kids. After bringing Aurora into her family, she'd pictured herself adopting.

But just the fact that Max had wanted to mention his vasectomy proved that he was actually considering their future relationship, what it might look like. Max wasn't sure he wanted kids at all, and that was something to consider.

Yet the real question was whether Max could commit to her. He was clearly struggling with the decision. She didn't think he was anywhere near as selfish as he liked to claim. He'd still been a kid at eighteen, scared to be tied down. Max wasn't a child anymore. And neither was she.

This decision wasn't something she could rush, certainly not something she could force him into. She could only decide for herself what she needed, and then ask herself whether he could provide it. And whether she could be patient enough to wait.

But as she walked through his apartment, not noticing its opulence, but simply all the little reminders of *Max*, she knew that she'd wait as long as it took.

Max Bennett had been her first love. Her only love. The way she felt about him had only grown deeper. She couldn't possibly turn away from him now.

Lana came back out of her bedroom in her comfiest leggings and a sweatshirt. After such a productive day, she was more than ready to decompress. She walked by the kitchen table and saw the package from the courier. She'd nearly forgotten about it.

She picked up the box. Every edge of it was covered with tape. That seemed strange. But it was addressed to "ADA Marchetti," which suggested it was connected to either this trial, or another case.

Lana got a knife from the kitchen to cut the tape. She pulled back the cardboard flaps and looked inside.

Then she screamed.

Someone had put sand into the box. That explained all the tape; it was to keep the grains of sand from slipping through the gaps in the cardboard.

Nestled into the sand was a torn piece of the scarf Max had bought her.

And a note.

Chapter Twenty-Five

$\mathcal{M}$ax had just stepped off the elevator when he heard Lana scream.

He ran into the living room. She had a cardboard box in her hands, and she was staring into it, horror on her face.

"Lana, what is it?"

He took the box and looked inside. It was a piece of the scarf that had gone missing from the beach yesterday. And there was a note pinned to the scrap of fabric.

I told you I'd be watching. Soon, I'll make you mine.

Max threw the box aside. It slid across the kitchen table.

"It was him," she whimpered. "He watched us together."

The stalker had stolen the scarf while they were in the water, and then used it to toy with her. Terrify her.

Max wrapped her in his embrace. He glanced at the box on the table, relieved that it hadn't tipped over and spilled its contents. Max had been too pissed off a moment ago to be careful. But they needed that box as intact as possible, so they could analyze it for clues.

He'd have his team check the delivery service that brought it, find out exactly who had sent it, and from where.

"This asshole's made a big mistake this time," Max said. "We'll be able to link this package back to his identity."

Her face was buried against his chest, her arms tied around him. She breathed deeply for a couple of minutes, then lifted her head. A stoic look of calm had now replaced the fear.

"Can we start now?"

She didn't even need to ask. "Of course, I will. Anything for my girl." He kissed her hair. "I'll get my team downstairs working on it, right away. I'll have someone come up here and get the box and start making calls." They would need to inform the police of this latest development as well.

"Will you stay here with me? I don't want you to go."

"That's where it pays to be the boss. I'm not going anywhere." Max wasn't about to leave her side.

Fifteen minutes later, the box was gone, and Lana was lying on the couch beneath a blanket.

He walked over and sat down beside her. "Everyone downstairs has dropped their other projects to work on this."

"I just keep thinking about how he was watching us. It makes me sick."

He caressed her forehead. "It makes me upset, too." He couldn't even begin to express how much. "I shouldn't have taken you out there. I thought nobody would pay any attention to us. I'm sorry."

"Don't be sorry. I'm not. I'm *pissed*. We should be able to have a few minutes of happiness together without some sicko ruining it. I've never been a vengeful person, but this guy is really testing me. I just want it to be over."

"It will be. We're going to find him."

But three hours later, it was almost midnight, and they'd made no progress. Sylvie and the others on his team had reached dead ends. The courier service said a man wearing a hat and sunglasses had brought in the package, but he apparently used a fake name. Max couldn't believe the people were so unprofessional as to not even require an ID. It wasn't how he'd ever run his business. But there wasn't anything he could do.

Nor had the box itself revealed any more clues. No fingerprints, no distinctive features that would allow either the box or its sender to be traced.

Max sat at his kitchen table, talking to Sylvie on his cell phone. "What about Dominic Crane? He said he was going to look into the burner phone connection. You spoke to his lawyer, right?"

"Yeah, we got through to Sandford's office. But so far, they've got nothing."

Max wasn't sure what to make of that. If Dominic Crane was behind this, wouldn't he swoop in with information at the exact moment that Lana needed it? Crane would want to manipulate her, make Lana feel that she owed him.

But that hadn't happened, which suggested that Crane wasn't actually involved.

Max still wondered if it was someone else inside the Syndicate. The stalker had been so careful. The man's skills suggested he was a pro. He'd evaded both the police and Max's own investigation.

Lana was getting ready for bed. She had the trial tomorrow, and Max would be testifying. Neither of them could spend any more time focused on the stalker.

"Okay, let's all of us get some sleep," he said to Sylvie. "While Lana and I are at the courthouse tomorrow, your group can keep working on this."

"Got it, boss."

Max went into the bedroom to find Lana sitting in a chair, calmly paging through her trial prep notebook. She looked up. "No luck?"

He shook his head, frustrated beyond belief that he hadn't solved this for her yet. "I'm sorry. I'm going to keep working on it tomorrow after I testify, I promise."

She got up and circled her arms around his neck. "I know you will. Let's just get through tomorrow. I'm not letting that asshole do anything that could compromise the trial."

They got into bed. Max remembered that it was their third night since they'd started sleeping together again. Usually, when it came to a third night with a woman, he was mentally saying goodbye. Either he was feeling a bit nostalgic about a few nights of satisfaction, or he was glad to move on. But that wasn't how he felt with Lana at all.

Tonight felt like only the beginning with her. He knew they weren't going to have sex, because they were both too upset and too tired for that. But it didn't remotely matter. He cared much more about just being here with her, making sure she felt comfortable. He could imagine so many more nights like this. Hopefully, not this stressful, but with the same level of closeness. He wanted to be around for the highs and the lows. To share everything with her.

He'd always thought that he wasn't boyfriend material. That he couldn't give up his freedom for anyone. But for Lana, he was ready to give up pretty much anything to have her by his side.

"L, I've been thinking about what I said last night. I don't want to take things one day at a time. Or one night at a time, either. I just want to be with you."

"Do you mean, like a relationship?"

He heard so many different things in her voice. A little humor, a little skepticism. And a lot of hope.

"I think so." Then, "Yes. Yes, I do."

"You don't sound very sure. We don't have to rush into this."

"This is the opposite of a rush. This is me taking ten years to tell you how I feel. I care about you. I want a relationship with you."

I love you, he added silently, though he wanted a more

perfect moment to say it. Not one that was marred by a stalker or by the distraction of the Hearst trial.

"Lana, will you be my girlfriend?"

"*Yes*, Max," she whispered.

He pulled her against him, smiling into the dark.

On Max's last full day in West Oaks, Aurora moped all day. She didn't want to go anywhere or do anything. Lana tried to convince her that she was just wasting the remainder of her time with her brother. But Aurora didn't want to listen. She shut herself in her room and went to bed early.

"Thanks for trying," Max said when Lana returned to the living room. "She's always like this when I'm about to go back."

"I know. But tomorrow she's going to be bummed that she didn't spend more time with you today."

After her brother went back to his unit, Aurora usually spent a full week depressed. Lana was used to that by now. But she didn't want to make Max feel worse.

"At least you had the day at the beach yesterday. I know she loved that."

Max shrugged. "I guess so." He was looking away, as if something weighed on his mind.

Lana wasn't sure if he wanted her to stay.

Last night with him had been incredible. Different from their first night, but somehow even better. She'd been getting a sense of the way Max liked to be touched. It was all about observation and experimentation. She'd been learning his body, and her own, and she was eager to get more data points tonight.

But although Max had been smiling at her and sneaking touches to her hand and back whenever Aurora wouldn't notice, he'd seemed distracted. Probably worrying about his sister or the real-life responsibilities he was about to return to.

Lana couldn't imagine that he regretted anything. But what if he'd already decided they were finished, and she just didn't know it yet?

She went into the kitchen to tidy up, even though they'd already finished all the dishes. Then Max came in behind her and kissed her neck. She leaned back against him, closing her eyes with relief.

"We have one more night," he murmured. "How do you want to spend it?"

"With you."

She spun around and found him grinning, though it wasn't the same lopsided grin he'd given her before. There was nothing teasing about it. Only sweetness.

"I was hoping you'd say that."

Everything between them moved half as slow that night. Every kiss was long and deep, like he was drinking her in. They lay down on the blanket in her parents' room, the door locked, and touched every inch of each other all over again. She didn't think she'd ever get enough of Max's tongue, his hands, his absurdly gorgeous body. Every time he groaned with pleasure, she couldn't believe he was making that sound for her.

After they made love, they just lay on the blanket, still touching and kissing. She had no idea what time it was, and she didn't feel tired. There were so many more things she wanted to try with him. How could he be leaving in the morning?

How, after she'd had Max Bennett, could she ever not want him?

Eventually, they both got quiet. Lana thought he was asleep. But then he turned to face her. Max slid his arm beneath her and rolled her onto him. He was hard again. Thank goodness Max had brought his own condoms in his travel bag, because they'd needed a lot more than one.

"You want me?"

She'd lost count of how many times he'd asked.

"Yes. Yes."

This time, she sat on top of him and lowered herself onto his cock, relishing this new experience. He ran his hands over her hips and her legs as she rode him.

"I don't want this night to end," he said.

"Me, neither."

Max lifted onto his elbows so he could kiss her. "Then let's stay here, together, as long as we can."

Chapter Twenty-Six

"Thank you, Mr. Bennett," Lana said. "I have no further questions."

Judge Vaughn looked up from the bench. "My apologies everyone, I need a ten-minute break before we proceed." The judge stood and took the door to her chambers.

Max got up as the jurors filed out of the courtroom. Lana nodded her head toward the doorway. He followed her out to the hall, where small groups of people were whispering.

Wayfair and the other defense lawyers had exited the courtroom and were talking with Ryan Hearst. The defendant was dressed in a trim suit by a designer that Max recognized. Max smirked at the man, but Hearst simply returned a glassy-eyed gaze.

Quickly, Max checked his phone for messages. Sylvie hadn't written with any updates. No progress yet on finding the stalker's identity. Damn.

Lana was down at the other end of the hall, murmuring to Trevor. Her underling nodded and dashed off on an errand. She gave Max just a hint of a smile as he approached.

"Ms. Marchetti."

"Mr. Bennett."

They'd spent all morning on Max's direct testimony. Lana had asked him question by painstaking question, first establishing his background in the military and the personal security industry. He'd explained how he had a private investigator's license and sometimes consulted with the local authorities on cases.

Then Lana had walked Max through his investigation into Ryan Hearst and his eventual discovery of Heather's necklace in Hearst's bedroom.

While on the stand, Max had stayed completely focused on answering Lana's questions. But now that they had a brief moment of rest, he let himself feel the simple pleasure of being near her. He couldn't wait for this to be finished so he could take her home.

My girlfriend. The more he said that, the more he liked it.

"How am I doing?"

"The jury likes you. Trevor told me they were leaning forward in their seats when you described seeing the necklace. You're quite the dramatic storyteller."

"Just telling it like it happened."

"And that's what we need." She pushed air through her mouth. "But it's Wayfair's turn with you. He's going to try to piss you off."

"I know, we've been over this."

Max recalled what Wayfair had called Lana on the phone. *A corrupt prosecutor who can't keep her legs closed.* But he brushed off the brief simmer of anger. Lana hadn't let Wayfair get to her, and neither would Max.

"He's going to imply—once again—that I planted the evidence," Max recited. "And he's going to ask about our relationship."

Max wasn't an expert on evidence rules. But apparently, Wayfair had plenty of leeway to make Lana's witnesses look bad on the stand. Max's job was to sit there and calmly take it. But he'd handled worse than that smarmy lawyer.

"Yes, he's going to ask about us," Lana said. "And you'll answer honestly. I could've brought it up on direct, but I still think it was better to focus on Heather's necklace. This way, Wayfair comes off as desperate, grasping for a distraction. When I question you on redirect, you can explain that it's a recent development, but we weren't seeing each other during your investigation into Hearst."

"I've got it. I promise." He didn't mind admitting his feelings for Lana. But Max didn't like that Wayfair could force him to discuss his love life in public. If Lana could deal with this, though, then so could he.

Max swung by the restroom and grabbed a glass of water. Then it was back to the stand.

Judge Vaughn took her seat. "Defense, any cross-examination of the witness?"

Wayfair stood and walked forward into the well. "Mr. Bennett, you aren't a police officer, are you?"

"No. I'm not."

"It's never been your job to investigate the death of Heather Barnes, correct?"

"That's true."

Wayfair adjusted his tie. "Then how did you get involved in this case at all?"

"Lana Marchetti asked me to look at the evidence and give my advice."

"Oh." Wayfair's thick eyebrows lifted. "Ms. Marchetti? The prosecutor in this case?"

"Yes," Max sighed. He'd already gone over all this earlier with Lana. *Just get to it*, he thought. *Ask me the damned question you really want.*

"You have a close friendship with Ms. Marchetti, isn't that correct?"

"I guess so."

"She told you she wanted Mr. Hearst prosecuted for murder?"

"No, she wanted the truth."

"And she just needed one more piece of evidence to go after Ryan Hearst, didn't she? So, you planted it?"

"No, I did not."

"But you *did* want to help her, right? Make her look good?"

"Not by lying."

"Have you ever had a romantic relationship with Ms. Marchetti?"

"Yes."

"Are you currently in a relationship with Ms. Marchetti?"

Lana nodded from her seat, almost imperceptibly.

Calm. I'm totally calm. "Yes."

Wayfair eyed him. Yet he didn't look surprised. "But when I asked you that same question in a hearing before this court, you said no, didn't you? Were you lying then?"

"No, I was not. I—"

"You were lying, weren't you? In fact, you've been carrying on a sexual relationship with Ms. Marchetti this entire time, haven't you?"

"That's not correct. But I'm happy to explain."

"Oh, you will? Would you care to explain these, Mr. Bennett?"

Wayfair opened his jacket, pulled out a stack of papers, and handed them to Max.

At first, he didn't understand what he was seeing.

Photos.

Photos of him and Lana, together. They were in the ocean, arms around each other.

"Objection," Lana said. "Is Mr. Wayfair introducing evidence? I don't even know what this is."

"It shows Mr. Bennett's bias," the defense lawyer replied. "Those images speak for themselves."

"Let Ms. Marchetti see what you're introducing, counsel."

Max kept flipping through the photos. He couldn't stop

himself. His skin heated at the intimacy of the moments this camera had captured. There was Max lifting Lana out of the water, her legs around his waist. The two of them with their lips locked, their chemistry written in their body language.

And then, Lana herself. Close-ups of her body. Her thighs and stomach and breasts, beaded with saltwater, barely covered by her skimpy bikini.

What the fuck.

"What the hell is this?" Max growled, only realizing he'd spoken aloud when he heard the fury in his voice.

Wayfair's smug face turned toward him. "Proof that you're a liar."

Lana and the judge were saying something, but it was all static in Max's ears. He could only stare at these photos of him. Of Lana.

The beach on Sunday.

Wayfair had these pictures taken. And the scarf…the box Lana had gotten last night, the note…

That fucking note.

I told you I'd be watching.

"It was you." Somehow, the lawyer was behind all of it.

"I'm sorry, what was that, Mr. Bennett?" Wayfair came closer, pretending he couldn't hear. Or maybe he couldn't over the other talking. The judge was saying something about silence, but Max's vision had tunneled to the sleazy, despicable man in front of him.

The note. The calls. The threats. The car that rear-ended Lana and Aurora, that could've killed them if they'd crashed.

"It was *you*." Wayfair was the stalker. Or he'd hired the guy.

The lawyer smiled, his eyes glinting. He knew exactly what Max meant.

"You've been terrorizing her. She could've been *killed*." Max shot up from his seat, photos scattering, and grabbed a fistful of Wayfair's shirt.

He'd expected Wayfair to cower. But the man's smile only grew.

Then Max realized the rest of the courtroom had gone quiet. Lana and the judge were staring at him in abject horror. A juror whispered. Then another.

The bailiff was hurrying toward the witness stand.

"Mr. Bennett," Judge Vaughn seethed. "That is enough."

Wayfair extricated himself from Max's grip. "This is outrageous, Your Honor. I've just been assaulted by the prosecution's witness, in full view of the jury."

Judge Vaughn motioned to the bailiff. "Please escort the jury from the room." She sent a furious glance toward Max. "The witness stays."

Max lowered himself to his seat. *Oh, shit. What did I just do?*

Lana slumped in her chair, eyes glazed. Wayfair stooped to gather up the photographs.

Once the bailiff had escorted the jurors out, the judge turned back to Max. "Young man, in all my years on this bench, I've never seen such behavior."

"Your Honor—"

Lana snapped to attention now. Her eyes sent daggers in his direction. *Not another word.* Max clamped his mouth shut.

"Your Honor, the People apologize on behalf of Mr. Bennett," Lana said. "I'm just as shocked as you are. But I'm sure that the witness's outburst was not intentional. This was an unfortunate reaction to some events outside this courtroom. If Your Honor could allow me to explain?"

"I don't see what explanation there could be. He just tried to strangle defense counsel."

Bullshit. I barely wrinkled his tie. But he wasn't dumb enough to say that, despite other evidence to the contrary.

"It was a momentary aberration," Lana said. "A limiting instruction…"

"Ms. Marchetti, no limiting instruction is going to fix what the jurors just saw. You know better than that."

Max looked from one person to the next as they spoke, trying to follow. He knew he'd fucked up royally. That was clear. But how badly would this mess up Lana's case? What was the judge planning to do?

Wayfair was whispering to his co-counsel and the defendant. Then he straightened. "Your Honor, the prosecution is responsible for its witness. But this goes far beyond negligence or inadvertence. We hereby move for a mistrial and a finding that it was caused by prosecutorial bad faith."

Lana jumped up. "No, *please.*"

"I'll hear from the prosecution. But first, bailiff, I'd like Mr. Bennett removed from my courtroom. He's lucky I don't appoint a special prosecutor to charge him. If he steps a toe out of line inside this building, I'll do just that."

~

MAX SAT on a bench in the hallway, head back against the wall. A few reporters had tried to speak to him, but he'd ignored them until they left him alone.

How could he have been so stupid as to let Wayfair manipulate him? Because that had obviously been the lawyer's goal all along. Max saw that now. Wayfair had been sowing these seeds for weeks at least.

And I walked right into it. What the hell is wrong with me?

He'd seen those pictures of Lana. Known that the man had not only scared her. He'd *enjoyed* it. Wayfair had gotten off on Lana's fear, on the control. Max had seen red and lashed out.

Why didn't I stop myself?

Finally, Lana stepped out into the hall. She saw him down at the end. Her heels clicked as she came toward him.

She wasn't looking at him. She had no expression at all on her face, but Max knew her. He knew Lana so well that he could feel her anguish, right underneath his own skin.

"I'm so sorry," he began.

"Not here. I need you to drive."

She wouldn't say anything else until they were in his car, pulling out of the parking garage.

Lana was typing onto her phone. "Take me to this address." She held up her screen, displaying a location on the other side of town.

"We're not going home?"

Even as he said that word—home—he felt it slipping away. Like the refuge they'd created together over the last few days was already gone. Destroyed by what he'd just done.

You ruined it. Just like you knew you would.

But he didn't want to believe that. He loved her, and he hoped that maybe she felt the same about him. What they had together was stronger than one mistake.

"I need to go talk to Heather Barnes's sister. Claire. She skipped the trial today and thank god for that. She didn't have to witness what just went on."

"L, please tell me what the judge said. What's going to happen with the trial?"

"There is no trial, Max. There is no case. The judge granted everything Wayfair asked for. The mistrial, everything."

Max cursed. "Tell me what I can do. I'll help get every-thing ready for the new trial. I'll pay for your department to hire a new lawyer to assist you. Something."

"There won't *be* a new trial. The judge ruled that the mistrial was my fault. Double jeopardy has attached, and that means that Ryan Hearst can never be tried again for Heather's murder. Unless I can somehow fix this, he's going free for good."

Lana had spoken in a monotone. Like she could hardly believe any of this herself.

"*Your* fault? That's ridiculous. I admit that I really messed up, but the judge can't possibly blame you. Didn't you tell her what Wayfair did?"

"I tried to explain that someone's been stalking me. She didn't want to hear it. I asked for time to brief the issues, for a formal hearing, anything at all to somehow give us a chance of changing her mind. Which any other judge would've permitted. But Vaughn wasn't having it."

Max slammed the flat of his hand against the steering wheel. "But that's not fair! Did you see those pictures? Wayfair was the stalker. Or he hired him."

"Of course, he did. I thought it was Wayfair from the start, from those first phone calls. I should have said something to the judge back then. But today? It was too late. I'm sure Wayfair just intended to put me off balance at first, but once he realized how close you and I really were? Wayfair set up a trap. He played you like a piano."

Max's face flushed with shame. "You're absolutely right. This is on me. I'll write to Judge Vaughn, apologize, and try to explain. I'll tell her she can't blame you for this."

She covered her eyes with her hand. "You think she'd listen? The judge thinks I told you to lie at the previous hearing about our relationship. She made a finding that I acted in bad faith. We know I didn't do that, but this is still my fault as much as anyone's."

"Why?"

She just shook her head.

He wished that Lana would yell at him. Get angry. Scream. But she wasn't. She was just sitting there, talking to him quietly but calmly. Maybe it was shock. Or maybe it was the opposite. Maybe some part of her wasn't surprised at all.

"I'm going to appeal," Lana said. "I've got a decent argument that the judge abused her discretion. She should've let me present evidence, or at least required Wayfair to prove his claim that I acted in bad faith. I'm hoping the appellate court will remand the case back to Judge Vaughn for a formal hearing. If that happens, I need you to testify about our side of the story. Just put it all out there. Our relationship and everything that Wayfair did."

Max took the full first full breath he'd had in the last hour. "Okay, yeah. I'll do whatever you say."

He glanced at her side-on and caught the skepticism that passed across her expression.

Max reached over and put his hand on her leg. "We are not giving up yet. I'm going to help you fix this."

She crossed her leg, pulling away from him. "I can't talk about it anymore right now. I have to think about what I'm going to say to Claire."

Max pulled up to the address Lana had given him. He parked at the curb and turned off the engine. "Can I come up with you?"

"No. This was my trial, my responsibility. I shouldn't have…"

She trailed off, but Max felt in his bones what she'd been about to say.

I shouldn't have trusted anyone else with this. Shouldn't have trusted you.

She got out of the car, not sparing him a single glance on her way to Claire Barnes's building.

Chapter Twenty-Seven

*T*his was going to be the hardest conversation of Lana's life.

Claire invited Lana into her kitchen, and they sat at the table. "What is it?" Claire asked. "Just tell me."

Over twenty years ago, this woman had opened her door to detectives bearing the news of her sister's death. Lana couldn't imagine how awful that day had been. Claire was tough now. She could sense bad news coming at her and was instinctively bracing herself.

But Lana knew, deep down, that Claire's wounds had never fully healed. She might look stoic, but she was living in a terrible limbo, waiting for the justice that was so long overdue.

There was no way to sugar coat this.

"I lost the case. The judge declared a mistrial."

Claire just sat there, not moving. Not breathing.

"It happened during Max Bennett's testimony today. Max and I are…in a relationship."

It felt bizarre saying that. What did it even mean?

"Paxton Wayfair, Hearst's lawyer, tried to introduce some improper evidence. Pictures of Max and me together. Supposedly, he wanted to prove Max is a biased witness and planted

Heather's necklace. But really, he just wanted to provoke an angry reaction from Max. Unfortunately, Wayfair got his wish."

She didn't want to get into the stalker angle. That might seem like she was fishing for sympathy. Claire had no sympathy to spare, and Lana didn't want it.

"So, the judge declared a mistrial," Claire repeated.

"Yes. Because she believes seeing Max's outburst against Wayfair would irreparably taint the jury. I don't agree with that. But that's Judge Vaughn's ruling."

"What happens next? A new trial?"

"Usually that would happen. But Judge Vaughn also ruled the mistrial was my fault. Again, I think she's wrong." Lana might feel morally responsible for the circumstances that led to the confrontation today, but legally, she thought the judge's ruling was Twilight Zone-level absurd.

Lana forced herself to say the next sentence. "But the judge's decision means we can't retry Ryan for Heather's murder."

Again, silence.

"But this isn't the end. We're going to appeal." Though right now, it was hard to feel hopeful.

In some ways, Lana thought Wayfair's behavior had been far worse than Max's. Wayfair knew better than to introduce those photos in such a theatrical manner, without any proper foundation. Plus, the photos were completely irrelevant and inappropriate. Especially those smutty images of Lana herself in her bikini, which had made her stomach twist. She'd seen them when they'd scattered onto the floor.

Even the photos of her and Max kissing were unnecessary. Max had already admitted to their current relationship. Wayfair's photos had zero relevance to the case, instead designed to humiliate Lana and get the worst reaction out of Max.

But Wayfair's strategy had worked. Max had blown up,

just like he did on the phone with Wayfair a few weeks ago. Only today, he'd had the lawyer standing right in front of him, within easy reach. Wayfair made sure of that.

Now, she essentially had proof that Wayfair had been stalking her and trying to interfere with the trial proceedings. But unless an appellate court saw her side of things, she couldn't do much about it. She could try to urge the DA to press charges against Wayfair, but that alone wouldn't fix this case.

And it wouldn't necessarily help Claire Barnes.

After the first few days of the trial, Lana had been so confident about their chances. Overconfident. All weekend, she should've been going over her trial notebook again. Staying focused on Heather and Claire. Not letting her attention waver for one single second.

Instead, she'd been running around like some horny teenager, blinded by her infatuation with Max. What had she been thinking, going to the beach with him on Sunday? Parading around with him in public while she knew, *she knew*, that she had a stalker and Wayfair was probably behind it?

I let this happen. I did this.

But as Max had said, she couldn't just give up. Claire deserved better than that.

"I'm going to fight this on appeal. I promise you."

Claire smiled sadly. "You've made me a lot of promises, Lana. We both know how that goes by now."

That was a knife to the heart. But it was a knife that Lana herself had placed.

"I don't even blame you," Claire said. "If that helps. I always knew it was a long shot. But I was really starting to believe…" She shook off the thought. "I don't think I can go through this again. Appeals take a long time, right? Months? Even years? And then a new trial. Testifying again. Going through all this again. I don't think I'm strong enough to do it."

"I get that it feels that way right now. This is a blow, and it's devastating. But I am not going to stop." The more she spoke, the more Lana felt her resolve strengthening. "We're going to get up and fight back."

"I'm so sorry. I just can't."

Lana knew that Claire wasn't apologizing to her. She was apologizing to her sister.

~

MAX WAS WAITING for her at the curb. But Lana wasn't ready to face him again yet.

She sat in the stairwell of Claire's apartment building and called Stephen Abrams. The district attorney answered. "Lana, how are you?"

She could already tell he'd heard the news. "I've been better. I just got done with Claire Barnes."

Stephen sighed. "That must've been awful. You told her we're going to appeal?"

"Of course. I told her that we're not giving up. I'll be filing our notice of appeal within days. But right now, Claire doesn't think she can go through another trial." Lana certainly couldn't blame her.

"Give her time. This is a shock to all of us. I'm still hazy on what exactly happened. I heard some of it from Trevor. I would've preferred speaking to you first, but I'm sure he was only trying to help. He said Judge Vaughn blamed you for the mistrial, but that it wasn't your fault. That it was some game Wayfair was playing? Something about a stalker?"

"It's a long story. I can tell you everything that I know. But could it be another day? I'm running out of steam."

"No problem. I just want to make sure that you're safe. Has someone been threatening you?"

"Like you said, it was a game Wayfair was playing. He's gotten what he wants now, so there's no reason for him to keep bothering me. I suspected he could be behind it, but I had no proof until now."

"I'm not inclined to take this lying down. I can go after Wayfair in all kinds of ways. You say the word."

"Thank you, Stephen. I'll think about it. But I just want to get back to work tomorrow. I want to draft the Hearst appeal and focus on my other cases." If she didn't, Lana was worried she'd buckle under the weight of all her mistakes.

She never should've lost sight of her responsibilities. So now, she had to get back to them. Getting back to work was the only thing that might soothe her mind.

"I don't think that's a good idea. You should take a few days."

"That's the last thing I want."

"But it's what we all need. What the office needs. There's going to be a media firestorm around this, Lana. You know that."

She shut her eyes. "And you want the office to have a little distance from me. No worries. I get it."

"Please don't see this as me pushing you aside. That is not going to happen. This office has your back, one hundred percent. But for the next few days, I think it would be better if I handle what's coming at us personally. And I'm sure you could use a mental break. Especially with this stalker thing you've been dealing with. Anybody's nerves would be frayed."

"Sure." That was the only response she could manage. A sob was right there at the top of her throat, begging to get out.

"Let's talk soon," her boss said. "Vaughn has gone way too far, and there's no way this can stand. We'll strategize about what we should do next. But until then, take care of yourself. All right? You're my second in command, and I don't want to lose you. You'll be right back to work before you know it."

Lana had heard everything that her boss wasn't saying. At this moment, she was a liability to the office. All of West Oaks, maybe even all of Southern California, would be talking about the Hearst case. Especially when Wayfair started winding up the media, as he no doubt was already plotting. He'd humiliated her in open court, but he wouldn't be satisfied until he'd assassinated her character to the entire state.

A corrupt prosecutor who can't keep her legs closed.

No matter what happened on appeal, Lana's potential run for DA in the next election wasn't even worth mentioning anymore. Wasn't even a thought.

She hadn't known until this moment that she truly wanted to run. But she did. She wanted to take Stephen's place and run the office officially, and now she would never get that chance.

So many things had been ruined today. And it wasn't even over yet.

AS SOON AS Lana stepped out of the building, Max started the car. She got into the passenger seat and buckled in.

"How did it go?"

"About as shitty as you'd expect."

Max pulled away from the curb. He opened his hand like he was offering it. But she didn't take it.

He drove them back toward the Bennett Security building. Neither of them said anything on the way. Lana didn't know what else she *could* say.

She didn't want to throw away what she and Max had. But she was so numb right now. If he pushed her, she might start getting angry. She might say things she couldn't take back.

They got to his apartment, and Lana went straight to her bedroom. She grabbed her suitcase.

She never would've expected when she arrived here, less than a week ago, that she and Max would reconnect. That she'd finally get so much of what she'd wanted all these years. Max in her bed. Max as her boyfriend.

And she'd certainly never expected her relationship with Max to cost her the Hearst case. Maybe even cost her career.

She started throwing clothes into the bag. She felt Max there in the doorway, watching her.

"You're leaving?" There was pain in his voice. Disbelief. An exact mirror to what she felt.

"The trial is over. We know who the stalker is. That was always the deal."

He came into the room, stopping her hands from pulling anything else from the drawer. "Whoa, wait a minute. We both know it's gone way beyond that. This isn't some convenient arrangement. Not anymore. So don't act like our conversation last night didn't happen."

"I need to be home, in my own space, so I can think about things. You don't realize how screwed I am, Max. I let my feelings for you distract me from my job, and I'm going to pay for it. But much worse is that Claire Barnes is paying for it. I let her down."

He wrapped her in his arms. "We're going to make this okay."

She hugged him back, taking a tiny bit of comfort from his embrace. "That's what I keep saying, too. To Claire. To Stephen Abrams. But honestly? I don't see how. Claire's too exhausted with this entire process to go through it again."

She didn't bring up the other issue. How was Max supposed to testify again after what happened? Wayfair was probably going to file a restraining order against him. Talk about a source of impeachment.

There was also zero possibility that Lana would get to prosecute a retrial of Hearst. As far as this case was concerned, she was tainted. Poison.

"All right," Max said. "I agree with you that it's bad. But

please don't punish us both by pulling away. Stay with me. Let me be here for you."

She couldn't handle his guilt right now. Could barely handle her own. "I'm overwhelmed. I can't discuss what happened in that courtroom anymore. I just need to be alone for a while." She pushed back from him and started packing again.

"For how long?"

"I don't know."

"L, are you breaking up with me?"

Chapter Twenty-Eight

"*I* don't want to," she said.

But that wasn't a *no*.

Part of Max didn't believe this could be happening. Lana couldn't be leaving him like this.

But the other part of Max? Not fucking surprised one bit.

You always knew it would happen. Just maybe not so soon. One day as her boyfriend. That's all you lasted.

But he wasn't going down that easy. He had to defend himself, if only so she'd understand where he was coming from.

"I know you're angry with me…"

"I told you I can't discuss this right now."

"And I told you I was sorry. I still am. But how many times can I say it? That man hurt you. He went after you and got off on your fear. Yes, I lost my temper. But only because it killed me to know what he'd done to you."

Lana didn't look up. "You lost your temper," she repeated. "Because you wanted to protect me."

"*Yes*. I reacted impulsively. I wish I could take it back because I've caused so many problems for you. But Wayfair deserved it. Isn't he the one who should get most of your anger?"

She walked back and forth across her bedroom, hands on her hips, the muscle in her jaw clenching. Like she was fighting to keep back a torrent of words.

In her eyes, he saw the moment that the dam broke.

Then she opened her mouth.

"Your problem is not impulse control. That's bullshit. You have impeccable control over your impulses. That stupid 'rule of three' is proof. Your company and your accomplishments are proof. It's your *ego* you can't control, Max. You claim that you wanted to protect *me*, but that tantrum in court was all about *you*."

He threw his arms out to his sides. "I'm an arrogant asshole. That's true. But you already knew that. I have never once hidden who I am from you."

Stop talking. You are making this worse.

Lana's stare was unyielding. "So, you do think this is my fault."

You see? So much worse.

"No. I'm not blaming you at all. I just don't want you to blame me." Not for everything. He was the one getting punished, not Wayfair.

She tipped her head back and laughed. "You've never wanted anyone to blame you. That's why you make sure every woman has low expectations of you from the start. 'I can't be your boyfriend.' 'I'm shitty at relationships.' Just so you can say, 'I told you so' later. Well, you're right Max. You did tell me. Over and over. I guess I should have listened."

She threw clothes into the bag, then stalked into the other room, where she'd set up her office. Papers and files got dumped into a box.

No. No, no, no.

"Lana, talk to me. Don't leave like this."

"I'm so tired of talking."

"I love you."

She froze.

This wasn't the way he'd wanted to say it. But this was all he had. The one single hope he had left.

A tear escaped from her eye, streaking down her cheek. "You wait until now to tell me? Like just saying those words means everything else gets erased?"

"It's all I've got. *You're* all I've got."

He had Aurora, but she didn't really need him. And everything else—this apartment, this building and his other investments, Bennett Security—none of that made him feel whole the way Lana did.

"I love you," he said again. "I've loved you for a while. I wish I'd been brave enough to say it before."

She took a stuttering breath. "I love you too, Max. I've loved you for ten fucking years. I think some part of me has always been waiting for you. Never giving my heart to anyone else, always hoping. I was *desperate* for you to want me back, and the minute you did, I pushed all my other responsibilities to the side. I'm trying to figure out how to deal with the consequences. At this moment, what I feel is confused."

The tears kept falling as she boxed up her makeshift office and carried it out to the living room. Lana grabbed her suitcase and wheeled it to the door.

"Just please don't go, L. Please."

"I can't think right now. I need space. I need..." She shook her head. "Something. Just not you."

Of all the things Lana had ever said to him, that had to be the worst.

Chapter Twenty-Nine

*L*ana spent the next three days in bed. She didn't shower. She barely ate. Instead, she replayed her fight with Max over and over again, questioning everything she'd said. Wishing he hadn't insisted on having that conversation. And wishing that she had found some way to separate her disappointment in herself from her feelings for him.

She didn't think they'd broken up, but she figured Max believed it. Yet she wasn't ready to talk to him again, either. She would probably just end up saying the wrong things. She needed more time to get her thoughts in order. And to grieve over what she'd lost.

And maybe a small part of her knew that being with Max right now would be a comfort, but it was a comfort she didn't deserve.

The very hardest part was that she couldn't lean on her best friend. Aurora had come by the house twice, first when she heard the news about the mistrial, and again with groceries. But Lana had refused as kindly as possible to see her.

If she told Aurora about everything that happened with

Max, then Aurora was going to take her side. But if Aurora sided against her brother, that would just end up hurting Max even more. Lana loved him too much to do that to him.

Early on the fourth day, Lana's doorbell rang. She checked the app on her phone, where she could see the feed from the doorbell camera.

It was Devon.

He spoke, and the microphone picked up what he said. "Lana, you're going to have to open up. If you don't, I'll assume that you're in distress, and I'll have to break down the door."

She grabbed her robe and padded over to let him in. The door creaked as it opened. "I'm just warning you, there are some very strong smells in here."

"I've lived in a barracks full of soldiers. I promise you, whatever you've got, I've smelled worse."

They went into the living room. Lana plopped onto the couch, crossing her arms. "Did Aurora send you?"

Or maybe it had been Max. But she couldn't bring herself to say his name.

Devon took an armchair. He wasn't facing Lana head on, which she appreciated. "Aurora's been worried. But so have I. You and I are friends, right? I wanted to make sure you haven't had any more trouble from the stalker."

She rubbed a crust of sleep and dried tears from her eyes. "Wayfair has no more reason to bother me. He's already won."

That was the only tiny silver lining in all of this. She didn't have to worry about the stupid stalker anymore. It had all been a farce from the beginning. A show. But she'd genuinely been scared and was relieved it was over.

Devon nodded. "That's what we thought, but I'm glad to have it confirmed. I also wanted to check on how you were doing otherwise. I'm really sorry about the trial. That was messed up, what went down."

"Yup. It definitely was. I feel awful, and it's not getting better. And my boss doesn't want me in the office, so I have nothing else to focus on."

"Damn, that sucks. Really sucks."

"Yeah. Sucks hard."

"Fuck that Paxton Wayfair guy. Fuck that guy right up the ass."

She could almost feel the glimmer of an urge to smile. It wasn't much, but it was an improvement.

"Is there more bothering you than the trial?" Devon asked. "Not that this Wayfair guy and losing the trial isn't reason enough to be upset. But it's hard to believe you'd let a sleazeball like that keep you down."

Devon wasn't great at subtle hinting. His intention was obvious. He already knew about Max. "Did he say something to you?"

Devon cringed. "It was Sylvie. We all noticed you'd left, but she's the one who first guessed the reason. She wanted to call you, but she didn't feel like it was her place. If you want, we can talk about him. Or, I don't have to mention that subject again. It's up to you. I totally get why you're not able discuss this with Aurora. But I wanted you to know that I'm available. As a stand-in best friend."

That statement was so sweet she almost cried. But after the past few days, she was cried out.

"I'm not ready to talk about…that. But a stand-in best friend sounds pretty nice. If that means you'll watch trashy reality TV with me."

"You think I don't with Aurora? Let's see what those housewives are up to."

They cued up a new season of a show on demand and started a binge watch. At some point around the third episode, Lana got up and took a shower. When she came out, Devon was still sitting there, absorbed in the cat fighting and name-calling.

"You can't say that about her man and not expect to get slapped," he muttered at the TV.

Lana heard herself laugh. She was tempted to take a picture of the burly bodyguard watching trash TV in her living room and send it to Aurora. "Want to order pizza for lunch?"

He looked over. "Can I get the one with pineapple? Aurora never lets me order it."

Lana laughed again. "Let's get all the pineapple. And the garlic and anchovies. As long as they're not on the same pizza."

Two more episodes and a pizza delivery later, Lana turned down the volume on the TV.

"How's Max?" she asked quietly.

His name on her lips sent shivers down her skin. She missed him so much.

"Torn up. He's only come down to the workroom once since the mistrial, and when he did, he looked...hollow. I haven't known him that long, but Sylvie said she's never seen him like this."

She hated the thought of Max upset. But at least he hadn't moved on, just acting like their relationship never happened. She couldn't have taken that.

"I wish I could talk to him. But what could I say?"

"Are you mad at him?"

"Not really. I was a little at first, but that burned out quick."

"Last time I talked to you, you and Max seemed happy. You weren't sure where it was going, but you seemed eager to get there."

"I was. I have a history with Max." She debated admitting the rest, since Aurora didn't know yet. But it was the truth, and Aurora would find out eventually. "I've been in love with him since forever."

"Then maybe you're punishing yourself? No offense, I just

don't see why you're sitting here alone and sad. If you were with Max, at least you could be miserable together."

The man had a point.

So, why couldn't she pick up her phone and call the guy she loved?

"I hope you don't think I'm talking out of my ass here," Devon added. "Before Aurora, I knew a few things about being lonely and miserable, even though I had my mom and sister around me. I was holding myself to an impossible standard. Like the whole world would collapse if I wasn't there, single-handedly holding it up. I thought that my responsibilities were more important than my own dreams or desires. But there's a way to take care of both. It might be messy, and you might even fuck some things up. I know I did. But you can't put the weight of all the world's problems or injustices on your shoulders, Lana. You'll lose your mind that way."

"I ruined any chance that Ryan Hearst would be held accountable for murdering Heather Barnes. Ruined most of the chances, anyway. How can I get over that?"

"But you're the entire reason Ryan Hearst was brought to trial in the first place. If you weren't working on that case, if you hadn't brought Max in to help, then nobody would really know for sure that Hearst did it. You got closer than anybody else. Doesn't that count for something, too? And like you said, there's still a chance. But you're not the only lawyer out there. You're not the only person who's capable of solving this. Wouldn't it be slightly arrogant to think that you were?"

Arrogant. Like Max had called himself so many times. Had she been arrogant to assume that if she'd failed to nail Hearst, everyone else would necessarily fail too?

"Maybe you're right," she said, "and I should just let the other people in the office handle this. But that's not me. My work has never been easy, but it matters to me. I can't give it up."

Devon had found a way to balance his duties with his

desires. But the problem was, Lana had no official duties anymore. Her boss had banished her.

"If I go back to Max now, I feel like I'll be admitting that I have nothing else left but him. He doesn't want that kind of pressure. And I don't want that kind of relationship."

"So, don't let anybody else keep you from working on the case. If you didn't get fired, then you still have a right to be there. Just don't take all the burden of winning onto yourself."

Stephen Abrams hadn't asked for her resignation yet. He'd claimed that he didn't want to lose her. And when he'd asked her to step aside, she hadn't put up much of a fight. She could've insisted on being a part of the team, but instead she'd been too busy feeling guilty.

She did want to fix things with Max. Somehow, she would, if he still wanted her. But first, she had to reclaim her place. She had to get back to work.

THAT AFTERNOON, after Devon had left, Lana got onto her computer and checked her work inbox.

It was ugly.

There were emails from reporters asking for comment. There were messages from concerned coworkers and her contacts in the legal community. Lana deleted most things, responding to those people she knew well. She tried to keep things vague, since she didn't know yet what Stephen and the rest of the office had been strategizing. But she was keeping up with her mantra: *I'm not going to give up.*

She didn't know if Claire Barnes would come around to the idea of testifying again. But even if she didn't, Lana was going to keep pushing forward. There had to be a way, and she would find it. Even if she couldn't see it yet.

And as for running for DA? She was still only twenty-nine. If she'd gotten elected, she would've been the youngest DA in

West Oaks history. She still had plenty of time to rebuild her reputation and run at some future point. If that was even what she ended up wanting. Because she had Max to think about now, too.

She wanted a life with him. And running for political office was definitely a decision that should include her partner.

Lana had fought for so much of what she wanted when it came to her career. But with Max, she'd simply let him slip away from her for so many years. She wasn't going to do that again.

But first things first. She picked up her phone and called Trevor.

Her second chair answered right away. "Lana! Thank god. Stephen just asked me for a fifty-state research memo, and I'm totally stuck."

She suppressed a smile. "Back up a minute. Can you give me an update on what's been happening in the office? I know I've been out of touch. Sorry I didn't call before."

"No, I totally understood. Everything that happened in the Hearst trial… It was wrong. Everybody here is saying it. We're all completely behind you. I didn't want to bother you because Stephen said we shouldn't. But now that you're back…"

She talked through the trouble Trevor was having. It felt good to flex her mind a little bit, dig into a specific legal question. And it had to do with another case, which gave her a much-needed break from thinking about the Hearst trial. But eventually, she brought the subject back to their ill-fated case.

"Has Stephen said anything about plans for the appeal on Hearst?"

"Not yet. We've all been scrambling here without you. Seriously, Lana, people have been panicking. We're so behind already. Everyone's going to be relieved to know you're back on the team. Honestly, I don't think even the DA knows what we should do about Hearst. Please tell me you have some ideas."

She bit her lip, drumming her fingers against the table in her home office. "I have a lot of ideas, actually." Since Devon had left, her brain had been pulling all kinds of strategies out of thin air. It was like she'd had a mental block the last few days, and she just needed a friend to help her clear it.

Lana checked the time. Almost three. If they moved fast, they'd have plenty of daylight left. "But first, do you want to ride shotgun with me to downtown L.A.? We can strategize on the way. Maybe grab a French dip sandwich while we're there."

"I guess so," Trevor said. "But why?

"I think we owe Paxton Wayfair a visit."

Chapter Thirty

*M*ax was lying on his couch, staring at the ceiling, when he heard his elevator ding. The doors opened.

"Max? Where are you? Oh—what the hell happened in here? It smells like whiskey and misery."

Pretty sure that's me. He turned his head, squinting. His sister was in his kitchen, messing around in the fridge, dumping dishes into the sink.

"Aurora? What are you doing here?"

"What does it look like? I'm checking up on you. Sylvie let me in using some override button thing? Since you had your floor locked out and haven't been answering any of your messages. I don't know how she did it, but whatever it was, I'm here. You're a mess, and your apartment is disgusting."

She shoveled empty cans and wrappers off his counter into the trash.

"I thought you'd be with Lana," he said.

"Well, I'm not. I'm with you. So, get off your ass and start helping."

Max stumbled over, wiping a hand over his face. His eyes were bleary, and he had several days' worth of beard growth on his chin. From the sun in the windows, he guessed it was morning. What day, he had no clue. But he did know he wasn't drunk anymore, and that was not a feeling he appreciated. His head was exploding with pressure.

He slumped onto a bar stool. "You don't have to do this. And it's beyond obvious you don't want to. So why bother?"

Aurora stopped, a trash bag in one hand, a half-empty liquor bottle in the other. "Because you're my brother. You've always been around for me, even when I didn't want you to be."

"Around for you? What are you talking about? I was gone all the time when you were a kid. You barely knew me."

She snickered. "Max, you were my freaking hero. Maybe our sibling relationship has been tense since I had my first boyfriend, but I always knew I could count on you. I'm trying to return the favor here. And I *do* know you. I know you don't want to be babied or told that you're a precious, beautiful flower."

He made a face.

"So, stop feeling sorry for yourself and clean up the mess you've made."

Aurora was right. This was exactly what he needed to hear.

Max drank some orange juice, took some pain killers, and got to work, helping to clear away the rest of the trash and dirty clothes he'd strewn across the living room.

He didn't remember much from the days since Lana had left. He'd managed to tell Devon to watch over her townhouse that first night, making sure Wayfair left her alone. There'd been messages from Devon reporting Lana was safe, that she hadn't left her home. Calls from Sylvie and from the new assistant he'd recently hired, reminding him of appointments he'd blown off. Emails that he'd failed to open.

He hadn't been able to sleep in his bed because it made him think of Lana.

Of course, that hadn't stopped him from sitting in her former bedroom, breaking open that case of absurdly expensive Japanese whiskey he'd been saving for clients, and wallowing in his failings.

'Have you seen Lana?" he asked his sister.

"I tried. She won't let me. She probably doesn't want me to choose sides."

"But is anyone with her? Is she alone?" His stomach wrenched. Not over worries for her safety, because it did seem that Wayfair had called off his terror campaign. But Max didn't want her to be isolated from her best friend because of him.

"Devon went to visit her this morning. He texted that she let him inside, so that's progress."

Max nodded. "Do you already know what I did to fuck up her entire life? Or are you waiting for the right moment to ask."

"I've heard some things. But does that matter? You didn't mean to hurt her, right?"

"God, no. I've never meant to hurt her." *Even though I keep on doing it.*

"Then I don't need to know the gory details. I don't *want* to choose sides, Max. I want you both to be happy. And right now, you are both absolutely destroyed."

He sat on the couch, resting his head in his hands. "I'm in love with her."

"I kind of guessed that, you know. From all this. I know what heartbreak looks like." Aurora sat down and put her arm around him. "You want to talk about it?"

"I asked her to be my girlfriend."

She did a comical double-take. "Hold up. You. Asked Lana. To be your girlfriend?"

"Yeah. It's not *that* absurd. She did say yes."

"But you've never had a girlfriend. You don't date. Right? That's what I thought."

"I haven't had a girlfriend since high school. But yeah, otherwise you're right. I'm in my thirties and haven't had a girlfriend since I was eighteen. Not until Lana, which lasted for a day. That's how pathetic I am."

"Maybe if you hadn't gotten laid since you were eighteen, one could make a case that you were pathetic. Depending on the reasons. But I may have heard that you, in fact, have gotten laid since then. Perhaps more than once."

He got up from the couch, scratching the back of his neck. "I am not discussing my sex life with you."

"Because you've been so respectful of mine? But you're distracting me. Gosh, who was it you decided to bone down with, when I was just a sweet, innocent kid..." Aurora tapped her finger on her chin. "Could it have been my babysitter, Lana Marchetti?"

"She wasn't your babysitter anymore by then."

"No, she was practically my big sister. And you two got busier than an elementary school lunchroom when Lana was still a teenager, and you were a big, strong manly man."

He gave her an infuriated look. "She was in college."

"Oh my god, calm down. I know it was all legally and ethically acceptable, I'm just teasing you. But I do seem to remember someone coming down really hard on me about my boy-crazy ways. I was supposed to be more responsible? 'Sex is not something to jump into lightly.' Who could have said that?"

"I know. I was a hypocrite."

"I'm sorry, I didn't quite catch that."

"I was a hypocrite," he said through gritted teeth.

"Is it my birthday already? Because that, dear brother, was a gift."

He picked up a dirty undershirt and threw it at her. Aurora took one sniff and tossed it into the trash.

"So, Lana's your girlfriend."

"Was."

"She definitely broke up with you?"

"I...don't actually know." That part was hazy. He hadn't been feeling very optimistic since she left. But she hadn't said anything definitive. "She was really angry."

"Lana knows how to choose her words. If she wanted to end things, I'm sure you would be aware. You probably just had a fight. Lana and I have had plenty of fights. Sometimes, we both need time to cool down. Same with me and Devon. Except, my fights with Devon usually lead to a *very* different kind of making up..."

Max scowled, and she cracked up.

"So let's assume you two didn't break up. What do you want from Lana? You say you love her. But how serious are you about this?"

"You're asking for my intentions?"

"She's my best friend. And you're the guy who hasn't dated since high school. You don't have a clue what you're doing, and your track record is shit. Can you blame me?"

"No. I can't." What did he want from Lana? Everything. And he wanted to give her everything. All his heart. He wouldn't have broken all his rules for anything less. "I'm very serious about Lana."

"Marriage serious? Family serious?"

Once, he'd panicked at even the thought of being tied down. But with Lana, the idea wasn't so scary. It was maybe even something he wanted. "I think so. Yes."

"Wow. Then you have my blessing." Aurora nudged him with her foot. "Now go get yourself cleaned up. Your smell is making my eyes water."

MAX STEPPED out of the elevators and into the workroom. A dozen pairs of eyes turned to him as his employees stopped, mid-task and mid-sentence. He lifted his chin, both in greeting and dismissal. Nothing to see here.

Luckily, they got the message and work resumed. He breathed in the ozone-scent of the computers, the starch of button-down shirts.

This is more like it, he thought. *I'm back.*

He strode to his new assistant's desk, hand tucked into his pants pocket. He'd worn a suit today, sans tie. His hair was slicked back, and his face was freshly shaved. The dark circles remained under his eyes, but there was only so much that a shower and a pot of coffee could do. But he'd had a full meal and sent Aurora on her way. He was ready to catch up on all that he'd neglected the last few days.

"Morning, Nancy. I need a list of all the meetings, calls, and emails I missed while I was sick, prioritized by importance. Please work on rescheduling anything that's urgent. Send the list and come by my office as soon as it's ready."

"Yes, Mr. Bennett. Of course. I've already been working on that."

"Perfect."

Next, he visited Sylvie in her corner of the workroom. She glanced up, spinning in her desk chair. "Look who's among the living."

"Reports of my death have been slightly exaggerated."

"When I said you should take some time off work, I was thinking Mexico. Tahiti. Not locking yourself in your apartment for the saddest staycation in written history."

"I already have Aurora on my case. She's family, so I put up with it, but I seem to remember you have a performance review coming up."

"Yep. Moving on."

"All kidding aside, Sylv," he said, lowering his voice, "how badly did things get screwed up while I was out?"

"I've seen worse dumpster fires. But it wasn't great." She

gave him an update on the damage. Clients pissed off that they suddenly had to deal with an underling, instead of the boss. Decisions without anyone to make them. "But once we all realized we were on our own? The team stepped up. Things are back on track. Against all odds, we survived without you for a few days. And learned a whole lot. Next time, especially if you give us notice instead of just disappearing, it'll be even smoother."

"I'll try." He glanced around at his employees. All working diligently, nobody pulling out their hair. His company hadn't fallen apart without him. "Any alarms from our clients' systems?"

"One. Tanner led a team to check on it. All good, paperwork submitted."

"Anything with…Lana's system?"

Sylvie eyed him. "Not a peep. But I'm sure you're not asking for details about who's been coming or going. Or, god forbid, a look at her cameras."

"I'm not going to spy on her."

"I'm sure you wouldn't."

Though they both knew he'd think about it. He was tempted, just to see if any creeps had been hanging around her door. But he wasn't going to give in to the urge.

"What happened with her? You two seemed cozy before she left."

He thought about deflecting the question and reminding Sylvie of that performance review. But she was also a friend. He didn't have many of those, not genuine ones. He knew she cared.

"We've all heard about the Hearst trial," Sylvie added. "How it blew up pretty bad?"

How I blew up, you mean? "Lana and I had a fight. But I'm going to fix it."

"Good to hear."

"She's my girlfriend now." At least, he hoped she still was.

But who was he, if not a confident bastard? He'd win her back. "In case you were wondering."

"Oh, I was." Sylvie smiled. "Happy for you."

"If there's nothing else, I'm going to head to my office."

"Got it, boss. Glad to have you back."

He jogged up the steps. His assistant Nancy was already waiting for him. "I sent you the list as you requested, Mr. Bennett. There's only one urgent item. A lawyer named Sandford has called multiple times. Apparently he tried Lana first at the DA's office, but heard she was unavailable. Says his client has information he needs to share with you?"

Dominic Crane's lawyer. Interesting. Max took a seat behind his desk, cracking his knuckles. "Then get Sandford on the line, please." He didn't know what Crane was up to. But he wanted to find out.

Chapter Thirty-One

*W*ayfair's assistant showed them into his office. "Lana, Trevor, what a pleasant surprise." The man stood up from his desk, holding out his hand like they were all great friends.

Lana stared at his offered hand but didn't return the gesture. Wayfair's smile didn't falter.

"Won't you sit down?" He was all smugness with the knowledge that he'd won. But Lana wasn't just going to take it. She knew what Wayfair had done.

And she needed to look this man in the face and show him that he couldn't intimidate her. She'd been so terrified by the stalker when she'd believed he could be an actual threat. Now she knew the truth. But the fear she'd experienced *had* been real, and she would make sure Paxton suffered real consequences for it.

"We had quite a battle, didn't we?" the man said. "It's too bad only one of us could come out the victor. But you know what they say, the fun is all in the journey."

Lana crossed her legs. "I like your battle analogy. It acknowledges this war isn't over. So, did you take those pictures on the beach yourself? Or did you send your little helper, the one who tried to get me into a car accident?"

"I don't know what you're talking about, Lana. I didn't take those pictures. And I certainly didn't force you to pose for them with your witness. You're the one who falsified evidence and tried to frame my client." He shrugged, his sleeve inching up over his Rolex. "I guess this time the justice system worked."

"Cut the crap, Paxton. I didn't falsify one damn thing, and neither did Max. Your client is guilty. You got that mistrial through manipulation. You knew the only way you could win was by playing dirty."

His cool exterior was slipping. "How exactly did I play dirty? I didn't do anything that was out of bounds. I'm a zealous advocate, but I always stay on the correct side of the rules. It's not my fault you had your witness lie about your relationship, and then paraded around with him in public."

"So, you won't admit what you did? Setting up those phone calls? The threats?"

Wayfair looked at Trevor. "Do you have an idea what this woman is babbling about? Because she's not making any sense."

Lana gripped the arms of her chair. She'd sworn to herself that she wouldn't get angry, but Wayfair was testing her. This must've been how Max had felt on the stand.

"I know you were behind it. You made me believe I had a stalker."

"A stalker?"

"You told him to threaten to hurt me. And that day, when he chased me in his car, he nearly did. Did you write the scripts for him? Or did you just give him creative license."

"Lana told me all about it," Trevor chimed in. "You might as well admit it now."

She smiled. "I know how you love deals, Paxton. I've got all the evidence I need that you were stalking me. That you set up that farce in Vaughn's courtroom. So, make me an offer. Give me a reason not to tell the police and the appeals court and attorney regulation everything you did."

Wayfair was sputtering, loosening the knot of his tie from his throat. "I got the pictures from an anonymous source. It came in a courier envelope and just had a note saying, '*You'll know how to use this.*' Which I did. But this stalker stuff? I haven't got a clue what you're talking about."

Lana couldn't believe he was holding out this long. "Then how did you know that Max and I had a history in the first place? You were having me followed."

"Where you go in public is fair game. It was obvious you were spending a lot of time with that guy. My instincts told me there was more to it, and I was dead-on. But the rest of this nonsense, these supposed phone calls, this car chase or whatever it was. None of it has anything to do with me."

Wayfair stood up, bracing his hands against his desk. "So why don't you go for it. Do your worst. Tell the appellate court whatever make-believe you want. If it's a war you're after, Lana, then you can have one. I was willing to keep this all professional, and just forget about your ample ethical violations and promiscuous tendencies. But if you insist—"

Lana shot up to standing. "I'm not going to sit here and listen to this. I came here as a professional courtesy, but courtesy is lost on you, Paxton. The next time I see you, it'll be in court."

ON THE WAY back to West Oaks, they got stuck in traffic, just as Lana had expected. But she still bounced her knees impatiently, wanting to be home. She was going to call Max as soon as she got there.

She didn't know what to make of Wayfair's denials. He

could still be playing his little games. Yet he'd been so adamant, so shocked and confused by her accusations.

Could he seriously have no idea about the stalker?

No. She just didn't believe it.

"I'm sorry I didn't stand up for you more in there," Trevor said.

"Don't worry about it." Lana squeezed her car into the next lane over, hoping it might somehow move faster. The 101 was a freaking parking lot.

Maybe she should've called Wayfair by phone, instead. But she'd wanted to face him in person, and it had felt good to show him she wasn't afraid.

"No, I should have defended you," Trevor insisted. "Calling you names? It's just not right."

"I can't disagree with you there."

"Are you going to the police about him stalking you?"

"I already have. They have an open file on the issue. But I'm not sure exactly how I want to pursue it. I've got people at Bennett Security working on tracing the stalking incidents to Wayfair, so I can prove his involvement without a doubt." She'd exaggerated the solidity of her evidence in Wayfair's office. But they'd get there. "And I'm going to nail whoever was working with him, because he had help."

"Oh." Trevor screwed up his lips, thinking. "I wish I'd known before about the stalker thing. I could've done something."

"I don't think so," Lana said gently. "Though I really appreciate the sentiment. Max is one of the only people I told, because he deals with stuff like this for a living. But I didn't want a lot of people to know. I really thought it wouldn't affect the trial, and that I could handle it."

Trevor looked out the passenger side window, but she caught his frown. "So, you're really seeing Max Bennett."

"It was very recent. He didn't lie at the hearing."

"Oh, I know. You would never have told him to lie. But

that day at the beach, when you and Max were there together—"

"What do *you* know about that day?"

"I just saw the pictures that Wayfair had, that's all I mean. And I think that Max should never have taken you there. He should've protected you better than that."

She squeezed her hands around the steering wheel. "Trevor, this isn't any of your business."

"I just don't think he deserves you. He's the reason we lost the trial."

She tried to keep her annoyance in check. Trevor probably felt grief over losing the Hearst case, too. He'd been the second chair. It would be a stain on Trevor's career, though to a lesser degree than hers. And she'd only been focused on her own pain.

"I do understand that you feel upset about what happened. Max apologized, and it was Wayfair who orchestrated the whole situation. Beyond that, I'm not going to discuss my personal life with you. So please don't bring it up again."

They drove the rest of the way in awkward silence. It was night when they pulled up to the DA building, where Trevor had left his car.

He hesitated before getting out. "I'm sorry that I offended you. I felt like I should speak my mind, but you're right, it's not my concern."

Lana sighed. "The meeting with Wayfair was stressful. Let's just forget about the ride home and what was said. I'll see you in the office tomorrow."

Trevor nodded. He opened the door and slid out, his skin sallow under the harsh security lights.

Chapter Thirty-Two

*T*he day had worn on, turning to night, and Max still hadn't heard from Dominic Crane's lawyer. He sat at his desk answering emails, but his mind was really on Crane's last conversation with Lana.

When they'd had that video conference with Crane and his lawyer, Sylvie had just discovered that the burner phone used to call Lana was connected to the Silverlake Syndicate. Max had been convinced that Crane was involved, despite the man's claim that he knew nothing of any attempts to harass Lana.

Of course, now Max knew that Wayfair had been behind the whole stalker facade. But what was the Silverlake Syndicate's connection? Was it just a coincidence, and that burner phone had ended up in Wayfair's hands by chance?

Or did Wayfair really have help, and he'd hired someone inside the Syndicate to do it?

Max recalled Lana's description of the man who'd been driving the car that chased her. How she'd been sure that it couldn't be Wayfair himself. It made sense that the little weasel wouldn't do his own dirty work. He was a coward. So perhaps he'd hired a Syndicate enforcer to run around town for him. Make the calls, take the pictures.

Yet, as far as Max knew, Wayfair didn't have a prior Syndicate connection. The man was scum, but he wasn't a mob lawyer.

Max glanced at his phone again, which still sat quiet on his desk. If he could just get Sandford or Crane himself on the phone.

Crane had claimed to have real information. Max was no fan of the guy, but he doubted the former leader of the Syndicate would waste his time. Crane wanted to get a deal out of Lana, and he'd know he had to provide something extremely valuable in exchange.

If Max could get Wayfair's enforcer to flip, testify against him, that would be huge. Lana could take that evidence straight to the appellate court.

And if I make it happen, he thought, *then I'll have fixed the whole shitstorm that I caused by losing my temper.*

Max wasn't above using this situation to score brownie points with Lana. He'd take whatever advantage he could get if it would make her forgive him.

Max's phone rang, and he pounced on it.

But it wasn't Crane's lawyer calling.

"Lana?" he asked hesitantly.

"Hey. How've you been?"

A wave of emotions crashed through him. Joy to hear her voice. Regret over their last fight and all his mistakes. But most of all, longing. Her voice just made him yearn to have her in his arms again.

"I've been a wreck without you." He figured it wouldn't pay to be subtle about his feelings.

"I've been a wreck, too. I miss you. So much."

He closed his eyes, just trying to breathe. "I miss you, too. I love you."

"Same here."

"I'm so sorry about everything."

"I want to see you."

Relief made him lightheaded. "That's what I want, too."

"So, we're agreed?" she asked.

His mouth broke into a smile. "This has been a productive meeting."

"If only all my conferences could be this efficient."

Max got up and went over to his couch, switching the walls to opaque on the way. He lay down, tucking a pillow under his head. "Aurora came by to force me out of my funk. I told her about us. That I'm serious about you. She had some reservations, but in the end, she gave me her blessing."

"I'm glad to hear that. I saw Devon this morning. He was helpful, too. Made me realize some things."

"I told him to keep an eye outside your townhouse. I'm sorry for not asking you first."

"Devon told me already. Thank you for the extra protection. But everything's been fine. I mean, no one's bothered me. *I* haven't been fine. I keep thinking of those awful things I said to you."

"Which were totally justified."

"No, they weren't. I called you egotistical."

"Because it's true."

She pushed out an exasperated sigh. "Max, you're so kind and giving that you feel guilty when you can't give even more of yourself. As if it's some personal failing of yours that you have your own ambitions and needs. But that's the opposite of selfish. The idea of causing anyone else pain is so intolerable to you that you've chosen to be alone. You've been so worried all these years about hurting someone else—hurting me—that you didn't let yourself be loved. But you deserve to be loved. I want to love you."

"I want you to love me, too. Tonight, if possible."

"I'm serious."

"I know." Max wanted to see himself the way she'd described. Generous instead of selfish. He wasn't so sure.

"You gave so much to Aurora when she was growing up, but instead of feeling proud of it, you beat yourself up over having your own life. As if pursuing a career in the army, serving your country, was anywhere close to self-centered."

"I guess."

"Max, you told me you wanted me to know the real you. But *I do*. I know you. I fell in love with you because you're a good man who takes care of other people. I stayed in love with you for the same reason. You're the *best* kind of man."

He closed his eyes. Too many things were bubbling up inside of him.

"Do you believe me?" she asked.

"I'll try." He was quiet for a minute or two, letting her words sink in.

"I got back to work today," Lana said. "I went to see Wayfair at his office in L.A."

Tension knotted the muscles at Max's shoulders. "Alone?"

"No, Trevor came with me. I just wanted to see Wayfair in person, look him in the face. He had the nerve to deny everything about the stalker. He acted like he didn't even know what I was talking about."

Max pinched the skin between his eyes. "That's surprising. The guy is kind of a coward, but he also struck me as someone who likes to gloat. I would've thought he'd be crowing about how smart he was."

"That's what I expected, too. Maybe he thought I was going to record the conversation. Who knows. All I can say is, I'm not backing down. I'm going to work with the DA's office to put together our appeal. I'll start on it first thing tomorrow morning."

"Let me know what I can do. I've been waiting to hear back from Crane's lawyer. He couldn't reach you, so he's been trying me. Apparently, the guy came back with some information. I'm hoping it'll help us prove what Wayfair did to you. If we can build a solid case, then we can really make him squirm."

"I love the sounds of that. Let me know what Crane says when you find out."

"Or you could be right next to me when he says it. Why don't come over, right now? You can pack an overnight bag and stay with me here tonight."

"Just tonight? Why not two nights? Or three?"

"If it's my choice, I'd say all the nights."

Her voice softened. "I'd like that, too." Then she made a sound of dismay. "Crap, Trevor is calling. I'd better see what he wants."

Max sat up. Suddenly, the thought of being apart from Lana for even a minute more was intolerable. He had to hold her and kiss her and tell her everything he felt face to face, all over again. To make sure she didn't have any doubt.

"How about you handle your phone call, and I'll come to you? That way I'll see you sooner. I can drive you back here."

"How long will you be? Maybe ten minutes?"

"I've made it there in five. Let's see if I can beat my record."

He wanted to tell her a lot more, too. Every detail of his conversation with Aurora. About the new idea he'd just had about taking Lana on vacation to a beach in Mexico, a private one where nobody else in the world would bother them.

But first, he had to get to her.

Max grabbed his keys and ran for the door.

Chapter Thirty-Three

"revor? What is it?"

"Um, hi."

He sounded strange. Lana was surprised he'd be calling, especially this late. They'd already spent hours together today. But maybe he wanted to apologize again about stepping out of bounds, as unnecessary as that was. She was perfectly willing to let his comments about Max go.

"What's going on?"

Lana was halfway done packing her bag. She'd thrown in work clothes, loungewear, a few toiletries. She'd be leaving for work from Max's, so she had to be ready to go in. It was hard to think about practicalities, though. Not when Max was on his way here.

Max loves me, she thought. Lana had been waiting so long for this, hoping, and now it was really happening. Max was hers. She couldn't wait to see him.

But she had to get rid of Trevor first. As he spoke, she kept tossing items into her bag with her free hand.

"I found out some...new information. About the judge. Judge Vaughn. I need to tell you."

Lana paused in her packing and stood. "Judge Vaughn? What do you mean?"

"Not on the phone. In person."

"But Trevor." She glanced around, trying to think. "This isn't a good time. Can we discuss this at the office tomorrow morning?"

"No. Please, Lana. I'm here. Outside. Just come out here, and we'll talk."

Trevor was out of breath. It was weird.

She went to her front window and looked out, pushing the curtain aside. Trevor's giant Mercedes was there, parked on the opposite curb from her house. What the hell was he doing here? At her *house*?

"You shouldn't have come here. I don't under——"

"Lana, *please*. Just five minutes. You'll understand when I tell you. It's important."

"Fine."

Max would be here any minute. He'd see her when he pulled up, and he could talk to Trevor, too. About…whatever this was. She lowered her phone, slipped on a pair of shoes, and opened the front door.

The street was quiet as she crossed to Trevor's car. It was a beautiful night, just a hint of a breeze carrying marine-scented air. It was late enough that many of her neighbors had gone to bed or were watching TV. Blueish lights flickered behind closed curtains.

Lana reached the driver's side door and knocked. But it was dark inside the car. "Trevor?" She leaned over to look.

There was nobody here. What was going on?

Then she heard a thumping sound. She looked around.

It was coming from the trunk.

Lana rounded the car to the back. The trunk was just barely popped open. She reached for the lid, pulled it open, and bit back a gasp.

Trevor was lying in the trunk. He had a black eye and a bloody lip. His arms were clasped behind his back.

"I'm sorry, Lana. I'm so sorry."

Something whooshed down over Lana's face, blocking the light. Fabric. A bag. Someone had put a bag over her head. She tried to scream and back up, but she bumped against something solid. Arms clamped around her, lifting her and pushing her forward. She tumbled into the trunk and heard the lid slam closed like a coffin.

~

"LANA, HOLD ON, OKAY? STAY STILL."

She'd been crying out for help, punching and kicking at the inside of the trunk lid. The car was driving. She felt the vibrations, heard the noise of the road.

The black fabric pulled away from her face. She could still barely see, but there was a tiny bit more light.

Trevor spit out the black hood. He'd used his teeth to grab hold of it and pull it off her.

"He made me do it. He said he'd kill me if I didn't get you outside. I'm so sorry."

The car rumbled beneath them. "Who is he?"

"I don't know. I don't know." Trevor was crying. She could smell his sweat in the tiny space. "He was hiding behind my car in the parking area when you dropped me off."

Lana's mind worked. She forced her fear aside. That was easier with Trevor here. She'd let him be afraid for them both, while she figured out how to get them out of this.

Trevor's hands were tied, but the kidnapper hadn't bound hers. That was his mistake. Lana searched around for an emergency release lever. Then she remembered. Trevor's car was his pride and joy, but the thing was ancient. Too old for modern upgrades like a trunk release. Shit.

"Turn over. Let me see if I can get your hands free."

His wrists were bound with rope. She tugged at the knot, but it wouldn't budge.

Okay, that hadn't worked either. But the minute the guy opened the trunk, though, she'd be kicking and clawing. She remembered what Max had told her. Go for anything sensitive. Eyes, throat, balls.

But just moments ago, when the guy pinned her arms down, she hadn't done a thing, had she? Despite Max's lessons, all that practice… It hadn't made an ounce of difference in the real world, not with the violence of that man's grip. She'd frozen, just like she'd worried she would. One single self-defense class wasn't going to turn her into a warrior.

But that was just round one, she told herself. *You'll do better next time. You'll be ready.*

"I didn't see the guy. Tell me what he looks like."

"Wearing sunglasses. Even though it's night. A h—hat," Trevor stuttered. "He's tall and thin."

It had to be the driver of the car who'd come after her before.

She felt around for her phone, but it seemed to be gone. The guy must've taken it out of her pocket.

"But he probably works for Wayfair," she said. Was the lawyer trying to get back at them for their visit to his office? "They're just trying scare us. That's it."

"I don't think so. He hit me really bad. This is fucked up."

Lana forced her lungs to work. Breathe in. Out. "We need to stay calm. It's the stalker Wayfair sent after me. It's the same game he's been playing all along."

"Wayfair didn't even know, Lana! This is somebody else. He's going to kill us. I know it. Oh, god. We're going to die."

"We're *not* going to die." *Max will be looking for me. He'll find us.*

Trevor kept whimpering, and the car kept moving. She could smell the ocean. It was much stronger now. They were on the coast. But where were they going? North? South?

Finally, the car pulled to a stop.

The sudden silence outside was deafening. All she could hear was Trevor's fevered breathing.

And then, faintly, the crash of waves against rocks.

The car door slammed. The trunk popped open, and the man calmly aimed a gun down at her. "Don't make me spoil that pretty face."

It was the voice from the phone call weeks ago. She recognized it, though he wasn't trying to disguise his tone anymore.

Yet it was familiar in a different way, too. Familiar in a way that sent fear rocketing through her insides, turning her bowels to water.

It can't be. No, please.

"Turn over," he ordered.

"No."

"If you don't, I'll shoot you."

He said this so matter-of-factly that she had to believe it. Lana rotated in the tight space so that she was face down. Trevor was sobbing beside her. The fear kept ratcheting up in her body, so she tried to sit with it and think past it.

This guy wasn't going to kill her yet. He had something else in mind. It couldn't be good. She'd worked with enough victims to have ample ideas of what could be coming. But others had survived terrible things. So would she. She was strong.

The kidnapper wrenched her hands behind her. Something tight cinched around her wrists. It felt like rope.

Then the man grabbed hold of Trevor's arm and yanked him up. "Out. You first."

Trevor blubbered. His knee dug into Lana's back as he struggled. The man pulled him out of the trunk, and Lana heard Trevor hit the ground. She got up into a seated position so she could see out.

They were on a secluded piece of shoreline. A rocky beach, rough waves. There were no streetlights nearby. She spotted a wooden building not far away. A shack. The sky was gray, the moon visible behind clouds.

"Get up," the man said to Trevor.

Her co-worker stood awkwardly, hands still tied behind his back. He started backing away. Lana expected the man to say something, to order him not to move. But the kidnapper just stood there in sunglasses, pointing the gun at Trevor. Almost like he was taunting him.

Go ahead. Try it. See how far you'll get.

Then, as if Trevor had heard those exact thoughts, he ran. There was a loud pop, and Lana flinched.

Trevor collapsed onto the dirt.

The man walked over to the slumped form and shot him again. The urge to cry balled in Lana's throat, but somehow, she kept it down.

Then the kidnapper turned back to the car, lowering his gun to his side.

"Now it's just you and me. I've been waiting for this moment. I told you I'd make you mine."

He took off his hat. His sunglasses.

She'd already known it was him. That it *had* to be him.

But still, she couldn't hold back her scream.

Chapter Thirty-Four

*M*ax pulled up to Lana's house. He hopped out of his car and jogged up her front walkway, whistling to himself. It had taken him a whole seven minutes to get here, which had annoyed him. But there'd been a lot of activity around the waterfront, people out enjoying themselves and clogging up a couple of the intersections, despite the late hour.

He'd passed the time thinking about Lana, anticipating her kisses, the taste of her skin. As soon as he got ahold of her tonight, there was no way he was letting her go until he absolutely had to.

He went to knock on her door. He was surprised that Lana wasn't outside already, bag packed and ready to go. But maybe she hadn't finished that phone call with her work colleague.

Then he noticed that her door was cracked open. That didn't seem like Lana. It wasn't exactly safe. But maybe he was overthinking things. She was probably just as anxious to see him as he was. And she'd known he was just minutes away.

Max nudged the door open. "Lana?" He walked into her kitchen. He didn't hear anything from further in the house.

He walked toward her bedroom and spotted the suitcase on the floor, the lid still open, the contents neatly folded.

Tingles of worry shot through him. Something wasn't right.

"Lana?" he shouted.

Max made a quick circuit of the rest of the rooms. She wasn't anywhere. His heart was beating faster and faster as the terrible realization sank in.

She was gone.

She was really gone.

She'd left her bag here, her purse on the counter, her front door open.

Jesus. Someone had taken her.

Cursing, he fumbled his phone out of his pocket and dialed a detective he knew with West Oaks P.D. Adrenaline was taking over, clearing his head and pushing his terror away. He explained to the detective what had happened. The man promised to send units immediately, and then follow himself.

"Any indication of who might've taken her? Any suspects?"

Max had already mentioned that Lana had a stalker. This detective was well aware of her file. "We think it's a man named Paxton Wayfair, or someone who's working for him."

Max remembered the phone call from Lana's work colleague. It must've happened right before she disappeared. "And there's a man named Trevor who works with her at the DA's office. I want to know where he is. It's possible he has something to do with this. I can't remember his last name."

"I think it's Trevor Allen. I know him. You stay put. We'll be there soon."

Max remembered the doorbell camera as he was speaking to the detective. He went to the panel by Lana's door and woke up the screen.

It was possible the doorbell camera had recorded Lana's

kidnapping. But he didn't know her security code to gain access to the system. Fuck.

Max dialed Sylvie's number. Thank god she worked the same kind of hours he did. He explained to her as quickly as possible what had happened, and he was grateful that she kept her emotion tamped down. She was all business.

"I don't see any alarms triggered, and her panic button hasn't been activated."

Max paced across Lana's kitchen. "I don't think she had time. Either the guy tricked her into coming outside, or he had some other way in. There was no forced entry. But I believe she left through the front door."

"Accessing the doorbell camera now."

Agonizing seconds passed as Max waited for Sylvie to speak again. Then he heard her curse under her breath. "I've got it, boss. Sending the clip to your phone now."

Max hit play on the video she'd sent. It showed Lana walking away from her front door, crossing the street. She stopped at a car that had been parked on the opposite curb. He saw her peer into the driver's seat, then go around to the trunk. Open it.

A man wearing a baseball cap and sunglasses lunged out of the shadows. Max bit down on his tongue, tasting blood. The man put a dark bag over Lana's head and tossed her into the trunk before getting into the car and driving off.

Max had stopped breathing.

"I'm isolating the image of the license plate," Sylvie said. "I'll send the tag, plus the make and model, over to the police so they can issue a BOLO. The timestamp is just a few minutes old."

"Can you access any other surveillance camera feeds to show where they might have gone?"

"Working on that now. I'll try to have something for you soon."

Max heard a siren. The first squad car roared up to the curb outside the house.

Half an hour later, Lana's townhouse was swarming with police.

His detective friend had contacted L.A.P.D., who sent someone to Paxton Wayfair's home to question the man. But so far, that hadn't turned up anything useful. The lawyer admitted he'd seen Lana earlier in the day but claimed to know nothing about her stalker.

Sylvie had identified the kidnapper's car as belonging to Trevor Allen. The police had tried Trevor's home, too, but there was no sign of him. The man on the video certainly hadn't matched the younger attorney's build, though. Trevor was stocky and short. Max guessed that Trevor was either in on it, or he'd been kidnapped, too.

Which explained how the kidnapper got Lana outside. The phone call from Trevor.

Sylvie had reported that the suspect vehicle was seen traveling south on the freeway along the coast. But it exited from there, and Sylvie had seen no further sign of it on surveillance or traffic cameras. There were all kinds of twisty old roads down there, isolated houses. Police vehicles were out driving the area just in case they spotted something. But there was no way to know where the guy was taking Lana.

Half an hour gone. Trevor Allen's car could be anywhere. And Max was barely holding his shit together.

Max's phone rang. Sylvie was calling again.

"Please tell me you've spotted Trevor's car somewhere."

"Not yet. But Dominic Crane called our main line. He's been trying to reach you. He says it's about Lana. Should I connect him through to your cell?"

"Do it."

Max walked away from Lana's house toward a small patch of quiet, where curious neighbors and police officers weren't congregating.

"Bennett?"

"I swear to god, Crane, if you're fucking with me right now, I'm going to—"

"Jeez, everyone knows you're a hot head. But shouldn't you wait until you're provoked? What are you already so upset about, apart from my general existence?"

"Lana's been kidnapped."

"Oh. Shit. I understand now. What's happened?"

"It's her stalker. The one my team linked to your Syndicate. If you have anything to do with this..."

"I don't. I wouldn't. I'd have nothing to gain."

"So, what's your information?" Max prayed it would help them find her.

"I asked around. Called in some favors from people who don't actively wish me dead. I found a low-level guy who was hired to keep tabs on you, way back at the end of last year."

"Wait. On *me*?"

"Yep. You. He was supposed to get to know your schedule, who you spent time with. The client seemed to have a real hard-on for you. But in the last few months, the orders changed to focus on a female West Oaks DA: Lana. Follow her around, take pictures. Report back whatever he saw. *Especially* anything involving you."

"Report to whom?"

"He didn't know. He had a phone number for the client and a drop location."

Okay. So this explained the Silverlake connection. But why would this client want to go after Max himself?

"Did your guy make the harassing phone calls to Lana?"

"Not personally. He did say he took some pictures. But he provided a burner phone to the client. I'm guessing the same phone used to call Lana."

"The stalker also rear-ended her. Chased her in his car. Was that your guy, too?"

"If it was, he didn't mention it. And believe me, he was

spilling. Some of my former associates in the Syndicate don't find me intimidating, but I can be persuasive when I choose to be."

Max's brain worked, trying to fit all these pieces together. The low-level Syndicate guy hadn't done much, apparently, aside from recon for his client. The client was the real stalker, and he'd done most of his own dirty work. Calling Lana, chasing her. Maybe sending the scarf.

First, he'd been after Max. Then Lana.

But he hadn't actively stalked Max. Max hadn't even known anybody was watching him. Why step up the threats and the harassment with Lana? Just because she was a beautiful woman?

No. Not only that. Because she was close to Max.

The stalker hadn't just been getting off on Lana's fear. He'd been targeting *Max*, too. Going after someone Max cared about.

And now this, the kidnapping. The stalker had taken the woman Max loved. As if he wanted Max to suffer.

Like this guy wanted *revenge*.

"So, let's say this client wanted to hurt Lana to get some kind of revenge on me. What else did your guy say about his client? There had to be something. Was the client old? Young? Did he have an accent?"

Crane made a humming sound. "Rich. But local. My guy said the client sounded like a rich asshole from around here. Southern California. But he probably says that about me. The description fits you too, Bennett. No offense."

Max stopped fidgeting. Cold spread through his veins. "Rich," he repeated. "From around here."

Oh, fuck me.

Max had nearly forgotten the other thing he knew about this stalker. The man had been helping Wayfair win the Hearst case.

Maybe Wayfair truly hadn't known his source's identity.

But the stalker hadn't just wanted to target Lana or get revenge on Max. He'd wanted to manipulate the Hearst trial. He'd had the financial means to hire the Silverlake Syndicate for help.

And this fucker was so sadistic that he'd enjoyed terrifying a woman. Like it was just one extra perk.

Who else could it be but Ryan Hearst himself?

Chapter Thirty-Five

*R*yan Hearst dragged Lana out of the trunk. She screamed and kicked at him, but he didn't even seem to feel it. He carried her to the small building she'd seen. It was made of dark, weathered planks of wood.

They went inside. It had an empty front room that looked abandoned.

But a doorway led into another room at the back.

There, Ryan dumped Lana onto a cot. It was too dark to see much. She scrambled upright. She was going to run at him, fight. But before she could, he stepped out of the door and slammed it closed.

She heard a lock snapping into place on the other side. *Damn it.* She kicked the door in frustration.

"Let me out of here!"

No answer.

Lana walked around the tiny space, hands bound behind her back. She could still hear the waves crashing into shore outside.

She found a lantern hanging from a wall. With some effort, she used her mouth to flip the switch on the light. The room came into view.

Shabby, rough, dirty.

But the walls were covered in glossy pictures.

Pictures of *her*.

She saw the images of herself at the beach, wearing the string bikini, many of the same ones Wayfair had produced at the trial. Close-ups of her body, her face. There were photos of her and Max at the beach as well, but Max's face was scribbled out.

Other pictures showed her walking into the judicial building. Into her townhouse. Walking down the street, driving her car, shopping at the grocery store.

Bile rose as she realized how much this monster had been watching her. Not on his own, clearly, because she would've recognized Hearst at some point, and she'd have noticed if a man in sunglasses started tracking her everywhere. No, he'd hired someone else to help him. A pro who wasn't so easily spotted.

The police had been unofficially keeping an eye on Hearst's movements. But Ryan had clearly been able to slip away from the off-duty cops' surveillance the day he chased her and Aurora. That had been him, she was sure of it.

Why hadn't she recognized his jawline? Why hadn't she thought of him being the stalker before? Lana was furious at herself. She'd been so focused on Wayfair, when she should've remembered it was Wayfair's *client* who was the sick murderer.

And he was a free man, now. No more bail. No more surveillance.

Ryan Hearst. The killer of Heather Barnes. The man so confident, so smug, that he'd displayed Heather's necklace in his own bedroom until Max had found it.

Max would know Lana was missing by now. He'd been on his way to her house just before Ryan arrived. As soon as Max saw she was gone, he would realize the stalker had kidnapped her. The doorbell camera had probably caught it on video, too, how Hearst stuffed her into the trunk of Trevor's car.

Poor Trevor. Tears filled her eyes. He'd been so terrified, and there'd been nothing she could do to save him.

She didn't know what Hearst planned to do to her, but he clearly didn't intend to leave any witnesses alive.

The room had a couple of small windows, but they'd been covered with plywood. She couldn't find anything that would function as a weapon. There was a leather trunk, but it was locked and bolted to the floor. Even the cot was screwed into the wall, so it couldn't be lifted.

Lana yanked at the ropes around her wrists. There was a tiny amount of give. She started twisting her hands to enlarge the gap.

Max, I need you. Please find me.

~

LANA HEARD a key in the lock. The door opened.

"I know you're standing behind the door right now," Ryan said. "Back out of there, or I'll shoot you through the wall."

Lana cursed silently. She'd been hoping to catch him by surprise. She moved out into the room, careful to keep her back turned away from him. The ropes were looser now. Her wrists were bleeding from the chafing, and the extra lubrication helped her move them even more. But she still hadn't made a large enough gap to slip her hand through.

Ryan waited in the doorway, holding the gun down by his side. "I'm sure your mind's been busy while I was gone. I was getting rid of Trevor."

"Someone's going to find him. They'll tie his death to you."

"Maybe they'll find him, but blame me? Nah. He's in the water, and that'll destroy most any evidence. There's the bullet, but this gun isn't registered to me."

He walked into the room and sat on the leather trunk, resting the gun on his thigh. Ryan looked much the way he had every day of the trial. Hair parted neatly, clean-shaven, preppy good looks. He was wearing shorts and a tee instead of a suit.

"Don't you want to sit down?" He nodded at the cot. "Get better acquainted?"

"Go fuck yourself."

"Such a dirty mouth, Lana. Who knows where it's been? Except Max Bennett. I'll bet *he* knows."

She didn't respond. Just glared. And twisted her wrists against the rope.

Ryan's eyes narrowed. "Do you know what this place is? This room?"

Lana refused to acknowledge the photos on the walls. She wouldn't give him the satisfaction.

He stood and walked toward her. "This is where I brought Heather. All those years ago. Nobody could hear her scream, and they won't hear you."

Lana gagged. Stomach acid filled her mouth. "You like to hurt people who are weaker than you so you can pretend to feel strong. You're pathetic."

Ryan pulled back his arm and slapped her.

The blow stunned her. She'd never been hit before, not by anyone. Stars danced across her watering eyes, and blood trickled from her mouth. But the pain was like a hit of speed, making her intensely alert.

"What do you want?" she choked out.

"Payback. But shouldn't I have some fun while I'm at it?"

He retreated, sitting back down on the leather trunk. Her lungs started to work again, relieved that he wasn't close enough to touch her. Even though she knew he was just pacing himself. Enjoying this.

"Payback against me? For prosecuting your case? Or against Max, for outsmarting you?"

"He had no business getting involved. I don't see why anyone still cared about that little whore dying. Heather was worthless, no use to anybody but me. You at least have some value, even though you're just as much of a slut."

"What value is that?"

The longer they kept talking, the more time Lana had to invent a way out of this. Or for Max to find her. She had to believe he was coming.

And if she could just slip her hand free...

"Showing Max that I win. I'll always win. He invaded my home, made me look like an idiot. For a while, at least. But when he finds out what I did to you, and knows it was all because of *him*, he'll wish he'd never even heard my name."

Ryan stood again, looking down at the gun on his open palm. "I thought about going after Max's sister at first, but as you got more involved in my case, I realized you could use a lesson of your own. And I figured the two of you were screwing, from all the time you spent together. Why else would Max have helped you with the investigation in the first place?"

"Because he's a good person?"

"Yeah, whatever. Either way, I just knew it was perfect. I could punish you and Bennett in one go. Scare you with my phone calls, rile you up. Have my fun. Like chasing you and his sister that day in the car. I almost never got moments away from home without any cops tailing me, which is too bad, because I'd love to have made you more personal visits. But at least I could pass on anything useful for the case to Wayfair."

"Like those pictures from the beach."

He laughed. "Yeah, that was a stroke of brilliance on my friend's part. He was the one who followed you, saw the opportunity. Then I teed up the ball and Wayfair hit it out of the park, even if he didn't really know all I'd done to make it happen. Wayfair got Max to lose his mind, right there on the stand. Which only proved how satisfying it would be to take you away from him permanently."

"But you've already won. Your charges were dismissed.

Why come after me now? You're just exposing yourself to a greater risk of getting caught again."

"You think you *ever* had a chance of convicting me? There was always going to be a mistrial. Of course, we had to make it look good. We can thank Max for playing his part so well."

"What do you mean, there was always going to be a mistrial? How…"

"Come on, Lana. You're smarter than that. Don't tell me you haven't guessed."

Indignation roiled in her stomach. "Judge Vaughn. Did you threaten her? Or buy her off?"

"Do I have to pick just one?" He stood up, leaving the gun on the windowsill behind him. Ryan advanced toward her, a slow step at a time.

"You and I were *always* going to end up here after the trial was over. I've been looking forward to this from those first phone calls. And when Wayfair told me this afternoon about your little visit to his office? I knew it needed to be today."

Ryan dipped his fingers into his pocket. He pulled out a long, silky piece of lightweight material. Her scarf, the one that had been stolen from the beach. The end of it was frayed, a piece ripped away.

"I wasn't at the beach that day myself, which is really too bad. I would've loved to see you in that bikini, simply as a connoisseur of beautiful things. But honestly? Scantily clad women don't do it for me. I have more demanding tastes."

Lana pressed herself against the wall. There was nowhere to go. A vein in her neck throbbed, but the rest of her body was paralyzed with fear.

He wrapped the ends of the fabric in each fist, holding it out, as his grin spread wide.

"Let's put your scarf back on you, Lana, and see how pretty you look. Let's put it on nice and *tight*."

Chapter Thirty-Six

*M*ax followed the detectives in his car to the Hearst residence. There, he watched them go to the front door. He sat behind the wheel, hands shaking, his throat closing.

Ryan Hearst had taken Lana. That murderer had her. Max knew that now. Dominic Crane had helped him make the connection. Maybe someday, he'd thank the man for that. But only if he got to Lana in time.

If anything happened to her, then nothing was going to hold back his rage. Max was going to burn down the entire world, and Crane would be first—for failing to respond to his calls earlier, when there'd still been time.

He saw the detectives talking to Ryan's sister, Bethany. The woman was shaking her head. Max couldn't stay put any longer. He pushed out of the car and walked over to the grand front entrance.

Bethany saw him coming. "No way. What is he doing here? That man is not welcome here."

"Ryan kidnapped Lana Marchetti, the prosecutor on his case. I need to know where he's taking her."

"You're insane! I want you to leave me alone."

The detectives tried to get Max to go back to his car, but he refused. "Bethany, please. I'm begging you. Do you want me to get on my knees? I'll do it."

She came out of the house and walked right up to him, standing toe to toe. "Why should I believe a word you say? You tricked me before. You made a fool of me."

"I didn't say one thing that wasn't true. I told you that I was here investigating Ryan for the murder of Heather Barnes. You chose to let me in. You took me upstairs."

"But you made me believe——" Bethany glanced at the detectives, who were closely watching all of this unfold. She grabbed Max's sleeve and pulled him around the side of the house. They were in a concrete driveway, and Max could see fancy cars lined up inside a garage with glass doors.

She whirled on him. "You acted like you didn't care about the investigation. You made me think you *liked me*."

"I wish that hadn't been necessary. But it was still your choice to allow me in."

"Do you have any idea what it's been like for me since that day? My brother and my family think I betrayed him. They hate me for letting you into the house. I can't believe you'd even show your face here, after what you did."

Max had flirted with her that day. Shamelessly. He'd encouraged her assumption that he wanted inside the house to be alone with her.

Almost always in his life, Max had made sure that women knew what to expect from him, so that they didn't get their hopes up. But that day, he didn't feel any sympathy for Bethany Hearst or concern for her feelings. He'd manipulated her without any regard for what might happen to her afterward.

"If I've made your life more difficult," Max said, "I'm sorry. I had a compelling reason. But I should've made sure that you were okay after what happened."

"No. I won't believe you. You're just trying to trick me

again. Pretending to be nice, confusing me. *You* planted that necklace in Ryan's room. You're just trying to find a new way to cause trouble for him, since he proved his innocence at trial."

"That's not even close to what happened at the trial. But you can believe that if it makes you sleep better." Max pulled out his phone and hit play on the video of Lana being kidnapping. He held up the device. "Do you recognize him? It's Ryan. That's your brother, isn't it? Pushing Lana into that trunk."

Bethany barely glanced at the screen. Her expression was hard. Max hit play again, holding the small device in front of her face. This time, she looked for a bit longer. Her eyes widened.

She recognized Ryan. He was sure of it.

"This was only about an hour ago. Where would he have taken her?"

Her face shut down again. Bethany walked back and forth across the driveway. "You planted that necklace. Ryan was going to call me as a witness, and I was going to testify that I had never seen that necklace in his room before. Then the mistrial happened, so I didn't get a chance."

"I didn't plant anything. I think you know that. But I don't blame you for being afraid of him. Has Ryan threatened you? Hurt you?"

She stepped back, rage marring her features. "You don't know a damned thing. *All of this* is your fault."

"Think about it, Bethany. Let's say that you're right, that I did plant the evidence. Ryan's case has already been dismissed. He's a free man. If he wanted to confront me about what he thinks I did, why not come at me directly? Why not have it out with me, man-to-man? But that's not what he chose. He went after Lana. He put a bag over her head and threw her into a trunk. He's going to *hurt her*." Max could barely get those words out. "Why do you think that is?"

Bethany kept walking back and forth. She covered her face. "I never wanted any of this to happen."

"You know something. Maybe it's way deep down, somewhere that you don't have to see it. So that you're able to get through each day and pretend your brother isn't a monster. But you've lived with him all these years. You must've seen that he likes to hurt people. Likes to hurt *women*."

"No. No."

But she sounded more like she was begging for release from this pressure than denying that Max's words were true.

"The woman he took, Lana? I love her. She means everything to me, and Ryan figured that out. He wants to punish me in the worst possible way for finding Heather's necklace. Don't let him do it."

"I really didn't know," she muttered. "I swear. I didn't. I thought, sometimes...but I didn't *know*. And I didn't remember the necklace. I really..."

She was losing focus. Max held up his phone yet again, freezing the image on the screen. "The man on the video is your brother, isn't he? You recognize him. You might as well admit it because I already know I'm right."

Bethany stopped pacing.

"He'll kill me if I tell you," she whispered.

"Then we'll protect you."

"You can't." She sank to the ground, right there on the concrete.

He knelt beside her. "I own a private security company. I have a team of bodyguards at my disposal. And the detectives waiting outside your door have their own resources, too."

"You can't help me. But I'll tell you. Because it's the right thing." Tears streamed over her cheeks. "It's Ryan on the video. It's him."

Max exhaled, wiping his hand over his face. "Okay. Thank you, Bethany. Now I need your help figuring out where Ryan's taken her."

For another minute, she could only cry. Then she spoke.

"There's a tiny old house in the coastal wildlife refuge. Abandoned. There's no nice beach there, hardly any roads nearby. Really wild. We used to have parties there, way back in high school. But ever since, it's been a spot for Ryan to get away that not many people know about. If he didn't want to be found, I think that's where he would go."

Chapter Thirty-Seven

*R*yan grabbed her. Spun her around so she was pushed against the wall. He looped the scarf around Lana's neck and yanked it taut.

She couldn't breathe.

Max's face appeared in her memory, kindness in his eyes. His hands, so gentle when she needed it, and firm exactly when she wanted. Lana thought of all those years wasted on being lonely. They'd both waited so long.

She couldn't let Hearst take that away from them. It couldn't end like this.

Be angry, Max's voice said in her memory. *Be explosive.*

Lana threw her head back. She connected with Ryan's nose. He shouted, losing his grip on her, and stumbled back a few steps.

Lana pivoted and charged at him. She yanked at her wrists, but her hand still couldn't pull free. So she threw her knee forward, straight into his groin. Soft flesh gave beneath her knee cap.

Ryan howled in pain, sinking to the ground.

Lana ran for the open door. His fingers closed over her ankle. She toppled to the floor. *No. I'm down.* Max had said that was the worst position. On the ground with a stronger opponent. And she didn't even have her hands.

Ryan rolled her so she was face up. He straddled her, his face contorted with fury. Blood streamed over his teeth from his nose.

He put his hands around her neck and squeezed.

"You're going to die. Just like Heather."

Lana's hand burst free of the ropes, her skin tearing. She jabbed her thumb into Ryan's eye. He emitted a high-pitched screech. She wrestled her other hand out from beneath her and punched at his testicles again. His weight fell to one side. She wriggled free.

Lana sprinted across the tiny room. But she didn't go for the door this time.

She went for Ryan's gun.

She grabbed the weapon, turned around, and aimed.

"Get away from me." Her voice was hoarse.

Ryan got up, smiling with his blood-soaked teeth. "You're tougher than I gave you credit for. But you're not going to shoot me."

Her whole body was trembling. Her throat aching, her wrists torn.

He licked his teeth. "If you had the guts, you'd have already done it."

She wanted to see this man dead for what he'd done. Ryan had murdered Heather. Murdered Trevor. Tried to kill her.

Ryan took a step closer.

Yet her finger wouldn't tighten on the trigger.

Chapter Thirty-Eight

*M*ax's flashlight roved across the expanse of wilderness. To his left and right, Devon and Tanner waded through tall grass as they searched. The lights of other searchers shone from farther away. Nothing was audible over the crashing waves. The moon was half full, just peeking out from behind the clouds.

He couldn't stop picturing the photos in Heather Barnes's murder book. The livid marks on her neck.

And the cold cruelty of Ryan Hearst's expression in the courtroom.

The police, along with Max's team, had converged on the wildlife refuge south of town. Bethany had only given them a general description of the location of the wooden house. She hadn't been there in years. But the refuge was a hundred and fifty square miles in size, spanning twenty miles of coastline. It was a lot to cover.

Two hours had now passed since Lana's abduction.

Max's eyes stung, and he told himself it was just the salty spray from the ocean. He had to stay strong for Lana. They were almost there. Any minute, they'd find her.

Hold on a little longer, he thought. *I'm coming.*

Tanner signaled. Max ran over to him. There was an old wooden beach house up ahead.

Using hand signals, Max directed Devon and Tanner to spread out. They switched off their lights, keeping low.

But when they got close enough, Max noticed the caved-in roof. This was just a ruin. Nobody here.

"Shit." Max checked his phone. Nothing from his detective friends or the other searchers. Nothing but unhelpful status updates from Sylvie, who was still poring over video back at the office.

Devon and Tanner had already moved on, continuing their survey.

After ten more minutes, the terrain lifted slightly. A low hill appeared, with huge rocks deflecting the water's spray beneath.

There was a dark spot on the hill.

Max studied it with his monocular. It looked like another abandoned cabin. Then a flash of yellow light caught his attention.

The light had come from inside that structure.

Then Tanner texted that he'd spotted a car parked on a stretch of dirt road. It matched the description of Trevor Allen's vehicle, though Tanner wasn't close enough to get the plates.

This had to be it. Adrenaline flooded his body anew. Max texted the detectives that they might've found Hearst's hideout.

Do not engage, a detective wrote back. *Wait for us to get there.*

"Fuck that." Max signaled *Go* with his hands to Devon and Tanner.

His men fanned out to approach from different sides.

Devon and Tanner flanked around the back, while Max took the front. He kept to a slight angle to stay out of sight of the window. As he got closer, he crouched in the grass, listening. Then dashed forward again.

He reached the front door and pressed himself to one side of it. From inside, there came a muffled sound. Like quiet footsteps or knocking.

Someone howled. Then a grunt. A thump. Scuffling.

He had to hurry. From his shoulder holster, Max drew his M9 Beretta.

A glance in the window told him nobody was in the front of the building. There was a rectangle of light shining against the wall inside. Like a doorway to another room. The source of the light. But Max couldn't see more from this angle.

He twisted the knob on the cabin's front door. It opened by a centimeter. An inch. Voices spoke.

"If you had the guts, you'd have already done it." It was Hearst.

Max pushed the door wider, and there was Lana, her back framed in the next doorway. She had her arms extended in front of her, pointing at Hearst.

She held a pistol. "I'm leaving now. If you try to stop me, I swear, I'll kill you."

His arms were extended, palms out. Blood flowed from his nose, marring the lower part of his face and his shirt. Had Lana done that? Max's heart lifted in triumph, thinking of his girl fighting back against that twisted fucker.

Hearst took a step toward her. Max flinched, still holding himself back.

"Where will you go? We're miles away from anyone. You don't know where I put the car keys." Hearst's eyes flicked down to the gun. Lana's body was rigid with tension.

Max sensed Devon and Tanner beside him, but he waved his men away. He stayed low, still peeking through the front doorway. He was afraid to do anything that might distract Lana. Hearst was far closer to her than he was. If she looked away, Hearst would go for Lana's gun.

Yet Max couldn't line up a decent shot, either. Lana was in the way. He couldn't risk hitting her.

"Just hand that to me. In exchange, I'll make this quick and painless, I promise. You won't feel a thing." Hearst was openly staring at the gun now, hands flexing.

And Lana still hadn't moved. She was paralyzed.

If Max didn't do something right fucking now, Hearst was going to grab that weapon and kill her.

He made his decision. Max rose and stepped fully into the front room.

"Lana, get down!" Max aimed his M9, praying for an opening.

That same second, Hearst's eyes connected with Max. Hatred burned there. He lunged at Lana.

Max was about to squeeze the trigger.

But Lana's gun went off first.

Abruptly, Hearst's body froze. The man looked down at the mess of dark red in the middle of his stomach.

Lana fired again.

Another gory patch appeared, this one at his chest. Hearst sat backward onto the floor, going limp. His head bowed.

The pistol in Lana's hands was shaking.

"Hey." Max tucked his own weapon back into its holster, edging toward her. "L, it's me. Can you put the gun on the floor? Gently, okay?"

Her knees bent, and she set the pistol on the floorboards. "Max..." It was like all the energy had gone out of her. She looked ready to fall over. He crouched down to steady her shoulders. Lana was staring at Hearst's body, so Max turned her head to face him instead.

"It's over now. You did great. You made sure he can't hurt you anymore. He can't hurt anyone else ever again."

Max pulled her against him as she sobbed.

～

MAX DIDN'T LET her out of his sight while the paramedics bandaged her wrists and checked her other injuries, or when the detectives asked questions. Finally, the police agreed to let him take Lana straight home. Devon drove them, while Max sat with Lana in the back, holding her. Tanner was driving a separate car.

"You want to go to your place?" Max asked. "Or mine?"

"Yours." She had her arms around his waist, her cheek pressed to his chest. "Is it too late ask Aurora to come over?"

Devon smiled sadly in the rearview mirror. "I already called her. I'll let her know to meet us at headquarters. I'm sure she'll beat us there."

Lana nodded. Max ran a hand over her hair. "I'm so sorry I wasn't there," he whispered. "I should've stopped him."

"I had a gun on him, and I almost didn't stop him, either. My finger was on the trigger, but it wouldn't move. It took hearing your voice to give me the courage. Why couldn't I do it before?"

"Because that's not you, L. You're willing to give second chances to people who don't deserve it. Even people who've hurt you."

"Don't you dare compare yourself to…"

"I'm not. I'm just saying there's nothing wrong with you. The fault isn't yours. It takes a different kind of strength to face down the worst in people, and still leave room for mercy."

Max would've killed Ryan Hearst for what he'd done without a moment's doubt. But he was thankful that Lana was different from him. The world needed more idealists like her, even though it still needed defenders like Max, too.

But enough big thoughts. That was making his brain tired. He just wanted to hold his girl and love her and give her everything she needed.

When they stepped into Max's apartment, Aurora was waiting. She ran over. "Lana!"

The two women embraced, and they both dissolved into

tears. Lana and Aurora went over to the couch and lay down, arms around each other, talking quietly.

Max sat with Devon at his kitchen counter, drinking glasses of orange juice. Maybe, a very long time ago, he'd been a little jealous of Aurora's closeness with Lana. But now he was just thanking the stars that Aurora and Lana had each other.

"You okay, Max?" Devon asked.

"Trying to be. Thanks for being there tonight." It was Devon's job, but it was more than that, too. They both knew it.

Devon patted him on the arm. "Let me know if you need anything."

"I will." He managed a smile. "And thanks for not calling me 'sir.'"

"I figured we were finally past that."

They were a family. Max knew Lana didn't like hearing that because it implied they had a sibling relationship. But it was more like he and Lana were the stand-in parents, and Aurora was their grown-up, rebellious daughter. And Devon... yeah, he could hang around, too. A something-in-law.

They were a family, and they would all take care of each other.

Chapter Thirty-Nine

"*T*hank you all so much for being here." Claire Barnes stood on a small stage in front of a vacant lot, smiling at the audience of reporters and friends. "It's my great honor to dedicate this site. Soon, right where we're standing, we'll begin construction on the Heather Barnes Center for Women."

Claire caught Lana's eye. Lana subtly waved back, not wanting to take any of the attention away. This was such a big day for Claire.

"Over twenty years ago, my sister Heather was murdered. Losing her was the worst thing I've ever gone through. But there are so many women in our community dealing with trauma and tragedy every day. The Center for Women will provide services to help them in their hour of need, as well as with the healing after. I feel Heather's spirit with us today, and I know how much this would mean to her, too."

It had only been a couple of weeks since Ryan Hearst's death. But an anonymous donor had provided the lot for the center, as well as the funding, and Claire was already running with it.

Claire would act as the Center's director, which was a big

step-up in responsibilities from her current job as a social worker. But Lana was sure the woman would succeed. It was cathartic to have a task, to feel productive and useful. Lana understood exactly how Claire felt.

While Claire responded to questions from the reporters, Max leaned over to Lana's ear. "I hate to run, but I've got a meeting in fifteen minutes. You okay staying without me?"

"Of course. I'll see you later." She gave him a kiss on the cheek, and he took off toward his car.

After the official dedication ceremony was over, the audience grabbed burritos from a waiting food truck and milled around, chatting. Lana saw the mayor and members of City Council, along with Stephen Abrams, the District Attorney. But she kept to the sidelines, not in the mood to talk. She'd done so much of that already, lately.

Abrams had asked her again to run for DA, but Lana declined. She knew she'd want to try in the future, but there wasn't any rush. She had a lot more she wanted to do first. Abrams hadn't decided whether he'd run again after all, or whether he'd support someone else. Lana was okay either way, so long as she remained a key part of the team.

Before long, Claire tracked Lana down. "I'm so glad you could make it." They hugged.

"I wouldn't miss it. Max was here too, but he had to leave for a meeting. He sends his congratulations."

"I have the feeling it wasn't just a meeting. Has Max been avoiding me?"

"Why would he do that?"

Claire gave her a knowing look. "I know that Max was the anonymous donor. It was pretty obvious. This lot belonged to him before he suddenly gifted it to the LLC that donated it to me. I'm no detective but give me a *little* more credit."

"Okay, you're right. But he wanted this to be about you and Heather." Max had the money to spare, and he hadn't felt he had any right to a pat on the back for it.

"Without Max, you couldn't have brought Hearst to trial. And you…" Claire shook her head, her eyes shining. "Lana, what you went through is unimaginable."

Only Heather really knows, Lana thought. But that was way too dark a thought for this beautiful sunny day.

"I understand that Max would rather keep his role quiet, but the two of you made all this possible. I'm never going to forget that. I am so incredibly grateful for everything. For you."

They strolled further away from the crowd, heading toward the edge of the lot, where they could just make out the waterfront in the distance.

"How've you been doing?" Claire asked.

"I'm hanging in there."

Lana had been so swamped with work that she hadn't had time to dwell on the worst of it. She was now ethically walled-off from any casework related to Ryan Hearst, given her personal involvement. Stephen Abrams had taken over the casefile. But that meant she had to pick up the slack on their office's other filings. Her next trial, one for vehicular manslaughter and drunk driving, would begin in just a few days. Abrams had offered her more time off than that, but Lana was eager to keep busy.

Now that Hearst was dead, of course, any appeals relating to his trial were moot. But Abrams had given plenty of interviews in the media making the truth known: that the mistrial had been the result of Hearst's interference, Judge Vaughn's biased rulings, and Wayfair's improper manipulation.

Dominic Crane's contact within the Syndicate—the guy Ryan Hearst had hired—had confessed everything he'd done on Hearst's behalf in exchange for immunity. Wayfair hadn't known about most of it, but he had been involved in paying off the judge. The DA was going to seek criminal charges against Judge Vaughn and Paxton Wayfair relating to the bribery.

And as for Crane himself, Lana was grateful for the help he'd given Max, and she had hopes of working with Crane more cooperatively in the future. She and the DA were discussing a potential new plea deal for him.

Lana was still embarrassed by all the prying into her personal life. She also didn't like that the media now painted her as a victim, and *Max* the ultimate hero. At least she wasn't the seductress/villain anymore.

But none of that mattered compared to the whole world knowing the truth about Heather Barnes. Ryan Hearst murdered her. There wasn't any more doubt.

"I saw Trevor Allen's family for the funeral," Lana said. "It was tough."

"I'm sure." Claire hadn't gone to Trevor's funeral, which Lana completely understood. "It takes a really long time to even begin to heal from the loss. I've been meaning to write to the Allens. Do you think they'd welcome it?"

"Absolutely."

Lana was seeing a therapist, too, which was helping her to deal. But most of all, having Max, Aurora, and Devon nearby let her sleep soundly most nights.

"Lana, I've been meaning to say… I was too hard on you the day of the mistrial."

"Don't even mention it."

"No, I have to. It was so difficult to keep the faith. But you always have. You promised me we'd get justice for Heather, and you did it. I'm just sorry about what it cost."

Claire gave her another hug before heading back to her guests.

THAT NIGHT, Max came up to the roof where Lana was sitting. She'd been listening to the waves. Insomnia had been plaguing her on occasion, and she usually liked to come up here to reset her mind. The sound of the ocean made her think of Hearst's cabin, yet at the same time, it reminded her that this world had existed long before that sick man, and it would keep going long after. Hearst was dead, and Lana was still here.

Max settled onto the wicker couch beside her. "I didn't have a chance to ask you. How was Claire?"

"She's well. She totally knows that you donated the money."

"I figured she might guess. Does she seem…happy?"

"I think she's as close to happy as she's been in a while. She's moving on. I want to do that, too."

It was dark where they were sitting, but Lana could see enough of him. His strong profile, his broad shoulders. She put her hand on his thigh, reassured as always by the firm muscle underneath.

"There's no timeline for moving on. There's no rush."

Max was being so patient. They hadn't made love since everything that happened. Not since before the mistrial. Lana had felt desire for him, but whenever things got heated, she hadn't liked the places her mind had gone.

But tonight felt different. The waves soothed her. Her bruises had healed, her throat wasn't bothering her anymore, and she felt more like herself. Maybe not the exact same Lana she'd been before Ryan Hearst, but her mind wasn't stuck in that cabin, either.

She leaned forward and kissed Max's jaw. "I know there's no rush. But I'm ready. I want you."

He gently brushed the hair back from her cheek. "You want me how?"

"I want you inside of me."

He grinned, and she kissed his mouth. Max was holding back, so she nudged her tongue past his lips, coaxing him open. She straddled his lap, one of her favorite places to be, and felt him hardening against her.

"How is that?" he asked. "Okay?"

"So much better than okay."

She didn't want slow and gentle Max. She wanted him fast and aggressive. Lana wasn't going to break, and she wanted him to acknowledge that fact, too.

But Aurora and Devon were sleeping in the guestroom downstairs. They'd been staying at Max's off-and-on for the last couple weeks at Lana's request, and Max hadn't complained once.

Lana didn't want any unexpected interruptions, though. She'd had more than enough of being on public display.

She stood up, pulling on Max's hands. "Take me to bed."

The minute his door closed, they were shucking off clothing, their mouths colliding again and again. Lana pushed Max onto the mattress and bent down to suck on the tip of his cock. He let out a loud moan.

"Shhh. You're going to wake the kids."

Lana crawled up his big body, settling herself over him. One of his hands squeezed her breast while his other fingers stroked between her legs, growing slipperier by the second. Soon she was riding his hand, already so close.

She reached down, fisted the base of his shaft, and sat on him. His length filled her, the pressure almost turning to pain, but not quite. Max grabbed her hips, hissing. "Fuck. You feel so good."

Lana draped her upper body over his and let Max pump into her. She adjusted the angle of her pelvis, so he hit her just right, giving her exactly what she needed. Her mouth dropped kisses onto his chest and neck.

"I've missed this," she said into his chest hair.

He hummed in agreement.

"Now fuck me harder, Max. Don't hold back."

His dick pulled almost out of her, then slammed into her again.

"Yes. Just like that."

He thrust his hips, and she answered each movement, loving the filthy, primal sound of their bodies meeting. The bed shook. She felt her climax surging inside of her. It tipped right over the edge. Max put his knuckle in her mouth, and she bit down to cover her cries. Another few seconds, and he was shuddering underneath her.

She just lay there on top of him, panting, not moving. Eyes heavy, a lazy smile on her lips. Wow, she'd needed that.

"Do you think they heard?" Max asked.

Lana giggled.

Epilogue

ax put the finishing touches on dinner while he waited for Lana to get home. They were at her townhouse tonight, a Friday, and they'd be staying here all weekend. Max preferred having his own belongings at his fingertips, but Lana liked the same thing, so they'd been compromising. He also would've taken his ocean panoramas over her view of the neighbor's trash can, but no way was he bringing that up.

He'd been happy to escape work early. Bennett Security had several new hires now, all of whom needed training, but they were starting to meld with the rest of his team. Max had made progress on delegating more responsibilities, which freed up an extra hour here or there to spend on Lana.

Their schedules were hectic, always changing, and he cherished their time together. But Max was a greedy bastard, so of course he only wanted more.

That was where tonight's homemade dinner came in. Shrimp scampi, broccoli rabe, saffron-infused rice. Often, they had to settle for takeout, quick salads, or sandwiches. But Max had a couple of big questions for her, and he was totally buttering her up.

He heard her car pull up. Lana came inside, dumping her laptop bag and purse by the door. "Something smells amazing in here."

She gave him a kiss, sliding off her shoes.

Together they plated up dinner and poured glasses of wine. While they ate, they shared stories from work. This was Max's favorite part of any day. Well, maybe second favorite. He found himself saving up thoughts at the office in anticipation of telling Lana, hearing her laugh or her huff of indignation, asking for her advice.

"Is Sylvie still bugging you to take a vacation?"

"Only twice a day or so." Although Max had been working a more humane schedule, he still rarely took a whole day off. Neither did Lana.

"I know your trial goes through next week, but what would you say to a long weekend in the Caribbean afterward? I found this little resort, really private…" He was pushing his last piece of shrimp around his plate as he spoke. He lifted his eyes when Lana didn't answer.

"I don't know." She was biting her lip. "Are you bringing those tiny swim shorts of yours?"

"That could be arranged. If I get to pick your bikini."

"Then I'm in. I can't *wait* to go on vacation with you. As long as there's still Wi-Fi at this resort?"

"Oh, there's definitely Wi-Fi. Let's not get carried away."

She seemed pleased. And she'd be showing her appreciation in her bedroom later, if the small foot massaging his calf was any indication.

So far, so good. Now, for the bigger ask.

Max cleared his throat. He had his whole argument prepared. "So, I've been thinking."

"Uh oh."

"Hey, give me a chance."

"What? I'm listening."

"I've been *thinking*…"—he cut his eyes at her, daring her to interrupt— "that we've been wasting a lot of time driving between our places. And I know how annoying it is when you forget a file or a witness statement back at your place and have to go fetch it. I think it would be much more sensible if we just move in together."

Lana pushed her plate away, folding her hands on the table. "Go on."

"Well, that's it. I want all the time with you I can get."

"But that's not the same as your first argument. At first, you just said it was 'sensible.' Like any reasonable person might decide to have a roommate."

"Nope, I'm only talking about unreasonable people here. Such as me." He knew what she was after. "I love you. I want to share everything with you. Would you move in with me, please?"

She nodded thoughtfully, like this was just a mildly interesting business proposal. "Move in where? My place or yours?"

"I just assumed it would be mine. My apartment's a lot bigger. And...nicer."

Retreat. She's glaring.

"And I do own my place, while yours is a rental."

"All good points. But here's my issue. I don't want to live at your work. I don't want to see your employees every time I go in and out of the building or pick up the mail. And it's one thing for you to answer some emails on your laptop in the middle of the night. It's another for you to disappear downstairs like you were never off duty."

"You've never said that stuff bothered you."

"Because it wasn't my home. You're talking about sharing a space. But every space in that building will always be yours."

This wasn't going as well as he'd hoped. But he was a problem solver. He could improvise. "So, we find a new place. Together."

"Halfway between both of our workplaces? With ocean views?"

"Exactly what I was thinking."

She pushed back her chair and sat in his lap, circling her arms around his neck. "Can I be the one to decorate?"

"No problem."

"Can I have the bigger home office?"

He opened his mouth. "Sure," he said tightly.

"I was just kidding. But good to know." She ran her fingers through his hair. "Can I have you all to myself whenever I want you?"

Now that one was easy. "*Yes*, Lana."

She grinned. "That's just what I hoped you'd say."

Don't miss the next book in the series, HARD WIRED, Sylvie and Dominic's story!

Sylvie can't resist the bad boys. When her job with Bennett Security throws her into the path of Dominic, a former crime boss, she comes face-to-face with her greatest temptation. But as their attraction grows, their warring loyalties threaten to shatter Dominic's hopes—not just to win her over, but to save his soul.

Also by Hannah Shield

THE BENNETT SECURITY SERIES

HANDS OFF (Aurora & Devon)

He's protecting his former flame… But can he resist falling for her? A steamy, action-packed romantic suspense.

HARD WIRED (Sylvie & Dominic)

Can this bad boy find redemption in the arms of the enemy? A steamy, enemies-to-lovers romance with hacker intrigue and mafia drama.

HOLD TIGHT (Faith & Tanner)

He was supposed to be her wingman. She was never supposed to fall for him. A steamy, friends-to-lovers military romance.

HUNG UP (Noah & Danica)

Coming August 2022

Her brother's worst enemy is the only man who can protect her. A second-chance romantic suspense between a former Navy SEAL and a billionaire's daughter.

And more coming soon!

Acknowledgments

Many thanks to my editor and my criminal law consultants. Any mistakes—and creative license—when it comes to legal proceedings in this book are entirely my own.

I'm so grateful to my beta readers and advance reviewers! Your support means the world to me.

About the Author

Hannah Shield once worked as an attorney. Now, she loves thrilling readers on the page—in every possible way.

She's an author of steamy romantic suspense with feisty heroines, brooding heroes, and pulse-pounding action. Bennett Security is her debut series. Visit her website at www.hannahshield.com.